HOSTAGE

CINDY BONDS

Scrivenings PRESS
Quench your thirst for story.
www.ScriveningsPress.com

Dedicated to my loving husband. Without your support and constant encouragement, I never would've gotten this far. God's plan for us is so much more than I could've imagined. Thanks for pushing me to be who God made me to be.

ACKNOWLEDGMENTS

In this journey, God has led me to some amazing people. When I started writing, I asked God to show me where to go if this was what He wanted me to do.

Starting with a small gathering of writers fifteen minutes from my house, He has perfectly placed so many helpers in my circle.

Thanks to all my writing friends at my Arkansas ACFW chapter. Without your encouragement and knowledge, I never would've kept writing.

Thanks to my first publisher, Mantle Rock Publishing, for taking a chance on me and to my new publisher, Scrivenings Press.

Linda and Shannon, you two have helped me find my words among the ramblings and encouraged me through the entire process. You both have taught me so much, not just about writing, but great writing. I promise I will take your words to heart *as* I continue my writing journey!

Thanks to all my family and friends for your words of encouragement and prayers! They worked!

Published by Scrivenings Press LLC
15 Lucky Lane
Morrilton, Arkansas 72110
https://ScriveningsPress.com

Printed in the United States of America

Paperback ISBN 978-1-64917-062-0

eBook ISBN 978-1-64917-063-7

Library of Congress Control Number: 2020943144

Cover by Linda Fulkerson, bookmarketinggraphics.com

All characters are fictional, and any resemblance to real people, either factional or historical, is purely coincidental.

1

"Get down!" Macy Packer shoved the senator to the ground and took cover. Gunfire erupted around them.

Bullets ricocheted over her head, forcing her to wait before returning fire. Her com-link rang out with the voices of her five-man crew, nearly deafening her, but over a short time, their voices faded. The outcome of the battle became clear.

The smell of smoke stung at her eyes and throat. Fire engulfed their helo. She yelled, "Get that bird here now!"

"Two minutes out."

"Too long," she muttered. Macy reloaded and rained another torrent of bullets, pushing back the insurgents making their way across the rooftop.

She grabbed Senator Marstill and rolled him beneath her.

He cried out and grabbed his head.

"Don't move." Ducking down, she snagged a Glock from a deceased friend, noting the blood seeping through his shirt and pooling around his body.

There would be time to mourn later. Right now, she was intent on living through this day. A bullet tore past her shoulder as she stood to move the assailants back, firing and falling back to her position.

It had all happened so quickly—the procession from the offices of the governor in Mexico City to their secondary pickup location, the rocket launcher that blew up the waiting helicopter, and now, the hailstorm of gunfire. If Jasper hadn't answered her distress call, their chances of survival would be zero.

"Get ready."

She could barely hear the com-link in her ear as rotor wash from the helo pushed onto the rooftop.

"When I say run, you run." She gripped the senator's collar and pulled him to her.

His eyes were glazed as he gasped for air.

"Sir, you better run hard. Don't you dare let these men die for nothing!"

The terrified man nodded. She released him and reached for the Beretta at her ankle.

"Go! Go!" the static-filled order pounded in her ear.

"Go! Now!" She stood and offered cover as the senator ran to the hovering chopper.

The helo's gunner kept them protected while the senator safely climbed aboard. Macy reached up and felt a grasp on her wrist. She tried to kick her legs onboard.

"Gotta go!"

The copter rose.

She glanced over her shoulder and saw a rocket launcher aimed at the bird. The grip on her wrist loosened when the helo suddenly banked. Spinning her body around, she took aim at the launcher but felt the grip on her wrist give way.

"Macy!"

Jasper's wide eyes were the last thing she saw as she fell. She landed on her back. Shock rippled through her body, and she fought to catch her breath. Her back, arms, and head reverberated from the force, bouncing against whatever had broken her fall.

Dizziness overwhelmed Macy. Hands grabbed her arms. She

fought to stay conscious through the pain, but the pull on her shoulders and the scraping of her back forced a scream out of her. Her body was too worn down, her conscious dazed, and the flashes of light finally gave way to darkness.

2

Agent Kane Bledsoe watched the woman's breaths pick up. *Three days.* For three days, he waited next to her cot, wondering if she would ever wake. The dried blood on the back of her head proved she'd taken a hard hit. She probably had a concussion.

"If we take care of her shoulder now, it won't hurt as bad," murmured Jon.

One shoulder sat awkwardly lower than the other, proving it was dislocated.

Kane sighed. "If she's here, she has training. You might find yourself with a broken hand for even touching her."

"She still looks out to me." Jon shrugged.

With a grunt, he got on his knees beside her as Jon felt around the joint. The muscles around her mouth twitched.

"She's waking up, Jon," he whispered.

Jon grasped her shoulder, and the woman's hand suddenly flew up, gripping his throat with a grunt. Taking a small sharpened nail Kane had found, he pressed it gently to her neck.

"Let go," he mumbled.

Her eyes darted between them, wide and erratic.

"Jon's a medic." Kane sighed and removed the nail. "He's trying to help you."

The woman released Jon. He eased her back onto the cot, and she groaned.

"Get her something to bite on now that she's awake," Jon whispered.

"No," her gritty voice murmured.

"You yell out, they'll come get you." Kane frowned down at her dirty face.

Her bright blue eyes locked with his for a moment. She nodded, then turned face down in the old, moldy mattress. With the expertise of a trained doctor, Jon pulled and pushed the joint back into place. She let out a low grunt and moan.

"You did good. What's your name?" Kane's throat burned, his voice a strained whisper. He glanced around, checking to see if they'd attracted the guards' attention.

"My, my name?" she mumbled and pushed herself to sit.

He steadied her uninjured shoulder as she looked around.

"Who are you, and where are we?" Her brows furrowed.

He frowned at her questions. "I can try and help you."

She cleared her throat with a grimace. "Don't put yourself in harm's way because of me." Her bright eyes turned dark. Breaking contact, she gazed at the men behind him. "Who are they?" she whispered.

"None of your concern. You can speak to Jon and me. They'll stay over there." Not that he didn't think she couldn't handle herself with those men. But her situation was dire enough. He didn't want her to have to worry about anything but her own survival.

Her gaze shifted to Jon, then back on him. "Okay, Gruff." She smirked.

He smiled. Strong with a sense of humor. She'd need both to survive this.

"Where are we?"

"Doesn't really matter. You need to find a way out."

"I—our intel must've been wrong," She mumbled and shook her head slowly, knitting her brows together again.

"Intel? What intel? Who do you work for?"

"My boss." She gave him a smug look.

"And your boss is?"

"You think I'm giving up our intel to someone I met ten minutes ago?"

"Intel you've already admitted was wrong, by the way." Kane sighed. "Let's start over. If you want our help, tell me what you know. We didn't get locked in here because we're one of the bad guys."

She sucked in a deep breath as if considering her options. "Okay, fine." She released her breath and straightened. "Someone has been sending Senator Marstill threatening letters and calls. We were in Mexico and assumed one of the major drug cartels wanted to make a martyr of him."

"Why?"

"He's got a hard line on immigration as well as drugs," she muttered. Looking up, she narrowed her eyes. "Are we still in Mexico?"

He nodded. "And the senator?"

"He's safe." With a wince, she touched the wound on the back of her head. Her eyes widened as a gasp escaped her lips.

"I'm so sorry, they cut it all off," Jon mumbled.

Cut with scissors, patches of dirty blonde clumps hung around her head. She fingered the remaining tufts of hair.

"It-it's okay. It'll grow back." Her eyes closed as she took a few breaths. She gripped the edge of the mattress, her feet rocked back and forth on the dirt floor. The rough tunic and pants she wore were filthy, stained with dirt and muck.

"Are we … are we underground?"

He shook his head. Her eyes met his for a moment. Gripping her arm, he stood and helped her up, her body unsteady.

"How long have you been here?"

"Doesn't matter. You need to focus on getting yourself out."

She turned to Jon and teetered. Holding her elbow, Kane helped her sit back down on the cot. She held her head.

"Save your energy. You'll need it," he whispered.

"But where are—?"

"What's your name?" He purposely avoided her question. How could he tell her she was in the worst place he could think of on earth for a man or woman?

"I don't want to say." She leaned back against the rock wall with a grimace. "Does it sound stupid to think saying my name will just make it more real?"

He smirked. "Nope."

"Just call me Pack." She closed her eyes.

With a sigh, Kane scanned Jon's meager frame. After weeks of being here, they were starved, weak, and on edge. If they didn't get help soon ...

A clatter echoed through the hallway, and Jon retreated to the back wall. Kane stood, moving in front of Pack.

"No, I told you," she whispered.

He shook his head slowly, glaring at the men entering the cell. There was no way he'd let them get her easily.

"Get her up."

Kane stepped forward and took a blow to the gut. Gripping his middle, he doubled over, unable to breathe.

"Get back." The low, accent-laden voice of the head guard prickled his skin.

"I'm fine. It's fine."

He felt her hand grip his arm. She grunted and stood, shaking her head at him.

"Can you walk?"

"Of course." Her light-hearted tone made him hurt worse.

He knew what she might be facing.

As they took hold of her arms, he glared at the men who pulled her from his cell. The door slammed shut. Its echo caused bile to rise in his throat.

"She's tough," Jon whispered from behind.

"She doesn't know any better." He shook his head. "But she will by the time she gets back."

Jon clutched his arm to steady him.

Kane groaned and pulled his arm from Jon's grip. "I don't need help."

"We all need help. Especially in here."

He shook his head and collapsed onto the cot. Closing his eyes, he swallowed hard. He couldn't save himself or Jon, and now, he couldn't save her. She needed help— much more than he could give.

"What do I do now?" he whispered to the void. Ignoring the silence, he slipped into sleep.

———

A HAND PUSHED HER FORWARD. The man wearing khaki turned and dragged her out of the cell and into the corridor. Macy struggled to keep from falling, her feet not willing to work as she followed.

The man giving the orders apparently noticed her slow gait. "Help her."

Hands gripped her again and pulled her arms. She could barely lift her feet as they scraped and burned against the cement floor. Macy noticed the cells lining the walls. At least twenty men were imprisoned here, counting the two men from her cell. The stench from their bodies hung in the air. Her captors led her up a wooden staircase to a landing, and then down a hallway.

A guard dragged her down a carpeted passageway. She caught a glimpse of another wooden corridor to the left before the man forced her into an office on her right.

"Sit."

The khaki man shoved her into a hardback chair. She grimaced and tried to catch her breath. He sat on the edge of the desk facing her, grinning through missing teeth and a scruffy chin.

"Your name?"

"What's yours?"

He answered her question with a hard slap across her face. Shooting pain pulsed from her jaw and down the back of her neck. She leaned to her right and spat blood across the carpet.

"Jay, no more blood." A Spanish-laden accent graced the words.

She struggled to swallow the rest of the blood. Her gaze lifted. The chair at the other side of the desk spun around, revealing an older, distinguished man. He clasped his hands clasped in front of him. His face bore a stern look.

The man's white hair and matching mustache contrasted against jet-black eyebrows.

Jay moved to her left side. He wore a wide grin that made her want to reach out and smack him. But she held her hands in front of her. They weren't tied, and she didn't want to give them a reason to do so.

"My dear, I have some questions, your name being the first of many."

"How about you give me your name first?" She saw Jay's hand come at her again. This time, she grabbed his wrist with both hands before he could make contact. "Now, Jay, he said to go easy." She glowered at the guard, who glared as if he'd kill her the first chance he got.

Laughter came from the other side of the desk, and she released the man's wrist.

"Let her be and wait by the door, Jay."

Jay stepped away, and her focus returned to the man at the desk.

"My name is Señor Luis DeLuca. I am in the information business."

"How did I get here? I have no information for anyone."

"I doubt that." DeLuca stood and moved to her side of the desk. "When we bring someone here, it is because they know something, and I am tasked with getting that information from them. But, you see, we do not keep women here. So, I would like to find out what you know sooner rather than later. The men have orders to keep to themselves. No one will abuse you without consequence."

"How gracious of you." She did her best to smile, but the pain in her face kept her muscles from working.

"Now, what is your name, and what is it you know? Who do you work for?"

"I work for a senator who's probably resigning at the moment. There's nothing I can tell you that would help anyone. Once the senator escaped, he received a new protection detail, one that I have no information on whatsoever." She ignored the first question, not willing to give the man the pleasure of knowing her name.

DeLuca frowned.

Macy looked around the office, orienting herself. She had no clue where she'd ended up, and without that knowledge, escape could do little to help her.

"Take her back down. I have a call to make."

Jay's hand pulled her head back by the tufts of her hair and ripped her from the chair.

"Remember, I need her talking."

Jay's grunt proved he felt differently.

"Yeah, Jay, might want to rein in that temper." If she could push his buttons, maybe she could stall the interrogations.

The door closed, and another slap knocked her against the wall.

"Now, Jay, is that how you treat women?" She mumbled as her mouth filled with blood.

His fist in her stomach crumpled her to her knees. She wrapped her arm around her middle and gasped for breath. A sharp pain jabbed her leg. When she turned to see what caused the pain, a kick sent her back to the ground, face first. Her fingers moved beneath her body until she found a jagged nail.

She pulled it from the floor and pushed into her top, keeping it for later.

"Jay!" DeLuca's voice sounded.

Another blow came down on her head, slamming her into the ground. Her vision dimmed, and darkness washed over her.

3

"Pack?" Gruff's voice rumbled through her mind, coaxing her back to consciousness.

"Mmmm ..." She gripped her head and rolled to her side.

"Are you alive?"

She forced open her eyes. Darkness overshadowed the room. "Depends. Is it nighttime now?"

"Yeah."

"Then yeah, I'm alive." She heard a chuckle and smiled as much as she could manage from the pain that pushed through her face. "Where are you?"

"Next room. They put you in a cell by yourself."

Moonlight filtered in through the small slits across the top of the cell. The light ebbed as shadows moved next to the wall. "Can I see you?"

"Almost. There's a hole in the wall between us."

Several fingers moved through the small hole.

"Oh." She pushed herself to a sitting position and leaned against the adjoining wall, her breathing labored as she held her left side.

"You good?"

"Sure, cracked ribs and all," she murmured between breaths.

"Take shallow breaths. Deep breathing will just make it worse."

She lay back down on the cold floor, curled on her side. Her back ached. "Gruff, what information do they want from you?"

"Kane."

"What?" She closed her eyes and breathed slowly.

"My name is Kane."

"What? You didn't like Gruff?" She smiled when she heard another chuckle.

"You need to rest. I don't know what they have planned for you, but I know it won't be good."

"I'll be fine, one way or the other." She held her aching side and took short breaths.

"What does that mean?"

"Well, if I die, I'll be in a much better place. If I get out, then I'll make it home." Macy winced at the pain caused by speaking. Visions of her father and brother moved through her mind. She squeezed her eyes closed, refusing to wallow in memories right now.

"Oh, you're one of *those*."

"What's the matter, Gruff—I mean, Kane? No hope for the believer?"

"Not a believer." His deep voice rumbled.

"Too bad. You remind me of someone."

"Who's that?"

"Saul. You can ask Jon about him." She paused and grasped her side, her breathing labored. "Is Jon awake?"

After a few moments, she heard Jon's soft voice.

"Yes?"

"Jon, are you a believer?"

"Yes, dear, I am."

"Then help Kane out. Tell him about Saul."

A chuckle moved through the wall. "I've never thought about that. I'll tell him all about Saul and Paul. But I don't think he'll be interested."

She sighed. "Kane, you should listen to your friend."

"Get some rest." Kane's deep whisper stirred through her, giving her some form of comfort.

She shifted her body, and a cold sting burned her side. Fingering the fabric of her shirt, the nail poked her finger. She smiled.

"Kane?"

It took more energy than she imagined, stretching out her arm to push the long nail through the hole.

He took it from her. "But you might need it."

"Nah. Don't have the energy."

"Rest. You'll get your energy back."

She nodded to herself. Her voice left her, but shallow breaths eased in and out as she drifted off.

THE CELL CREAKED OPEN. Kane jumped.

"Get her up."

An unfamiliar voice. He frowned. A new jailer. That didn't bode well for her situation.

"Drink. You need your energy."

He coughed loudly and leaned against the wall. Hopefully, she heard him and would get it. When they were allowed water, it was drugged. Whatever it was made tongues go loose. There was no need for torture if you talked freely. The problem was, he and Jon had too many things they must keep quiet.

The sounds of her choking up the water made him blow out a relieved sigh. She must have understood his not so subtle signal.

"No more spitting it up. Drink it all."

Several moments ticked by while he waited. Her cell door finally slammed shut, and he moved to the hole in the wall to look.

She lay on her side, her face buried.

"How much did you take?"

"More than I should've," she whispered.

He frowned. "It might be a long shot, but this could be your chance to make a run for it. If you get out, you'll need coordinates."

"What?"

Her confused tone worried him, but he continued, "Just listen. 24, 14, 26."

"24, 14, 26." She groaned. "I'm … I'm not so great with numbers."

"Pack, you really need to clear your head. They drugged you. Gave you stuff to make you talk."

"Don't worry about me, Kane. I can talk and talk." She chuckled.

Kane sighed. "What are the coordinates?"

"24, 14, 26. This new guy—I'm not sure I can buy time," Macy whispered.

"Yeah, not sure the same tactic would work anyway. I don't think you could take another beating."

"Don't worry about me. I can take care of myself." She sucked in a deep breath and groaned in pain. "You just—you stay alive long enough for someone to find you."

"You find a way out. Don't worry about me."

Silence gave way as he leaned down and peered into the hole. She was on her side, eyes closed, breaths heavy.

He raised back up. "It's bad enough we're here, but how could your God allow her to be here?"

Jon sighed and shook his head. "God granted humans free will. Men make their own choices."

Kane leaned against the wall. He gritted his teeth and pulled his knees to his chest. The cuts across his stomach burned. She didn't deserve this. It wasn't just torture he worried about. For her to be here …

Swallowing hard against a dry throat, he did his best to halt his thoughts, his fear for her weighing on him. Her bright blue eyes resonated in Kane's mind, and he wanted nothing more than for her to be freed from this evil place.

He had to find a way to get her out, more than just some coordinates. Jailbreak was impossible. At this point, they were all too weak, too beaten down to make a push against the guards. He needed to think of something before she ended up in even more danger.

Maybe he could use the nail she gave him to pick the lock, get her to safety before dawn. Kane blew out a big breath. Exhaustion weighed on his shoulders. His job was to protect, and he had to find a way to protect her.

"I want to protect her," he whispered as he closed his eyes and leaned his head back against the wall.

4

Cool water washed over Macy's face. She flinched and carefully pushed up with her right arm to see the guards. They lifted her arms. She groaned and managed to stand. The new guard pushed into her, glaring down and sneering. Cigar smoke and alcohol filled her nostrils, just like with Jay. But unlike Jay, the new guard appeared younger. Clean-shaven and combed hair, the smell of cologne lingered on him.

"Either walk, or we'll drag you."

She nodded, attempting a smile, even though the left side of her face was numb. He turned to leave, and she followed, doing her best to keep up. The stairwell caused her trouble. She strained with each step to lift her legs.

Once in the hallway, she followed the man into DeLuca's office, and, once again, collapsed in the chair. She glanced over her right shoulder and found the crimson stain on the carpet from yesterday.

"I really am sorry about the blood, Señor, is that why Jay isn't here today?"

Señor DeLuca crossed the room from the large picture window on her left and glared at her.

"Jay is not here because he is dead. He disobeyed an order.

Besides, I will have new carpet tomorrow." DeLuca came back to the desk and sat on the edge in front of her.

"Now, what information do you have on the senator?"

"First of all, he's a weasel. I would never vote for him. After following him around for a month, he ended up being the biggest scumbag. You wouldn't—" she paused, "I mean, maybe you would believe how underhanded he is." She grinned, feeling more in control than when she passed out earlier, the drugs easing the ache in her side and shoulder.

If he wanted her to talk, she would talk.

"Anyway, he would hit on anything that walked. He tried me once, and I quickly put him in his place. He was married too—wife, kids, the whole family thing. Too bad—"

"Enough!"

She looked up.

DeLuca paced the floor. He wore a stern expression, and his face reddened. "You should have information about his plans."

"His plans? What? You mean besides being a weasel?"

The drugs slowed her movements. Her arms barely flinched as he stepped toward her, hands fisted as he breathed down on her.

"Give me something to stop him, or I will kill you myself." His white teeth glistened as he spoke through a clenched jaw.

"It's not just him you need to worry about. He's intent on stopping whatever's crossing the border, in every sense of the word. If he backs down, which I imagine he will now, they'll just send the next man in line. I'm only the protection detail, Señor, I have no information on their plans."

He paced a moment before sitting at his desk.

"I will see you in the morning. Your captors hoped you would have more information, but apparently, you are worthless. Take her back and put her in a cell. Alone."

The younger man grabbed her arm and yanked her to stand, dragging her around the chair and through the door. He pulled her down the stairwell to the prison floor. He shoved her into her cell. His hands firmly gripped her wrists, and he pushed her against the wall.

"You have no information, huh?" He stood only a few inches taller than her.

For a moment, she considered him. Kane had suggested she do whatever she could to get out, but she wasn't too sure about those stakes.

"No, I told him that yesterday. So, I'm guessing whoever brought me here will put a bullet in my head in the morning." She watched as he looked her over and attempted to control the shudder as his hands pushed under her tunic and grabbed her waist.

———

"I CAN GET you out tonight if it would be worth something to you."

Kane heard the guard's thick accent and pushed against the wall between the cells, his forehead against the cold stone.

"Get me out? How in the world would you do that? I'm sure your boss wouldn't want his reputation ruined with a missing inmate."

Macy's voice was weak. Kane fisted his hands at the thought of that man hurting her.

"I will be back tonight if it's worth it to you," the guard offered again.

"Tell you what, you get me out of this place, it would be worth pretty much anything to me."

The cell door slammed shut, and he heard her fall to the ground. Kane stooped to the hole. Tears ran down her cheeks, and her fists hit the packed dirt. His stomach churned as he did his best to calm his voice. "Save it for tonight. You'll need those fists to work."

She ignored him, shaking her head as she gripped her hands in her lap.

"Want this back?" He pushed the nail she'd given him back through the hole.

"No." She shook her head, wiping her cheek with a frown. "I want you to use it to get out," she whispered.

"I'm not getting my hopes up. Besides, it might do you some good later."

"Keep those hopes up, Kane." She sighed. "I'm not sure I'll have any strength to use it." She moved around on her side, her breaths strained.

His mind spun. How could he fix this? Do his job? Getting Jon out, getting Pack out—that was his job. And he was failing.

A hand fell on his shoulder, and he turned, Jon's weary form stood over him.

"I'm praying for all of us. Especially you."

"It hasn't helped so far," Kane muttered. He heard her breaths go short in the adjacent cell.

Her crying killed him.

"She wanted me to tell you about Saul."

"Not now," he gritted and stood to pace a moment, trying to get himself together enough to save her.

What that jailer had promised, well, he was all but certain the man would free her from the cell. But what would follow made bile burn the back of his throat.

"You can't do anything. None of us can."

He spun toward Jon and shook his head. "I don't want to hear it."

"It's not your fault she's here."

"I don't want to hear it." His voice strained as it rose, his breaths heavy in his aching chest.

Leaning his hands against the wall, Kane let out a long exhale and tried to think.

How could he do it? How could he get her to safety?

SILENCE LINGERED, and time stopped for a moment. Light filtered into the room through a slit close to the ceiling. Macy prayed as she rested, prayed for the energy and courage to do what she must do to escape, and bring back help.

Focusing on the others, she prayed for Jon and everyone held captive. And she prayed for Kane— a lost soul who could easily die in this place. The thought of him not joining her in heaven someday sickened her.

"Kane?" Her raspy and dry voice echoed in the empty room.

"Yeah?"

She smiled at the low growl and wondered if he always sounded that way. "Make me a deal."

"What's that?"

"You keep up hope that you'll get out." She took several short breaths. "And if I do get out tonight, you better stay alive long enough for me to come back and get you."

"Seems a bit one-sided."

She laughed, then groaned as pain pushed through her body. "Fine." With labored breaths, she lay there, staring at the hole in the wall. "What's your side?"

"Don't do anything stupid to get yourself killed, like come back here. Send the troops, but you stay back."

"I'll think about it."

He chuckled through the wall. "I figured you wouldn't go for it."

"My brother would say I'm stubborn—" She paused to catch her breath, each word increasing the ache in her side. "But I'd never admit to it."

"No more talking. Save it. You need to rest."

The hole between their cells was about four inches from the floor, and she could see him moving—a flash of his face, those green eyes as he watched her.

"Gruff, just keep yourself alive." She all but mouthed the words.

His head bobbed. Probably just to appease her.

Tears streamed down her face. Macy closed her eyes, attempted to slow her breathing. Feeling alone, she looked back through the hole, watched him moving. She wiped her face, forcing her body to relax and rest. Kane was right. She'd need all her strength tonight if the new guard were true to his word.

5

"Get up." The whispered words brought her through a fog. Rough hands pulled her upright.

Macy stood with a groan. The young guard tugged her through the cell door. She gripped her ribs with her left arm. Instead of going outside, he pulled her under the stairwell and into a room.

"I thought you were getting me out?"

"Too tight, there's no way I can leave with you in tow." He shoved her to the ground and straddled her hips, removing his shirt.

With his weight on top of her, struggling would only tire her. Bile burned the back of her throat. Her heart pounded. When he reached for his pants, she made a move.

Jerking a leg out from under him, she kicked him in the groin. The guard reeled back and crumpled to the ground, moaning. Rolling to her right, she tucked her elbow against her side, bracing wounded ribs, and kicked again, slamming her foot into his chest.

She searched the ground for anything she could use as a weapon and came up empty. Macy kicked one last time, nailing the man in the face. Pain seared her side and shoulder. She gasped a series of short breaths.

Lord, let that be enough.

The dim light allowed her to see the rise and fall of his chest. Breathing, but unconscious. Her body burned. Tremors moved through her, and adrenaline surged. Scouring the room, she found a length of rope. She moved quickly and tied his hands behind his back, shoved a rag in his mouth.

After tugging his oversized shirt over her clothes, she stripped his pants and pulled them on over hers, using the belt to cinch them. His boots were too big, but she shoved the too-long pants into them and tied the laces tight. Macy tucked what was left of her hair into his hat, then rubbed dirt across her face and wrapped a dirty bandana around her neck.

She cracked the door open. No one appeared, so she crept to a side entrance. Pulling out the phone from the pants pocket, she pretended to talk, bowing up as large as possible to impersonate one of their officers in case someone saw her. Hopefully, the bulk of her oversized top tucked into the large uniform would sell her size.

Macy found the outside doorway and opened it just enough to see out. The sun was rising, a sliver of light drifting through the sky from far away. She hoped the remaining darkness could be used for her advantage.

Lord, let this work!

She spotted a Jeep parked a few feet from the door. Keeping her head down with the phone to her ear, she made her way inside the vehicle. The keys were gone, but she leaned down and stripped two wires, making them spark. The engine came to life.

Driving toward the gate, she grabbed a pair of sunglasses from the seat and slid them on, her raspy voice yelling into the phone. Her limited Spanish would be an issue, but she could at least create a one-sided conversation.

A man stopped her at the gate, but she continued yelling into the phone. He simply opened it and nodded her through. As the compound fell into the background, she punched in Zander's number, observing the men on the towers and the firepower on the roof in the mirrors.

"Who is this?"

"Zander, it's Packer, get me zoned in and get a team here. Now."

"Macy? What? I mean—"

"Zander, snap out of it." She used a stern voice, pushing him out of his stupor. "Get a team here now. The compound's coordinates are 24, 14, 26. I'll keep the phone on, but I have to find a place to lay low."

"A team has been on standby since they took you. Give me ten minutes."

The line went dead, and a sigh escaped her lips. As long as the team had the coordinates, it didn't matter what happened to her. The captives would be released.

She really wanted to return to the compound and visit with the men who took her. And make sure Kane made it out alive.

———

AFTER DRIVING for what seemed like an hour through the dusty, arid land, Macy finally found civilization. She pulled into the back of a partially dismantled building on the outskirts of a town. The walls had collapsed in sections, the tin roof in shambles, and rubble piled high everywhere. The Jeep bumped and bounced as she drove over the debris and parked inside the mess. Her body throbbed from all the jostling.

Macy got out of the Jeep. She kept the phone, hat, and boots, but dumped the uniform. Holding her side, she slowly moved past the rubble and concrete barriers toward the buildings and market that already held a small crowd.

Noticing a length of fabric draped across a tree branch, she took it and wrapped it over her clothes. She tossed the hat and pulled the bandana around her head, leaving just the sunglasses and boots from the compound in view.

She moved through the town slowly, doing her best to walk upright, blend in, and go unseen. The smells of different foods made her stomach ache and mouth water. She couldn't remember the last time she'd eaten, and the adrenaline only amplified the need. Her energy dropped, the adrenaline gone, replaced by pain and exhaustion. She needed rest soon.

Macy leaned against the corner of a cobbled building. A light hit her face. She removed her sunglasses and glanced across the street at the building's roof. A man wearing Army fatigues watched her. Mostly hidden behind the brick, he gave a thumbs up. She followed the beam to the door below his nest and nodded.

Making her way through the vendors and townspeople, she paused at the door and gave it a gentle push. A man in a long gray tunic pulled the door open and stared down at her. He stepped aside. Macy hurried into the small room. The man led her down a narrow hallway and into a back room.

As she hobbled in, she counted eight men, fully armed and decked in military fatigues.

"You'll need more." She collapsed in a chair, pulled off the bandana, and leaned forward onto her knees.

"I assume you're Agent Packer?"

She raised her head. "Yes, and if you want to save the men they have locked up, you'll need help. A lot of it." She inhaled sharply, trying to get enough wind to speak. "They don't have many men, but the firepower on their border is more than you can handle."

"Let's take a look." An officer came and knelt next to her.

"I'm fine. There's nothing you can do here for me." She paused to catch her breath. "Tell me you have clothes I can wear, shoes too."

The officer nodded as a soldier handed a backpack.

"What time is it?"

"Almost seven."

"Good. They're expecting company, and I want to be there before they leave."

"Why is that?" The officer who'd done all the talking stepped closer as she unwrapped the fabric dress from around her tunic and dropped it on the floor.

"And you are?"

"Lieutenant Carver James, the officer in charge."

"Well, Lieutenant, the people who held me there will show up this morning to learn what information I've spilled and then kill me. I'd like to meet them in person."

He chuckled.

She kicked off the boots, wincing at the bloody scratches on the top of her feet. The medic moved in, and she pushed him away.

"Look, I want to get dressed and go back. At least twenty men are being held there, several Americans. I spoke to a medic named Jon and a man named Kane."

"Kane Bledsoe?" A man against the wall spoke up. His face bore a stern expression. The man's eyes widened, and he moved away from the wall, staring at her.

"He wouldn't tell me his last name or unit. I don't know anything more than that. But if we don't get them out, they'll be killed today, I'm sure."

"Wait a minute. There is no 'we.' You're not going back in."

She frowned, heaved a breath, and stood. The lieutenant stood taller than her, so much so, he practically had to lean down when he spoke to her. But she wouldn't let them leave her behind. She couldn't.

"You'll need me to get in and out. I know the lay of the land. I know where the cells are. Face it, Lieutenant, I'm in, whether you like it or not." She grabbed the pack and hobbled to another room to change. Her energy dead, she forced her legs to move.

Macy pulled the curtain, faced the corner, and undressed. She tugged the pants up quickly, then sucked in a breath before trying the shirt. Raising her arms to rid herself of the tunic, she groaned. A searing heat knifed through her shoulder and side.

She pulled the shirt down and collapsed onto the bench with a huff. When she leaned over to grab the boots, pain shot through her side.

A knock came, and the curtain parted.

"I heard you. What do you need?" The medic stood with a pack, ready to help.

"Not sure you can do anything." She leaned against the wall and grimaced.

The officer knelt and tied her boots.

"You don't have to do that." Her ragged words tumbled out as she held her side.

"You keep moving around, you'll make things worse. You need to rest and ice your side."

"Don't tell your boss."

He looked up at her and grinned. "I'm sure he already knows."

She frowned as he helped her to stand. Pulling out a hat to cover her missing hair, she ambled back into the room, feeling better now that she wore clean clothes. The lieutenant was on the phone when she returned and took a seat at the table.

The medic removed an ice pack, broke it, and pushed it into her hands. Macy held it against the bruised left side of her face and picked at the plate of food someone gave her.

The lieutenant ended the call, and she looked up at him. "Have you mentioned my name?"

He shook his head.

"Would you? Just say you've got me."

He frowned, furrowing his brow at her request. Moving back to the radio, he switched it off the phone recall and spoke into the mic. "Receiving Macy Packer, all is good." He waited a moment.

Nothing but static. She smiled.

"Macy? Macy, if you're there, pick up."

She bit the inside of her lip to keep from crying. The lieutenant handed her the mic, and she shook her head. "He'll ask me too many questions."

"Husband?"

"Brother."

He nodded and answered for her. "All is good, man. She's coming home."

"Is she hurt? Where are you?"

"Not to worry. Out." He turned it off and watched her for a moment.

Staring past him to the wall, she strained to hold in her emotions. Hearing Jasper's voice affected her more than she planned. The look on his face had stayed with her, him screaming her name when she fell. She couldn't bear to think about him blaming himself for her demise.

Sucking a deep breath, she bit back her tears, closed her eyes, and said a silent prayer.

Lord, guide me back to that prison, help me find and free all those men, and get me home safely.

In the whirlwind of events that led her here, survival had been her only thought, her only focus. But now, she could feel herself letting go, moving into weakness when she needed to be strong. Just a few more hours, only a few more hours.

6

With his hands cuffed, Kane saved his energy for what
was to come.

"Let's go."

He slowly exited the cell, Jon's meager frame in front of him.
He had lost count of how many times they'd been led away like
this. Now, he was ready for it to be over.

They neared the steps, and he looked for the man who'd
taken Macy this morning. He saw her leave out the side door,
hopeful that since she hadn't returned, she made it out.

His body burned—the cuts, the pain, it all amplified as they
moved up the stairs. He knew what was to come, and he'd
already told Jon what to do. If they killed him today, then Jon
could give in. But only after he was dead.

For the first time since captured, fear took over. What would
happen after he died? Would that be it? Or, like Jon continually
reminded him, would something worse await him?

While his mind moved into overdrive, the guard shoved him
into the room. Kane's adrenaline pumped as he collapsed in a
chair.

"Let's get this over with," he muttered.

Macy watched as the lieutenant unrolled a set of blueprints on the table in front of her. He leaned over them and stared at her. She finished a protein bar and started on a water bottle.

"Boss says it's my call. If you're too injured to go back in, you stay."

She shook her head. "I'm not staying."

"You will if I order you to."

"Wanna bet? Call my brother back and see how many of these arguments he's won. Or my boss. He can give you a number less than three." Her gaze held his.

He looked to the medic then back to her. "Your shoulder messed up?"

"Not anymore, besides, I shoot better right-handed."

"Fine." He frowned as a chuckle moved through the men. "But I'm not pulling you out."

"Wouldn't beg you to."

"Tell me where everyone is." A flush crept over his face, and he turned his attention back to the blueprints

She stood, leaning against the table, and oriented herself. Apparently, he noticed her hesitancy and pointed out the direction of their position.

"Okay. I came out here." She pointed to a side door. Finally, her brain kicked in, and she noticed the elevation change on the paper. "There are maybe seven cells that line these walls. Jon and Kane, along with five other men, are here." She pointed out the cell, swallowing as she ran her finger over the pathway to the stairwell. "Up these stairs, there are two hallways. I've only been down this one. It leads to the office."

"Who's running this thing? We've been watching this compound for a while and haven't figured it out. All we know is we have missing soldiers from different areas all over the country. They all have one thing in common—a distress call that describes a similar aggressor. When we received your coordinates, we were only a few clicks east of here, tracking someone we tagged who works inside."

"Señor Luis DeLuca." She sat back down, holding her side and easing her breaths to speak. "He says he's in the information business. Captives are sent to him, tortured until they talk, and then he gets paid for the information. You'll know when you're in his office. I left a bit of a blood trail he wasn't too happy about. He said they were getting new carpet delivered today."

"We could use that as cover."

"No." She frowned and shook her head. "Once he finds out I'm gone, the evidence will be destroyed. I'm not waiting that long, risking those men."

"Look, we need a better plan than to storm the gate."

"And we need more firepower than what you can provide. It seems we're both unhappy with the situation." She took a few shallow breaths.

"Wheels up in ten." Lieutenant James glared at her, ignoring the men standing around them.

Macy turned and hobbled through the room, needing some privacy. Making her way to a small alcove outside, she tried to breathe through the pain building in her body. She just needed to hold on a little longer, keep moving for a little longer, and then she could rest. Stretching her neck, she slowly returned, stopping as a reflection caught her attention.

A cracked, aged mirror hung on the wall as she came inside. Her eyes widened at the face staring back at her. She didn't even recognize herself. The left side of her face was bruised and swollen, unrecognizable under the dirt she'd slathered on earlier. Two trails snaked down her cheeks from tears she didn't even know she'd cried.

She held a breath, trying not to hyperventilate. Macy pulled off her hat and reached up to touch the remaining tufts of her hair. It was uneven and ugly.

Macy assumed that was their intention, hoping to disarm whatever devices she might use to entice an escape. She sighed and replaced the hat, keeping her eyes downward. When she entered the room, the men were checking their weapons.

Lieutenant James frowned as he handed her a rifle. "I was told you were a good shot. Hope so. You'll need to be on your game."

She took the weapon. He also handed her a backup that she slid into her waistband. The officer who spoke up at Kane's name earlier helped her into a vest, strapping it tightly. She groaned and loosened the straps.

"What did he look like?"

She looked up at the man who stared down on her. He wasn't as tall as Kane, but she noticed something similar. A smirk lifted the corner of her lip. "He won't look the same. Don't let him see you pitying on him."

"It's him, though? You're sure?" His green eyes widened.

She looked at his nametag, Bledsoe. "He's taller than you, gruff voice, and has a beard. But ..."

"But what?" The man's voice wavered.

"He's thinner than you. His face is gaunt. Your brother?"

Bledsoe nodded as he walked away, wiping his eyes with the back of his hand.

"Let's go." James's voice ripped through the tension.

Macy followed the others outside to a waiting truck. The men basically picked her up and threw her into the back of the covered bed. At least they were gentle about it.

"I don't like this. I need to see out."

"Look, this is a different operation than you're used to. Do it our way, okay?"

She heard the lieutenant's voice but could barely see him.

"You and Bledsoe are going in, the rest of us—we're the diversion."

"Tell me you have some air backup."

"On its way as we speak. You two are to go in, release the prisoners, and come out the same way you went in. Got it?"

"Yes, sir." Her answer sounded weak. She took several small breaths, working to calm her nerves.

Reentering the most terrifying place imaginable wasn't something she thought she could handle, but she had to. She had to save those men. Had to save Jon and Kane.

7

The team dropped off Macy and Bledsoe less than a mile from the gate she'd exited earlier that morning. The guards were still there. Nothing had changed. Hopefully, that meant no one knew she was missing.

"As soon as they start up, we go in. I'll take out anyone above and follow you." Bledsoe took charge. "Once inside, take me to the cells and cover me while I open them. Okay?"

"Yeah." She saved her voice, attempting to ease the tremors moving through her body.

Within minutes, a firefight echoed. Men left their posts and headed to the front of the compound, leaving only two guards on the back gate. Bledsoe took them out quickly and efficiently. She ran as fast as she could toward the gate but sensed Bledsoe's irritation at her slow movement.

"Sorry." Breathless, she entered the gate.

Slipping through the side entrance, Macy raised her weapon. Gunfire raged above her. Once inside, she kept the stairwell in her sights, moving toward the cells.

She tapped Bledsoe's shoulder and took watch as he released the cell doors.

"Go out the right-side door and run to the waiting truck," his voice whispered, rising as the men started to file out.

"Where is he?" The was cell empty, except for two men. "Where are Kane and Jon?"

"They took them this morning," one of the men answered. "Come on, I know where."

The man took the sidearm from Macy's waistband, and Bledsoe handed off his to the other captive. She hobbled up the stairwell. As they went through the doorway, a blood-curdling scream fill the air. Her heart leaped to her throat. She locked eyes with Bledsoe, who immediately froze, his face white.

Shaking, she followed the captive down the wooden corridor instead of the carpeted hallway. She counted down from three and pushed the door open. The men bolted inside, firing, and taking out the interrogator. The air left her lungs when she saw Kane tied to a chair. Bloody wounds enveloped his shirtless body.

"Kane!" His brother cut his bindings.

Macy forced her attention to the rest of the room. "Where's Jon?"

The man who'd taken her sidearm tapped her shoulder and pointed to another door. She pushed it open to find Jon with a gun to his head.

"Come any closer, and he's dead," the Hispanic man sneered. His gaze darted over her face.

She stood firm, feeling one of the men push behind her.

"Left side," she whispered slowly. She lowered her weapon to the right. The captor's gaze followed her gun.

The shot deafened her left ear as the man behind her shot the captor in the head. The guard fell in a heap, leaving Jon unharmed.

Macy turned and raised her eyebrows at the smiling man behind her. "Nice shooting."

"Bart." He nodded.

She smiled as Jon hobbled toward her. "Let's get out of here."

Jon nodded, and she took his arm. Bledsoe supported Kane's weight.

"Is he out?"

"Almost, we need to get him to a hospital."

She nodded.

Bart and his buddy covered their descent back down the steps and through the door they had entered. They found a truck parked outside, and Bart watched above them for anyone who might be waiting.

"Clear."

Macy supported Jon as Bledsoe carried his brother to the back of the truck. She got in the driver's seat, found the keys in the ignition, and started it. Jon looked pained as he closed his door. She watched the mirror, waiting for Bart and his buddy to climb in before she drove out of the compound.

"Go left, head for the east part of the town!" Bledsoe's voice sounded.

She turned the truck down the bumpy road.

The air assault James called in appeared as streaks of light drifting through the air and toward the compound. She wanted to cheer at seeing the compound engulfed in smoke, but they still had to make the extraction.

A truck barreling down the road in front of her braked and caught her attention. It was the same one they rode in on. James stuck his head out the window and waved her down.

"Did you pick up the other men?" Her voice barely rose above the airpower and the truck engines.

"Yeah, in the back. Follow us and stick close."

She nodded, waiting for the truck to pull in front of her.

"Are you all right?" Jon finally spoke, his voice soft and trembling.

"I'm fine. You?"

"I will be all right. How bad is Kane? I—I could only hear him screaming."

A lump formed in her throat as she tried to swallow, pushing down the need to have a full breakdown after seeing Kane bloody and passed out.

"He doesn't look good." Her voice barely rose above the sound of the truck.

A hard left sent Jon into the door. She checked her rearview, counting heads and making sure everyone made the turn. The truck in front braked suddenly, causing her to brake fast as well. Two large helos surfaced at the edge of the clearing just a few feet in front of them. She climbed out and grabbed Jon, who could barely walk. Snatching the shirt of one of the Marines, she pulled him to Jon.

"Help him!"

The Marine nodded, basically lifting Jon and carrying him to the copter. She turned back to see Bledsoe strong-arming Kane to the airlift. Kane woke up, and blood seeped through the shirt his brother had put on him. She followed the last of the men, praying everyone was accounted for.

"Mace?"

She shielded her eyes as she approached the helo, looking for him.

"Macy!"

A smile worked its way on her lips. Jasper ran and grabbed her up, carting her back to safety.

"I'm good, Jasper, easy," she groaned.

"No way, I'm not letting you go. I thought I lost you."

"I'm okay, but you're going to do more damage if you don't let go."

He lifted her aboard as the helo rose above the Mexican desert and away from the compound of Luis DeLuca.

She eased away from Jasper and looked around the cabin, finding Kane sitting in the back, his shirt gone. Gasping at the cuts, she watched as the medic applied bandages and pressure to close up the wounds. He finally opened his eyes and caught her gaze. She attempted a smile. He looked away, leaning forward on his knees. She turned back to Jasper, who stared wide-eyed at her.

"It's not as bad as it looks, I just need some rest."

He nodded, his face turning red as he frowned. She fell to her left, holding her side and leaning against Jasper as he gripped her arm, wrapping her hand in his. Her mind faded as the wind rushed around her, and she drifted off.

8

Macy sat up, blinking. She attempted to focus and ignore the pain surging through her body. The room's darkness scared her. She reached around and felt blankets and bed rails. The threat of the prison, torture, or getting killed washed away.

Her breathing picked up, causing pain to shoot through her side. She couldn't get enough oxygen. She searched for the nurse button.

"Macy?" Her brother ran into the room, yelling for help. "Just calm down. We're safe. We made it to Camp Pendleton Hospital in California."

She shook her head, trying to ease her breaths and the pull in her side. A nurse pushed Jasper aside and placed an oxygen mask over her face, giving her relief. Within minutes, her breathing calmed, and she rested back against the bed.

"Keep that mask on for a while. I'll be back later to check your vitals."

Macy nodded at the woman as she left the room.

"I didn't think you'd wake up so soon. The doctor said it might be a while."

"How long was I out?" She looked into her brother's weary face, her breaths morphing into sounds.

"Almost ten hours. The doctor wants to keep you here and let your ribs heal without surgery. You need rest before we can get you home to Virginia."

She leaned back again, lifting her hands to her head and frowned.

"They did a hack job, Mace."

"I know." She closed her eyes for a moment. "I need you to check and see how Jon and Kane are doing."

"Who are they?"

"The two men who helped me when I first woke up. Kane had the bad cuts." She opened her eyes to see another frown. "What?"

"I'm not sure I'll get much information. Everyone is really tight-lipped around here. I'll look into it, but no promises."

She closed her eyes, praying she hadn't been too late, that they would both be all right.

A KNOCK SOUNDED at the door, and Macy jerked awake. Her body felt rested but bruised, pain radiating every time she moved.

"Hey, how is she?"

Macy recognized her father's voice. She turned carefully to focus on him. "Hey, Dad."

The tears in her father's eyes almost did her in.

He leaned forward and gently pulled her to him. "I thought I'd lost you, Macy," he whispered.

His words made her heart pound again.

Stepping back, he wiped his face and sat down next to her on the bed. "You gave us a scare."

"Yeah, me too." She kept her breaths shallow so she wouldn't need the mask again.

Jasper sat in a chair, watching. The black circles around his eyes and face made him look as though he hadn't slept in weeks.

"How long has it been?"

"Six days," Jasper mumbled.

Gripping her side, she sat up, leaning to get into his line of sight. "It wasn't your fault, Jas. The bird moved, and I decided to take a shot. You couldn't hold me when I wasn't cooperating."

"Don't do that."

Her emotions surged. "Jasper Dale Packer, I can't get better if you spend the rest of your life thinking all this is on you. I had just as much a hand in it. I don't blame you, and neither does Dad."

"Son, I know you did all you could."

"But it wasn't enough." Jasper stood, his voice ringing in the room. "I let go, it's all my fault. I felt the helo turn, and I didn't compensate."

"I turned my whole body away from you to fire at the guys below. I turned."

"Why, Macy?"

"Maybe I didn't want you to get shot down, Jasper!" Her voice left her as she closed her eyes and steadied her breathing again. "I didn't want to lose anyone else. My entire team had already been taken out. As far as I know, no one else survived besides the senator. I couldn't let them take you too."

Tears welled in her eyes. "They had that launcher aimed right at you, and the pilot needed time to disengage. If you want to be mad, be mad at me for turning."

Her brother stood next to her, his eyes red with streaks down his face. He took her hand and squeezed her fingers.

Macy's father took both their hands. "Lord, thank You for the protection over Macy as she survived whatever it was that surrounded her. Thank You for Your continued protection and bringing both Macy and Jasper home to me. Please heal them both, inside and out. Amen."

"Did you find any information?" She gently tugged on Jasper's hand.

"No. No one will tell me anything."

"Find Lieutenant James. Maybe he'll talk to me."

Jasper shook his head. "Oh no, that guy has a rep. Plus, he doesn't like me very much."

"I'll talk to him. What do you need?" Her father asked.

She grinned up at her dad, realizing her face seemed to be working again. "Hey, is my cheek still swelled up?"

"No, all the swelling is gone, just some bruises." Jasper swallowed hard and shifted to sit down next to her, still gripping her hand.

"I'm trying to find out if two of the men are okay. The ones who helped me when I first woke up there."

"Speaking of there, are you going to tell me what happened?" Her father looked her over. A deep frown etched on his face.

"No, I'm not."

He sighed.

"Their names are Jon and Kane. They took care of me. They were both in bad shape when we left, and I just want to check on them. Jasper says no one is giving anything up."

"I'll make it work. I can play the poor father routine." He winked

She chuckled. Thank goodness one of them was in a good mood.

Her father left the room, and she rolled over with a grimace to face Jasper. "Tell me what to do to fix this. I don't want you mad. I need some positive attitudes around me—at least until my hair grows back."

Jasper grunted, and she pulled on his hand. "I need you to tell me."

"Tell you what?"

He stood with his arms crossed, staring down at her.

"No, I'm not telling you all that. It'll make things worse, and you'll act like everything is your fault."

"So, it was bad."

She frowned. "I had Jon and Kane to talk to. That's why I need to see if they're okay."

"You have to talk to someone about all this, Mace."

"No one did anything. Not like that." She sighed. "But maybe I will after I get out of the hospital."

A knock at the door got her hopes up. She sat up with a smile. The door opened to reveal Zander, her boss. She leaned back, feeling her smile fade.

"Well, it looks like I came at the wrong time. Expecting company?"

"Just hopeful. Sorry. It's not that I'm not glad to see you."

"I understand. Been a rough week." He placed a vase of flowers on the bedside table. "It's good to see you, Macy. We've all been worried sick, praying for you."

"Any other survivors from protection detail?"

He shook his head as he sat down next to her on the bed. "Sorry, Mace. There were two that made it to the hospital, but with their injuries, they didn't pull through. This whole operation went sideways fast, and I'm still grasping at straws trying to figure out what went wrong."

She shook her head, wiping the tears as the voices from that attack echoed in her mind. They were all gone, all of them. Men she'd worked with for years had been cut down doing their job. It was a risk they all knew could happen, but now, she was the only one left.

"Macy?"

Sniffing, she dried her face. "Someone leaked the information."

His brows furrowed.

She blew out a huff. "Look, Zander, they were waiting. They knew exactly where we'd be. There's no way they walked around with a rocket launcher just hoping to find the building we would be taking off from. Someone leaked it, and I'm surprised the senator even made it out."

His eyes dimmed.

"What do you know, Zander? You're holding back."

"I don't know, not really. I'm just finding out a few pieces here and there. I promise, you'll be the first to know when I put it together."

She frowned, but sat back in the bed, hating the fact her boss felt the need to hold out on her.

"If you need anything, let me know." He stood and shoved his hands into his pockets.

"Actually, I need some information."

His eyebrows shot up. "On who, exactly?"

"Kane Bledsoe and a man named Jon we brought back. I've been trying to find out if they're okay and where they are. They helped me, and I want to see them."

Biting her lip, she held her breath. *God, please let them be okay.*

Zander's eyes shifted between her and Jasper.

"Jasper, go see if Dad needs anything."

"Yep."

She never lost eye contact with Zander as Jasper left the room. Fortunately, her brother was well versed in the politics of information.

"Okay, but you didn't hear this from me."

She simply nodded.

"They're both fine, besides some malnourishment and dehydration issues. Bledsoe has some major cuts to his body, and Jon has some other issues, but they'll make full recoveries."

She let out the breath she'd been holding. "Okay, so can I see them?"

"Nope. Well above your pay grade."

"Seriously? Mine is as high as yours, and you know what's going on."

He shrugged. "Not really, just the rumors."

"Tell me the rumors."

Zander shook his head. "No, not going there. Bledsoe is well above both our pay grades. He isn't allowed to see anyone except his brother. His parents aren't even allowed in. He can talk to them on the phone with a supervisor in the room. It's all very hush-hush."

"But I want to see him." She strained as she sat up, hoping he understood how emphatic she felt about the situation.

"You can't. His brother is here. Maybe we can make that work."

She sat back with a grunt. Maybe she could find him on her own. In reality, she knew she was still too weak.

"Fine. Send his brother."

"I'll do my best."

"You haven't mentioned Jon."

"No, I haven't."

She frowned at Zander, who gave her a wave as he left. Her heart pounded at the memory of Kane, his body broken and bleeding in the back of the helo. And he wouldn't even look at her. The pain he must've been in, the fear.

The door opened again, and her father ushered in Lieutenant James.

"Well, well, if it isn't Macy Packer, back from the dead. At least your face seems better, more lifelike anyway."

She frowned.

Her dad pushed between them, his arms crossed and red pushing up his neck.

"Dad, give us a minute."

"I don't like him."

"Apparently, not too many people do. It's fine."

Her father glanced her way before he turned for the door, huffing as he walked out.

"What?" James looked confused. "I didn't say anything you wouldn't say."

"But I wouldn't say it in front of a parent."

"Yeah, I guess so." His face flushed. He paced the room a moment before facing her again. "What is it you want? Your dad can sure play the sympathy card."

She grinned, and a chuckle came out. "Yeah, he's good at that, the whole guilt thing. Actually, I want some information."

He shook his head.

"You don't even know what I'm going to ask."

"It's about Bledsoe or the other guy, and I'm not at liberty to discuss it."

"I don't want to discuss his job. I want to see him and see if he's okay. If it weren't for him and Jon, I'm not sure I would've made it."

"I understand, but my hands are tied."

She scoffed. "Really? Someone like you has tied hands? I don't believe it for a second. I'm sure you've bent a rule or two."

James shrugged. "Maybe, but nothing I'm confessing to." He winked.

She rolled her eyes.

"It's more than just rule-bending, Macy. This is national security territory. I can't talk about it, and neither can he."

"I just said I didn't want to talk about the job. So, what? Bledsoe has no contact with the outside world?"

"He does, but most people don't know his job."

"Well, what now?" She sighed and leaned back. "I never get to speak to either one?"

"Maybe, but it's not my decision or Bledsoe's."

"So, it's Jon, huh?"

"See you on the outside, Macy." James just grinned, shrugged his shoulders, and left the room.

She leaned back and attempted to relax, but the inability to talk to either man ate at her.

Jasper came back in with a tray. "The doctor has allowed you to eat." He set it on the bedside table and scooted it over to her.

"Great," she murmured.

"Sorry, Mace, I know you really wanted to see them."

"Yeah."

What could be so important that she couldn't speak to either one? What would involve national security, as James mentioned?

She let out a breath, and she stared at the practically empty tray containing broth, gelatin, and milk. Man, she was ready to get out of here.

9

K ane leaned back in his bed and groaned when his leg cramped up again. The IV pole held so many bags, he didn't know which was which, but one helped with the muscle pain. The cramp subsided, and he closed his eyes.

Pack had made it out and, in return, had rescued them. She'd done what he'd been unable to do for weeks—six weeks, he'd discovered.

With a grimace, he tried to shift in this bed, his body worn down and aching.

Pack's face came to mind, and he sighed. Those bright blue eyes of hers, that's what he saw when he closed his. Was she okay? How badly had she been hurt?

His anger surged at the thought of what that guard did before she escaped. But she'd been moving well, although he knew from experience that adrenaline could push a body beyond its limits.

"Hey."

Opening his eyes, he found his brother Collin standing at the foot of his bed. "Yeah?"

"Um, a guy came by, said a woman wanted to see you."

He furrowed his brows.

"I think it's that woman who escaped."

"She's okay?"

Collin shrugged. "I guess. But they said you couldn't go to see her, and she can't come in here. Not with you on lockdown and all."

He groaned as he pushed up in bed. "Give me something to write on, a pen too."

With his service to Jon and Jon's status, everything about this situation had become classified, and he wouldn't be able to explain that.

Leaning his head back, Jon's words about the story of Saul flowed through his mind. The story seemed so unreal, impossible, and he wondered why Pack had wanted Jon to explain it to him.

"Here."

He took the offered paper and tried to clear his mind enough to write a few words, wondering if he would ever get a chance to thank her in person for what she sacrificed to save him.

THE NEXT DAY, Macy woke as sunlight flooded her room, casting shadows all around her. She'd convinced Jasper and her father to go to a hotel, needing time to herself. Her internalization of what happened needed to stop, but she didn't want to talk about it with anyone. Not yet.

She stared out the window. The hum of the nurses in the hallway and the different machines filled the silence.

What was her life about to become? Between the briefings, the paperwork, and the mandatory psych and gun evaluations, she would be wading through the memory of this mess for the foreseeable future.

She always tried to keep an upbeat mentality. After all, with the trials she experienced growing up, she knew God used trials to give her a stronger faith.

But this time, she struggled to stay positive. Between her missing hair, the pain that moved through her body, and the nightmares that kept her awake, she couldn't find anything to cling to that could give her peace.

God, why did this happen?

A soft knock on her door surprised her. She sat up.

"Ms. Packer?" Kane's brother stood in the doorway, nervously clenching something in his hand.

"Hey, I'm so glad you could come by."

"It's not too early?"

"No, really, I've been up." She motioned for him to come inside, grabbed the hat the nurse had left for her, and slipped it on her head. "I've been worried about your brother and Jon, but no one will tell me anything."

"Yeah, it's a security disaster." He nervously shifted from one leg to the other.

"Do you want to sit?"

"No, no, I ... your boss asked me to stop by because you wanted to speak with Kane."

"Is he doing okay? I mean, his cuts—" She stopped and bit her lip.

Kane's brother only nodded and pursed his lips. "Yeah, he's okay. They stitched him up, and he's been able to sleep." He took a deep breath and finally looked her in the eye. He had the same color eyes as Kane, but they weren't nearly as intense.

"Look, I never thanked you for getting out and helping me to find him once we got inside. He said you did it all, you had a plan from the beginning, and if you hadn't shown up, they would've been dead sooner. Seems the head guy became distracted when you arrived, gave them a break."

Her jaw dropped. Everything he said was wrong. She had no plan, and if it weren't for Kane's insistence and her desire to free him and Jon, she might never have allowed her suitor so close or agreed to his plan.

"Anyway, I'm supposed to give you this." He handed her a piece of folded paper. "I didn't read it or anything, but I'm not allowed to stay." He turned to leave.

"Wait, I mean, that's it?"

He paused at the door. "I'm not allowed to talk about it."

"Hey, I don't care about his job. And he lied. If he hadn't pushed, I never would've made it out. I didn't have a plan."

Bledsoe only stood at the door, his lips a thin line across his face, his eyes bloodshot and sunken in from worry and lack of sleep.

"I'll see you around." He left through the door.

Her heart sank.

Unfolding the note, her jaw clenched as she read.

Pack—

I still don't know your real name. I think I heard that guy say Mace? Anyway, I'm not allowed to speak to anyone right now or for the foreseeable future. I'm glad you made it safely and wanted to say thanks for everything. It was more than you know. Been thinking about that Saul guy Jon told me about. It seems unreal, but I think we all just lived through unreal, so maybe I'm the one wrong. You didn't keep your promise, and I wish you had.

Take care-
Kane

She refrained from crumpling the letter up to throw it away. Here she'd been worried to no end about him, and he simply shrugged her off. Fine, she could find a way to discard him too.

Pushing aside the blankets, she slid her feet to the floor, steadying herself before heading to the bathroom. Once inside, she tucked the letter in her bag, then leaned against the sink.

Her body shook, and her world collapsed around her. The sudden loss of someone she knew nothing about rocked her. She didn't understand why it affected her, but she couldn't stop it, either.

She closed the door and sat on the floor, holding her knees and letting her emotions go. Her body ached to hold everything in, but now she let her tears out.

"Macy? You okay?" Jasper asked from the other side of the door.

"No," she voiced through the sobs. "Just give me a minute," she mumbled.

Jasper would have to wait. Her disappointment in herself as well as Kane bubbled up, and she realized, somewhere during those two days, she'd become attached to the man. She cared about him deeply, much more than she wanted to admit. Those green eyes watching her, protecting her, his voice walking her through, and helping her body adjust to the pain.

He made her realize she needed to get out any way possible, something she couldn't have done on her own. But she was done now. No more wishing and hoping to see him again. All she wanted now was to be at home and for life to go back to normal, whatever that would now be.

"You okay?"

Kane opened his eyes, blowing out a breath at the pain. "Yeah. What'd she say? Did you get her name?"

"No name, just Packer on the door. But she seemed pretty worried about you. Are you sure she has a boyfriend?"

"He was on the chopper with her, don't you remember?"

"Sorry, I was trying to keep from getting sick at the sight of your cuts."

He frowned and leaned back in the bed. Pain seared through his skin as the cuts were stitched once again.

"She also said you lied."

"What?" He sat upright, staring at his brother and hating the look of pity on his face.

"I told her what you told me. She said she never had a plan, that if you hadn't pushed, she never would've made it out."

He closed his eyes. Her face was the only thing he saw anymore once his eyes closed. The nightmares always came when he drifted to sleep, but it was her face that let him live through that day. She'd made a deal for him to make it until she returned.

"Did you hear me, Kane?"

"Huh?"

"There wasn't anyone there in the room with her."

"I'm sure he just stepped out."

"Look, man," Collin sat down next to him, rubbing the hair on his head back and forth as if working up the courage to speak. "It's obvious you like her, just talk to her. See if she does have a guy."

"I'm not allowed to talk to anyone but you. Even if it's not her guy, it doesn't matter."

"So, you don't mind if I talk to her, right?" Collin's mouth turned up.

Without thinking, Kane grabbed his brother's wrist.

"See—see right there. You would never do that if you didn't really, really like her."

"Drop it," Kane growled and let go.

"You can't do this again. You know that, right?" Collin stood and stared down at him. "No more secret missions or special protection details at all, man. Not after this. It took us so long to find you. You went from Germany to Mexico, and we had no idea."

"I don't know what I'm going to do. Until Jon and I talk ..."

"Why does Jon get to call the shots? It's your life too."

"It's our life." His voice rose, and he leaned back in the bed to catch his breath. "You weren't there. It was over a month of torture, and we went through it together. He always had my back, and he fixed me up as best he could. I can't undo that bond, Collin. When I signed on, I signed on for life. I told him that. And then, after this—" He let his voice drop, unsure what else to say.

"So, you have no life now? Even if she wants one with you?" Collin's face turned red as he sighed.

"You can't know that. Man, it had to be the worst two days of her life. She probably wants to forget it."

"Then, why try so hard to see you? She didn't even mention Jon. She wanted to see *you*." Collin turned and walked out of the room

His brother's words left Kane with hope in his heart, a very dangerous thing for someone in his predicament. He closed his eyes. Her face appeared, bringing a grin to his lips. The joking voice, the nickname, the smile she had even after her face was so swollen he could barely recognize her. But her eyes, those blue eyes staring back at him through that hole in the wall. They shone brightly, even with her world crashing around her.

Wiping his face, he groaned. Hope would kill him—the hope she and Jon kept talking about. It wasn't for him, and he didn't believe God would look at him and see a man who could be forgiven, a man who could be saved.

His life was in shambles because he allowed it to be, allowed his life to be as reckless as possible. After all, no one else needed him. Jon could have had someone else there to protect him, someone who could have saved him. He had even failed his job.

Straining to reach his water, he pulled the bottle close and drank it all quickly.

Pack couldn't really want him or need him. She needed someone who could protect her, be there for her, and give her everything she ever wanted. He could do none of those things. In fact, he didn't even know how to begin to understand what she needed or wanted. He wished he did, wished he could learn about her, get to know her better.

The image of the guy wrapping his arms around her, crying,

and holding her made his gut churn. She was crying too, as he carried her to the helo. That's who she needed. He obviously had a great job and life for her to share. It was for the best. He wanted her to have the best life could offer, and he didn't really know what that was. But he was certain it wasn't with him.

10

After four weeks at his parents' home in Virginia and doing rehab, Kane gained a little weight. The scale still read thirty pounds less than before their imprisonment. So, he worked hard, trying to reshape his body and find a way back from the time he spent in prison.

But during the healing process, he found himself anxious and bitter. Something nagged at him, something more than the fact he survived such a horrific experience—something he couldn't quite explain.

Kane dug through his bag. He pulled on some shorts and frowned at the mess sitting in front of him on his bed. He'd moved in with Collin yesterday, needing some space and a break from the constant hovering of his parents. Collin's apartment was next to a park that ran the length of the river. The park had trails he could run and outdoor equipment he could use instead of going to a gym.

"Hey, Kane?"

He quickly pulled a T-shirt over his head before Collin entered. For the rest of his life, he would never be able to have his shirt off around anyone. The scars were too gruesome, and he didn't want to deal with the questions. And even though Collin knew the answers, he'd still stare, his eyes widening as he moved over each cut.

Kane realized his brother only saw his blood-stained body that day and figured there would be no way that picture would ever leave his mind.

"Yeah?"

Collin stuck his head through the door. "Your phone is going off in the living room."

"Oh, yeah."

"Did you sleep at all last night?"

"Some." Sleep still evaded him. He would get a few hours from sheer exhaustion, but then after that, a nightmare would rouse him, and he wouldn't be able to go back to sleep.

He rushed to the living room to get to his phone. Collin followed him. Jon's number glowed on the screen.

"Hey, Jon, sorry I missed your call." He went to the window that overlooked the park. It had a great view of the pond and the trails that pushed through the huge protected rec area.

"No problem. How are you doing, Kane?"

"Just fine, living the dream. How are you doin'?"

"Well, I'm not as fool hearty as you. I don't sleep and haven't gained much weight back. But, I am mentally a little better than when we last spoke."

"That's good." His eyes zoned in on a person walking the trail right in front of the apartment building. Something about the way the figure moved looked familiar.

"I wanted to see if you were available tomorrow morning. 10:30? There are a few things I want to discuss with you."

"Sounds good. Will they let me in the front gate?" He chuckled, knowing the security Jon had probably hired.

"I'll let them know you're coming. See you in the morning, Kane."

He ended the call, still focused on the walker who now sat on a bench. From across the street, he couldn't get a good view of her profile. He moved quickly from the window and pulled on his shoes, grabbed a ball cap, and tucked a gun at his waist.

"Where you goin'?"

"For a jog."

"And you need your weapon?"

"Never go anywhere without it." He shoved his phone and keys in his pocket, darted out the balcony doors, and climbed down the fire escape.

He crossed the street, scanning the path for the woman, but she was gone. He picked up his pace to a jog until he saw her back to him. Slowing, he stretched out his arms and followed, keeping his distance.

She settled on a bench where the trails divided, and he crossed the grass to the pathway leading away from her. Finding a set of workout equipment, he went through a routine, glancing up at her every now and then.

The woman kept her head down, holding it with both hands, the actions of someone upset. Frowning, he gave her a moment. She looked up and to her right, revealing the side profile he'd hoped to see. His mouth dropped. It was Pack.

She stood quickly and strode down the path that led back to the parking lot. As she left, he struggled with what to do. How could she be here, in Virginia, at the same park he lived next to?

Pack made her way to the rise in the path before he finally chased after her. It only took a minute for him to climb the rise and see her on the sidewalk in front of the parking lot, her head down.

An SUV caught his eye as it eased through the lot. The window lowered, and the barrel of a rifle came into view.

"Pack!" Yelling the only name he knew her by, he sprinted down the hill.

She looked up at him for only a second. Her eyes followed his gaze. She drew her weapon and fired several rounds at the car. The gun swung toward him as he pulled to a stop in front of her.

Her eyes widened, and her jaw dropped. "Kane?"

He tackled her, covering her body as the sound of the automatic rifle unloading echoed in the serene park. Kane pulled her gun from her hand and fired back, shifting to his knees. Once the attacker had been stopped, he looked down at her.

"Sorry, I ..."

"Sorry for what?" Her curt voice rang as she pushed him off balance, grabbing her weapon back and glared at him.

He watched from his sitting position as she edged to the vehicle to clear it. The sounds of sirens filled the air, and he retreated into the wooded area behind them.

Getting involved in a shooting would be a disaster. The incident in Mexico had at least been contained under a military guise, but here, a public attack where the police were involved would cause all sorts of problems for him and for Jon.

He watched while she waited for the police and then spoke with a man dressed in a suit and tie. She looked over her shoulder every now and then, searching. Even after the police had left, she waited on the bench.

After almost twenty minutes of sitting alone, she made her way back to the area where he hid.

"Okay, I know you're still here. Either come out now or the next time we see each other, I swear you're going to regret it."

He chuckled and stepped out from his hiding place. "You're kinda making me regret it now."

Despite his smile, she only glared back. Arms crossed over her chest, her gaze unnerved him. "Where did you come from?"

"Who was shooting at you?"

"I asked first." Her jaw clenched.

She didn't attempt to close the gap, and neither did he since she seemed pretty upset.

"I happened to see you running, and I wanted to catch up with you." He noticed the flinch, the hard swallow as her face paled.

"Why?"

"Why did I want to catch up with you?"

She only nodded.

"I wanted to see if you were okay. It's been a while."

"Yes, yes, it has." She paused, trying to pull the hat down over her face, but there wasn't much farther it could go. "I'm fine." She spun away from him, her tone icy.

"Hey, who was shooting at you?"

She paused and angled sideways.

His breath caught in his throat. He'd been so focused on seeing her profile that he didn't take inventory of her. With her slim tank top on and leggings, every curve stood out. Breathing out, he forced his gaze back to her eyes, those blue eyes burning into him.

"Not your concern."

"Hey—"

"Look, you can't just appear like this." She turned to fully face him, her arms crossed again.

He'd taken several steps toward her, but she moved farther away.

"What does that mean?" He frowned.

"Figure it out, Kane." She turned to leave again.

He sighed. "I figured you would be more straightforward, Pack."

She paused for a moment before she faced him. Her countenance changed, her bottom lip quivered, and her jaw clenched. Gripping her arms, her face tinged red. She looked up at him.

"Some things you need to figure out on your own. And if you don't, well, that says something too."

He watched her take off for her car. The image of the darkness around her eyes made him frown. It seemed sleep wasn't lost on only him.

Her words rolled around in his head while he jogged back to Collin's apartment. Could she possibly be upset with him? It wasn't like he could just call her up or come visit. She had a boyfriend, and he'd been under a gag order. Besides, he had no idea she'd end up in the same town, the same area where he lived.

Walking up the steps, he made his way into the apartment and headed to his bedroom.

"Hey, I heard sirens earlier, that wasn't you, right? Uh-oh." Collin froze in his doorway. "It was you wasn't it?" Collin's eyes widened as he stared.

"Not really."

"Seriously, man?"

"Look, someone started shooting, and I alerted her."

"Her who?"

He frowned as Collin's smile kicked into gear.

"Is that Packer girl here? What kind of weird coincidence is that?"

"Someone shot at her, Collin. Not exactly a great experience."

Collin grimaced. "Hey, I'm sorry. Was she hurt?"

"No."

"Then, what happened? Did you talk to her?"

"Not really. She didn't look happy to see me." He pushed past his brother with a change of clothes. He needed a shower.

"Did you tell her?"

"Tell her what?" He paused outside the bathroom door.

"That you like her." Collin's big grin made Kane want to punch him, just like when they were kids. But that wasn't happening. It would just give Collin more ammo.

"I don't like her like that. Just let me get a shower."

"Wanna go to lunch?"

"Sure." He smiled at the surprised look on his brother's face and slammed the door.

He let the hot water saturate his body while he leaned against the tile. Who was he kidding? Of course, he liked Pack. In that way. In pretty much every way he could like her. After their chance meeting, however, he wondered if the hope he'd been clinging to ever since his hospital stay was ill-advised.

The image of the shooter made his heart race. She was in trouble again, and this time, he wanted to be the one to help her. But, she didn't seem interested in a truce. Maybe he could find out where she lived.

He turned off the water, toweled dry, and got dressed quickly, then headed to his bedroom to find his shoes. If Jon let him go, he'd have to find another job. Even with a recommendation from Jon, being thirty-four and a recent hostage, a lot of agencies would pass on him.

He glanced at the Bible on his bedside table. After finding it at his parents' home, he looked up everything he could on Saul, who he discovered was also called Paul. It was an interesting story that Pack had Jon tell him. He and Saul did have some similar traits, a man doing what he thought was right, but was completely wrong. That's why Kane had left the military for the private sector.

He'd been wrong for so long and couldn't stand to look at himself if he ever fell back into the lifestyle and job he'd had. But unlike Saul, a conversion seemed unlikely. Jon had tried for a while, unsuccessfully, to talk to him about it. Kane had to admit, the stories he'd read were interesting. Just like he included in the letter he wrote Pack, they'd been through something that seemed unreal.

So much so, the stories he read in the Bible seemed plausible. He picked it up and tossed it on his bed. Kane strapped on his gun and shoved his phone in his pocket, then headed for the living room where Collin waited.

"You sure you want to go eat?"

"Yep, let's go." He followed Collin out, turned to lock the door, and took a deep breath.

Throwing himself back into social life felt impossible with his mind on Pack, but he wanted to move on, needed to move on. And Collin had a lot of friends who could help with that. He blew out another ragged breath. Because that's what he wanted, right? To move on? Hardly.

11

K ane woke early, hoping to get another chance to speak with Pack. He blew out a breath at the impossibility of it all, but considering their chance meeting, he shoved common sense aside and hoped for another coincidence.

He took the steps down the stairwell, crossed the street, and walked through the trails. It was barely eight o'clock on Friday morning, and he really didn't expect her to show up. At the parking lot, he scanned for her car but didn't see it. He jogged toward another lot and stopped mid-stride. Ahead of him on the opposite trail, he saw her walking with her back toward him

Grinning, he ambled behind her as she slowly walked, clad in sweatpants and T-shirt. Kane kept his distance, suddenly feeling nervous and awkward. He still didn't understand what she meant yesterday, and he didn't want her to reject him again.

Torn between his need to protect her and to get on her good side, he knew he should leave her alone. After all, it's not like she seemed interested in his help yesterday. The attack appeared personal, and she could use someone to watch her six, whether she knew it or not. He decided to follow her for her own good, and he picked up his pace.

Keeping his distance, he shadowed her, staying off the trail.

After thirty minutes, she turned and looked around. Her eyes wide, she glared right at his hiding place. She shook her head, turned, and headed to the parking lot.

He waited a moment before climbing the hill and turning toward the lot. Her car was still there, but she was nowhere in sight. Frowning, he circled the trailheads, looking for her, but came up empty.

Fear gripped him. What if someone had grabbed her? Kane dashed back to the parking lot. He found her sitting on a bench, arms crossed over her chest, and not looking happy.

"What're you doing?" Her tone sounded different today, not as harsh as yesterday.

"I—well, I was walking and ..." He rubbed the back of his neck as he approached. "I wasn't sure you'd want to see me." He sat on the bench next to her, calming his breathing, feeling her watching him.

"So, you thought following me through the whole park would be better?"

"I didn't think you'd notice." He chuckled

"I did tell you I had a protection detail, right? I may not be as secretive as you, but I do my job well." Macy wrapped her arms around her knees, hugging them into her chest. She looked away and pulled on her hat.

"I'm sure you do." He leaned forward, unsure what to say now that he'd been caught. "Yesterday—the shooting—I got worried." He looked her way, but she kept her eyes downward. "Would you at least tell me your name now?"

Her jaw flexed. She turned away from him.

"I think I need to go." Her whisper sounded familiar as she started to stand.

He stood too, but something inside him giving him more courage than he thought he had. "I want to see you again, Pack."

Macy froze, her back to him. She clenched and unclenched her hands at her sides.

"I'm sorry I couldn't call you. I was on lockdown, and I

figured, well, I figured you already had enough people helping you out, and maybe you didn't want to see me."

"I asked to see you." She faced him, crossed her arms, and glared at him from under her hat.

Collin was right.

"And then you give me that letter, blowing me off completely."

"What?" Confusion gripped him.

"I can't believe I let myself get so worried about you. I just don't get it. You wouldn't even look at me when we left, and then you write me a letter that ended with you saying you wished I'd kept our deal? What were you thinking?"

She stepped toward him, practically pushing into him. He stared down at her. Gently grabbing her upper arms, he tried to find the words, but she only pulled away.

"Don't do that." The warning was evident in her voice, her blue eyes staring a hole through him.

"Sorry." He pocketed his hands. "Look, I'm sorry about the letter too. I thought, well, I thought I'd written something much better than what I did. I didn't mean to upset you, I just—I was still reeling." He groaned, struggling to keep from reaching out to her again.

"Then, you show up after this long and act like you're worried about me?"

"I am worried about you. You didn't tell me what that shooting was about yesterday."

"Maybe I don't want you involved."

"So, it's something I need to be involved in?"

She frowned. "Don't do that."

"I'm trying to help."

"It's a little too late for trying to help me, Kane. You missed that by about six weeks."

He saw fear flash through her blue eyes and swallowed hard. Apparently, she'd been struggling with what happened, and she'd wanted to see him.

"I'm sorry. Please tell me your name. I don't want to keep calling you Pack."

The decision took longer than he wanted.

She lowered her gaze. "Macy."

Macy. He liked that name. It fit her well. "Macy, I'm sorry. My brother said you probably wanted to see me, but I figured ..." His words fumbled again as he struggled to come up with what he needed to say.

"Just forget about it. I have to go." She turned to leave again.

It hit him like a shot to the gut. His heart pounded in his ears. She walked to her car, and he jogged up and held the door before she could slide inside, effectively blocking her entrance. "I'm sorry, really."

"I said forget about it."

He groaned internally. "I don't want to. I have somewhere to be at ten thirty, and then I want to sit and talk if you have time. If not, I'm pretty much free most of the time, unless my meeting today changes things. There's no way I'm forgetting about any of it, Macy." He swallowed hard at his ramblings.

"So, for the past six weeks, you just what?" She wiped her face, hugged herself, gripping her upper arms. "Dismissed the fact you ignored me when all I wanted was to see if you were okay?"

He stepped in closer, grasping the door with one hand and the car with the other, determined to keep his hands back since her previous reaction proved she was uncomfortable being touched.

"No," he whispered the word.

Her hat couldn't hide the quiver of her chin.

"Macy, I've thought about you every single day. You're the last face I see at night before I go to sleep. When I wake up, I see your face, just like when I looked through that hole as you lay on the ground. I watched you sleep. I watched as you talked to me ..." His voice trailed off as he realized just how deeply he'd been thinking about her, how much she truly meant to him.

Leaning his head alongside hers, he stilled, his hands aching as he kept them back. She cried, sniffing and covering her face with her hands. He stepped forward until she finally leaned into him, his heart pounding as he wrapped first one arm around her, then the other when he was certain she wouldn't pull away.

For the first time in three months, he was able to breathe and relax. Throughout his captivity, the return trip, and constant contact with everyone from his parents to his brother and his doctors—he could never rest, really relax. He held her tight and closed his eyes. Feeling her against him was more than he thought possible.

As he opened his eyes, she was no longer crying, but tensed as she pulled away.

"I have to go," she murmured.

"No. Not until you agree to see me later today."

"I can't."

His stomach dropped. She must still be with her boyfriend.

"I've gone back to work, and I have a late shift. I can't."

"You're already back?"

"It was only two days for me. I'm fine."

"You don't act fine," he whispered.

She wiped her face with her hands and struggled to pull out of his arms, but he wasn't backing down. He'd come this far.

"You need to let me go. I told you to forget it, and—"

"I told you, that's not happening. I need to see you. When do you have some free time?"

"Kane, I can't."

"If you're still with that guy, that's fine. I just need to see you, talk to you."

"What guy?" She looked up, raising her face, pulling away from his arms.

"The guy from the rescue." He frowned and released her.

"Jasper?" She smiled.

He swallowed. Her smile brought back a comfort he'd found in her from the moment he'd first seen her.

"Jasper is my brother. He was the one that tried to pull me out before ..." She bit her lip as he grinned.

"Brother, huh?" He leaned forward, attempting to wrap her up again, but she stopped him, firmly gripping his wrists.

"I'm on another detail, one that, as you've seen, will cause problems for people I'm around."

"I think I can handle it."

"No, I don't want you to. You've handled more than your share of demons. I just can't, okay?" Her jaw clenched as she looked down again, her hat covering her face. She squeezed his wrists. "Are you healed, Kane?" Her voice softened.

The sound was more appealing than he wanted to admit. "Yeah. Stitches came out after a couple of weeks, and I've finally started gaining weight."

"I can tell."

He grinned. A red flush crept up her neck and ears.

"I'm still thirty pounds under."

"Thirty?" She looked up at him with a frown. "That's a lot to make up for."

"Yeah." He turned his wrists so he could hold her arms, feeling the need to grip something before he did something stupid and made her mad. "Macy, how are you, really?"

He took another step forward, and she stiffened again.

He sighed and moved back. "Sorry," he whispered.

"I'm okay. It's okay," she muttered. "This is the closest anyone has been since about two days after we got back. I just can't seem to deal with men being close, I guess."

A lump formed in his throat as his face burned. He didn't know how she got out of that room, but he'd seen the new guard drag her in, and minutes later, after hearing a few sounds from her, she'd snuck out. He cleared his throat.

"Then here, in the morning. Meet me here. What time?"

She squeezed his wrists and shook her head.

He leaned down again, his head next to hers, and whispered, "Please, Macy, I need to see you. I think you need it too." He squeezed her arms, running his thumbs back and forth on her smooth skin.

"Just tomorrow. Then that's it. I've tried to change my schedule since yesterday. I don't want you to get hurt."

"I carry a weapon too. I'm a pretty good shot. In fact, I'd feel better if you met me every morning someplace different until you're done. I don't want them tracking you again."

She shook her head.

He released one hand and pulled out his phone, setting up her name. "Give me your number, and then you can meet me someplace different in the morning."

"I thought you said you'd be working too?"

"Well, if that happens, I need a number I can call you at." He waited, trying his best to give her time to trust him.

After a moment, she rattled off her number.

"I'll text you when I get home, and then you can text me. Don't make me come looking for you. I have contacts, and I'm pretty sure I could find you if necessary." He hoped his voice sounded light-hearted.

She let go, crossed her arms, and leaned her head back. "Don't act like you need to protect me, Kane, I'm good on my own. Don't mess with that line. I'm not your responsibility."

"I won't. Just text me, okay?" He grinned. It usually worked on women.

Macy only frowned. She wasn't so easily charmed.

"Be careful tonight." His smile lessened. He gently gripped her elbow.

Touch wasn't something he usually craved, but after everything that happened and having her in front of him, it took great restraint to keep from wrapping her in another hug. Her flinch was enough to squelch that need too. At least she didn't stiffen like the last time.

"Tell Jon I've been worried about him."

His grin returned as hers surfaced. "What're you talking about?"

"I don't know much, no one will talk, but I do get the impression he's running your show anyway. Tell him I've been praying for him too."

"What? Why are you so kind toward him?"

"I don't know. Maybe you should figure that out." Her smile dropped as she turned to get into the car.

"Macy, don't. I was just ..."

"It's almost ten. You have a meeting, and I have to go."

He glanced at the time on his phone and frowned. "If you gave me a wrong number, I'll have Jon find you."

She smiled and started the car. "I guess you'll have to wait and see."

12

Kane texted her while he sat in his car, just to double-check her number. Response bubbles came up for a moment, then disappeared. It took great restraint to keep from calling, but that would push her too much. An emoji smiley face finally appeared. He figured that's all she'd do until she was more comfortable. He put the car in reverse and left the parking lot, pulling out on the highway.

Macy's smile hit him hard as he drove. Those blue eyes made her whole face shine. He didn't miss the dark circles around her eyes and the pale complexion. She needed sleep too. If he had just listened to Collin, maybe he could've found her sooner, and then, he would have been there for her during the past six weeks. Six weeks that he couldn't make up for. Six weeks when she had really needed him.

He blew out a breath and pulled up to the gate, noticing the new equipment Jon had installed. The simple gatehouse had been converted into a guard station, complete with monitors and surveillance systems. Extra cameras around the perimeter were a nice touch too. It all seemed like too much for the meager estate. However, considering the fact Jon had been targeted and kidnapped, Kane understood the response.

After showing his license, he waited several minutes before the guards allowed him entrance. Once in front of the house, another guard with a dog approached. The man led Kane to the side door that entered the sunroom.

"You made it." Jon nodded, a smirk on his face instead of his usual cheery smile.

"Barely. I was afraid they were going to strip search me."

Jon beamed. "You've had a good day. I haven't heard a joke from you in a while, nor seen you smile. Tell me, Kane, what changed your mood?" Jon leaned against the bar that faced the windows, his arms and legs crossed.

"Let's save that for after whatever you wanted to talk about."

As hard as he tried, Kane's smile was etched on. He could ease it, but it wasn't going anywhere.

"I won't forget." Jon's grin got bigger. He sat down in his chair, motioning for Kane to sit as well. "I've been doing a lot of thinking. My time overseas is done. As hard as I've worked, I can't bring myself to go overseas again."

"It's only been a few months since we returned. Give yourself a break."

"I understand, and there is a slim chance I'll change my mind. But for now, I'm done. Which brings me to you."

Kane sat back and studied Jon a moment. He'd worked for the man for five years without incident until their trip to Germany. He knew everything about Jon, his tics, his interests, and what he wouldn't allow.

"If you're ready, I'd like for you to come back to work for me. I don't have any plans for the rest of the year. All the funds and benefits will run without me there. If by the end of the year, I feel up to it, I'll go. But for now, I plan on being here."

Jon Warrick was an intelligent man. CEO of several technology and surveillance companies, his disappearance had created a lot of fear. If he were ever to release what he knew about the United States and their defense systems, the U.S.

would be at the mercy of whoever had the information. He was a bit eccentric, but when a person's brain operated well above everyone else's, a few strange habits were allowed.

"I know that will make the job boring for you, but I'm not going to lie. I feel better knowing you're around. I don't want to push you. We can either hold off completely or go to a three-day work week and move from there."

He seemed under control, but Kane could see fear still lingering. "What's going on? There's something else." He frowned. After five years, Jon should know better than to hide something from him.

Jon leaned forward. "I've received some disturbing threats."

"What? Why didn't you call me?"

"I didn't want you back until you were ready. I've hired more men outside, and I have someone that sorts through my mail now. I don't even read the letters. I've spoken with the police and have hired a PI with a stellar reputation, recommended by several officers. He's looking into the letters now."

"Living like a hermit isn't for you. We tried that, remember? It didn't go well." He frowned, remembering the longest three months of his life.

"I understand. That's why I hired the PI—to put a stop to this. Now, back to you. Whenever you're ready, just let me know. Although you seem better, you still look rough around the edges. Not sleeping, huh?"

He only nodded, looking over Jon's frail form. His friend looked almost the same as the last time they were together.

"Are you speaking with anyone? I have a therapist who comes to see me twice a week."

"Has the doctor been checked out?"

"Yes, by the PI, as well as my force here."

He nodded.

"But what about you?"

"Not there yet."

Jon leaned forward again, watching him. "Kane, you suffered terrible things. You can't function if you don't talk it out. You may have moments of levity, just like whatever put you in a good mood today. But it won't last. I won't push you, just like with my faith, but I need you to know how important it is."

Kane frowned. He sat back in the chair, crossing his arms.

"I've heard you call me the smartest man in the world several times. If I'm so smart, why won't you listen to me?"

"It's not that I won't. I'm just not there. I work it out differently. I get mad. I hit things. I go to the gym. I'm not to the talking stage yet."

"So, tell me, what or who has you in a good mood?"

"When did you become so insightful?"

"I've known you for five years. Don't you think I've picked up a few things about you?"

"Someone wanted me to tell you she's been praying for you."

Jon's eyes widened. "Amazing! She's here? Pack?"

"Her name is Macy" He chuckled. "And yes, she's here."

"How did you track her down?"

"I didn't. I just happened to see her out jogging. I moved in with my brother."

"Oh, by the lake? That's a wonderful area. And you saw her jogging there?" Jon's voice rose.

"Yes." He chuckled again. "Anyway, yesterday morning, I saw her, and after a brief gunfight, she and I spoke for all of two minutes before she left."

Jon's jaw dropped. "A gunfight? She's working already?"

"I don't know if you were aware, but she tried hard to talk to both of us once we made it to the hospital." He rubbed his hand across his chin, badly in need of a shave. "But no one would tell her anything. My brother spoke to her just to let her know I would be okay."

"I'll have to call her. She's an amazing woman. No fear, she had such courage when she spoke to those men."

Once again, fire burned up his neck at the thought of what they did to her.

"So, you spoke this morning too?" Jon grinned again.

"Yes. I made a big mistake, and it seemed she was upset, but I didn't understand."

"What did you do?"

"Well, the man that put her on the helicopter?"

"Yes, her brother."

Kane frowned. "How did you know it was her brother?"

"They share very similar familial traits."

He shook his head. Why hadn't he asked Jon about it sooner? "Yeah, well, I thought he was her boyfriend, so I kept my distance, and apparently she didn't like that I pushed her away. I didn't push, I just didn't—"

"She assumed you didn't want her. You know, as much as I want to believe she would've come back for me, I think the only reason she came back was because of you."

"What? She asked for both of us."

Jon sighed. "Don't do that. You're very good at creating distance. It's one of the things that makes you so good at your job. You can see things from the outside, whereas the rest of us only see things from where we stand.

"But don't do that with her," Jon continued. "It's obvious she wanted your approval when she returned. I saw her face when you turned away in the helicopter. That and whatever else you said or did, hurt her deeply."

"Just lay it all out. Good grief, I don't need to feel any worse." He stood and paced.

"Kane, I'm trying to help. You've told me several times the reason you don't have anyone in your life is because you don't understand women. I'm not claiming to, but I can see this very clearly."

"I wrote her a letter, and my brother gave it to her. I wasn't in my right mind when I wrote it, and whatever I said really ticked her off."

"You'd just been through such a terrible experience, and you tried to write her a letter? What were you thinking?" Jon stood and placed his hands on his hips.

"I wasn't, okay?" His phone chirped, and he pulled it from his pocket to silence it, not even thinking to do it before their meeting. It was one of those things Jon didn't like. "Sorry."

"Who is it?"

"I don't know."

"Check."

He pulled it back out and saw a text from Macy.

I hope I'm not interrupting your meeting with Jon. I just finally decided what I wanted to say. I don't think we should meet until after I'm done. I have two weeks left. Let's just leave it, okay?

He frowned. "It's just something from Macy."

"Oh, you have her number?"

"Yeah." He pocketed the cell phone and looked out the window, watching the guards move in rotation.

"What did she say?"

"She has two more weeks until she's done with her job and doesn't want to meet me until it's over. After yesterday's gunfight, she's afraid I'll get hurt. For some reason, she thinks she has to protect me." The words stung as he said them, leaving a bitter taste in his mouth.

"That's a good thing."

"What?" He spun around and glared at Jon.

Jon shook his head as he shoved his hands in his pockets. "She cares so much for you. She wants to keep you from danger. That's a good thing."

"But she doesn't need to. I can handle myself. She even mentioned me dealing with too much already. I don't want anyone to think that. Including you." He pointed at Jon.

Jon smirked.

"What's so funny?"

"I think you need to see a therapist more than you know."

Kane took a step toward him.

Jon put his hands up in defense. "Look, I've never known you to feel the need to be the most masculine man in the room. You aren't the typical military machine people think of when they see a large, muscled Marine.

"You've never cared what anyone thought of you until our capture. For the record, you're a stronger man than I realized. But I know it's not my admiration you seek."

He frowned and paced the room again, irritated that Jon once again made sense, and he wasn't prepared to be diagnosed.

"This might be a good time to get to know this woman. You can talk to her on the phone and text her. Maybe she can't handle in-person contact right now. We both know how bad she looked after they brought her back."

He heard the tremor in Jon's voice. Facing the window, he let out a breath.

"She said she wasn't doing good with men being close and pulled away every time I tried to touch her arm or hand." Gripping her elbow and holding her arms had been barely enough for him, but it might have been too much for her.

"Then, do this. Don't push her. God has given you a chance here."

"Jon ..." He turned to face him.

"Think about everything that's happened. Do you really think chance had something to do with this? Her being in the same town? The same park you live next to?"

Kane leaned against the wall, shoving his hands in his pockets. He attempted to ignore Jon's glare. As someone who worked the job he did, no. Coincidences didn't exactly fit into his belief system.

"So, take the next two weeks and let her handle it the way she wants."

He nodded. "Yeah, maybe you have a point." He sighed and turned to look out the window again, his mind bouncing between Macy and her job and the danger she could easily be in.

Jon was right, of course, but he felt the need to be there for her—more than just texting and talking. How would he navigate all of this?

13

"I wanted to talk to you about something before you start back." Jon joined him at the window, his meager frame reflected in the glass. "I don't know if you saw what they did ..."

"I saw the tracks, Jon." Kane remembered the needle marks vividly on Jon's arms after the first time they took them back. He also remembered the withdrawals Jon suffered that first night.

"I have to tell you something." Jon cleared his throat. "They always asked for information on you, anything they could use against you. I never gave them anything, but I ..." Jon began to tremble, turned to face him. "I never gave anything up, but I always prayed. I prayed that either God would kill me or take you.

"I hated to feel that way, but soon, I needed whatever they'd given me. I prayed they'd come so I could get another dose. I prayed that when they had you, they'd simply kill you so I wouldn't have to hear you. I—"

Kane held up his hand and pulled Jon gently to the couch by the arm, sat him down, and perched in front of him on the coffee table. "Jon, whatever they gave you made you different. They took your mind from you. Even if you would've given me up and said something to make it harder on me, I wouldn't blame you. *They* did this. It's all on them."

Jon trembled until his whole body shook.

"Tell me you have someone besides a therapist here."

"Y-yes." Jon took a deep breath. "A nurse from a prominent rehab facility is living here. I also have a doctor who comes in several times a week to manage my dosages."

"They're still giving you drugs?" He frowned.

"Not now. They gradually lowered the dosage, and yesterday was the first day to be completely off everything. My mind is finally feeling clear, although, I will admit, I have cravings for foods I don't normally eat."

"Eat whatever you want. You need the weight." He smiled.

Jon's frown eased. "You've been a great friend, Kane."

"You have too. Don't worry about any of this. Don't feel guilty because of me. Promise me."

"I promise."

He stood, eager to move past the subject and went back to the window. "I'll start back, three days a week. I need to see how much I can handle before I go full time. Is my room still available?"

"Of course. The nurse is on the first floor, next to me."

"How much longer will she be here?"

"At least another week. They're monitoring my weight and withdrawals. She's a very competent nurse."

He turned as Jon leaned back on the couch, his body drooping.

"Wednesday through Friday or Thursday through Saturday?"

"It's your choice."

"Jon, just tell me."

Jon had always been more nervous on Friday and Saturday night, mostly because all the events he attended were usually on one of those nights.

"Thursday through Saturday will be fine."

"I can bring my things and move in today."

"No, wait until next week. Take some more time. With Macy now in the picture, perhaps you need to focus on that relationship before coming back to work."

"You shouldn't be worried about my personal life."

"Do you really think you can keep pushing the employer-employee angle after what we've been through?" Jon glared up at him.

Kane shook his head and turned back to the window. Although Jon would always be his boss, they'd survived a life-changing experience, which made them more like brothers than the typical employer-employee relationship. He turned back around. His friend was fading, his eyes drooping.

"Go rest. I'll be here Thursday morning early. Call me if you need anything. Don't hesitate."

"I will."

An armed guard came to Jon's side as soon as Kane closed the door. Outside, he slid into his car and sat behind the wheel for a moment. The conversation about Macy rolled around in his head. He pulled out his phone, wanting to push call. Jon had said not to push Macy and this relationship. But he did want to push, at least a little.

> How about we meet in the morning? Then we can discuss everything.

It's not up for debate.

Kane frowned.

> Okay, then call me when you get off work.

It'll be late. We both know you need sleep.

> What about you?

The stall of texting bubbles at the bottom of the screen proved she wasn't so sure about her answer. He waited for a moment, but after several minutes without a reply, he started the car and headed toward the apartment.

Glancing down at the blank screen on his phone, he frowned and tapped her number to call.

"Hello?" The sound of her voice made him smile.

"Hey, Macy. Wasn't sure you'd pick up."

The pause at the end of the line proved she hadn't screened her call.

"W-why are you calling me?"

"It's lunchtime."

"So?"

"I wondered if you wanted to meet for lunch, a busy, crowded place where no one would notice us."

Another long pause. Had she hung up? A glance at his phone showed the call still active. "Macy?"

"Yeah, I'm here."

Her soft voice carried to him, and he swallowed. She had to have something more going on than what she wanted him to know.

"I just don't think it's a good idea, Kane."

"Then tell me what's going on. I know there's more to your job if you have active shooters out to find you. I'm not real happy about that." Showing concern without crossing the line she'd established was challenging. He heard her sigh, and he gripped the steering wheel tighter.

She cleared her throat. "I have a lot going on since yesterday. Things are complicated. This detail just turned into something else entirely, and I'm struggling to deal with everything. Throwing you in the mix just makes things harder."

"Then maybe you need to talk to your boss. Sounds like this might be too much, too soon." He eased his tone as much as he could with the lump swelling in his throat.

"This is my second assignment. Working has helped me. Although, I did ask to stay away from international assignments for now."

She chuckled, easing the knot forming in his gut.

"Besides, aren't you going back to work?"

"Not yet, Thursday. Don't change the subject."

"How's Jon? I was hoping he'd contact me."

"He's better. I'll pass along your number if you want. I know he wants to talk with you."

"Yeah, that sounds good." Her voice softened again.

"Macy, stop changing the subject." Parking in front of the apartment building, he leaned his head back and closed his eyes. "Don't say we can't meet because you're worried about me. Just give me some other reason besides that. I can't handle that."

"Oh, I can find other reasons, but I don't think you'd like any of them, Kane."

She had a point.

"But what's the real reason? I want to know the real reason."

He huffed and ran his hand through his hair. It needed cut.

"Well, there are too many of those. None of which I'm willing to share. Look, I'm heading out the door, my shift is starting."

"Call me when you get off."

"No, I don't want to risk waking you."

"I don't sleep much anyway, and I'm pretty sure I won't be sleeping at all until you call to tell me you made it through the day." He rested his head in his hand and leaned against the door, wondering if he'd revealed too much. But after six weeks of missing her, the feeling of desperation hit him. He couldn't risk losing her again.

"I'll try. I just can't promise ..." her voice faded for a moment. "You know how when there's a shift change and everything that could go wrong, does?"

"Yeah?"

"I've had a bad feeling all day about it. Something isn't sitting right, and I'm struggling with trusting myself again." She paused.

He heard shuffling through the line.

"Sometimes, I feel like I'm just paranoid."

"It could be. How long have you done protection detail?"

"Almost eight years."

Wow, that was a long career. Although now, he had more questions he wanted to ask. But he took a breath and focused on the topic at hand.

"That's a lot of experience. This isn't new to you, even if the situation is."

"It's not."

"Then trust your gut. If you've lasted this long, it's because you're good. Protection agencies won't keep personnel around who can't do their job. Take the precautions when you get there. Macy, don't second guess anything. Okay? Don't let your boss or anyone else try and convince you that you're just paranoid."

The silence lapsed again, but this time, he heard her car start.

"Macy, I'll make you a deal." He smiled as she chuckled.

"Sure, what's that?"

"You promise me to stick to your guns on this, and I promise not to call you tonight."

"That seems one-sided."

He grinned big, remembering their previous deal. The fact she brought it up, well, that spoke volumes.

"It's not. And it's the only way you're going to keep me from calling before the sun comes up in the morning. Otherwise, I'll be calling you starting at one in the morning."

"Fine, fine. No phone calls. And I'll take precautions."

"What's wrong?" He heard the doubt in her voice.

"It might be too late." She exhaled loudly. "I'll try and call tonight."

"Please be careful." He gripped the steering wheel again, his knuckles turning white as he struggled to keep himself seated and calm.

"Don't worry about me. Bye."

He dropped the phone in the cup holder and leaned into the steering wheel. If she'd been doing this job for eight years and felt her gut churning about something, he was worried. More than worried—he was terrified.

14

Taking the steps two at a time, Kane entered the apartment. After running errands, cleaning and then hitting the gym this afternoon, nothing seemed to divert his thoughts.

He paced around the kitchen. His mind was on overdrive about Macy. A woman he barely knew, but one who meant so much to him. This new friendship brought up issues, and he struggled to understand how to deal with them. If they were merely friends now, how would he cope later on, if they moved beyond friendship? An idea he found himself clinging to, chasing after, and thinking about nonstop since seeing her yesterday.

Kane groaned at the thought and finished off the takeout Collin had picked up. Settling on the couch, he flipped through channels, hoping to find something distracting. It was after six in the evening, and he had nothing left to do but wait for Macy to call him.

"Hey, what was that?" Collin walked over to the couch and stood behind him.

Flipping back a few channels, Kane found a news story breaking with a house blazing in the background. Firetrucks pulled up, and firefighters jumped out. They set up their hoses, attempting to salvage the residence.

"Police cruisers have set up a perimeter," a reporter explained. "The bomb blast was contained to the home of a man named Carlos Santiago. There is no word whether or not the blast was intended for him or was related to the company he works for, Sundance Incorporated."

The news reporter droned on as cameras zoomed in on the fire. Kane stared at the screen, and his mouth dropped when he saw Macy escorting a man from the burning home to an SUV. Her face down, she pulled on a man with a jacket covering his face.

He grabbed his phone, then froze. She obviously had a lot on her plate. Calling her would be a distraction. The short clip ended, and he sat back on the couch. She didn't appear injured, but what he saw had been so quick, it didn't show much.

"You okay?"

"I've got to go." He stood, pulled his keys out of his pocket, headed to the door, and rushed to his car. Since he couldn't call her, maybe he could drive by, just to see if everything was okay.

It wasn't hard to find the fire. The news had already given the approximate area, and the lights and smoke billowing from the house made a beacon. He pulled up a block out and parked. Walking to the perimeter, he glanced around to see if the SUV he'd seen Macy get into was still there. No luck.

News crews jockeyed for position, overwhelming the scene. Police kept the perimeter, and firefighters worked to contain the blaze. A dark sedan pulled through the tape. He moved to the far end of the property, closer to the driveway where fewer officers were watching.

Kane stood, arms crossed, taking in the chaos. Had she known there would be a bomb? If she had, then she could be in danger and probably knew who wanted to kill her employer.

Straining to see through the crowd, he noticed movement around the car. Someone emerged from the sedan, searching the crowd. His eyes focused as her form came into view. Uh-oh. She spotted him. Macy spoke to an officer, who emerged from the group of uniforms and walked up to him.

"Come on." The officer lifted the tape.

Kane ducked under, moving through the throng of officers and firefighters. Someone gripped his arm and pulled him to the side.

He turned to see the back of her head and the cute short haircut she sported, much better than a few months ago.

"What are you doing here?" she hissed and pushed him against the side of the garage, away from everyone.

"It's good to see you're all right."

"Kane," she mumbled, wiping her face with the back of her hand. "You can't be here."

"Look, I saw you on TV. I was simply watching the news, and there you were." He looked her up and down. The slacks and button-up shirt sat nicely on her form, and besides a few cuts, she seemed fine. He gripped her arm gently. "What's so bad about me being here?"

Macy shook her head and pulled away. Then, she grabbed his arm and led him down the side driveway, away from the crowds. He pulled arm away, gripping her hand instead.

She stopped and turned to him. "You have to leave. Someone might recognize you."

"Wait, why would anyone recognize me?" His attention turned to the scene. Was that the reason she'd been so evasive about her job?

"Let's just say there are ties here. I came back to get help from the police. My security detail is busted."

"So, you were right?"

She nodded. "Yeah, but a fat lot of good it did me to be right. I waited too long."

Her eyes were focused everywhere but his. Nervous wouldn't even begin to explain her demeanor. He pushed into her vision and her space, trying to get her focus.

"Tell me how I can help."

"You can't. You need to go—now." She lifted the police tape, urging him through.

He obliged, still gripping her hand. "I'm still expecting a call, Mace."

She released the tape. "Don't wait up." Macy pulled away, ripping her hand from his and keeping her head down.

He frowned as she left, her hands running through her hair. The short cut looked good on her, but she was still obviously dealing with it.

Kane strolled back to the crowd. He lingered on the edge and surveyed the people surrounding the police cruisers. If there were ties, he wanted to know about them. She wouldn't give them up, but maybe he would recognize someone.

His phone rang. Jon. "Hey, Jon."

"Have you seen Macy?"

"Yeah, just a second ago. You see the news too?"

"I did, and I'm worried. She shouldn't be involved in this. It hasn't been long enough for her to recover."

"Wait, what? What is she involved in? She won't tell me anything." He frowned as Jon chuckled.

"She's right. You shouldn't know."

"Just tell me." His voice dropped to a low growl.

"The man she's protecting works for a company associated with the man who held us prisoner."

"What?" His voice dropped, and he leaned over, attempting to catch his breath. "How do you know?"

"I had a phone call earlier this evening about a situation. The man in charge of us was never captured or killed. They never found his body and have been looking for him. She inadvertently ended up in the middle."

"What's his name?" He growled again as Jon sighed.

"Luis DeLuca."

Heat rose through his body as he fisted his empty hand. "Why am I just now hearing about this?"

"Because it's not your job. If I'd told you when I found out, you would've found a way into the situation before you were able. I don't think you're ready now, but they aren't looking for help now."

"Oh, yes, they are. Macy just told me her team has been scrapped. She needs some officers to help in protection detail."

"No, Kane. I won't help you do this."

"Don't you want the man responsible for what happened to us to be punished?" He did his best to keep his voice down, but a few turned heads, prompting him to move toward his car.

"The man responsible has already been captured. Two weeks ago, in Argentina. His name is Derek Lundvall, and he is currently serving several life sentences in a Brazilian jail. He was the man who planned our capture and sent us to DeLuca."

Slamming his car door, he sat behind the wheel, too upset to think. "But DeLuca ..."

"He isn't our concern. My discussion earlier was with the people in charge, and I have full trust that by using Santiago as bait, they will lure DeLuca out of hiding."

"What if it goes wrong? What if they get to her again? You have to call them and get me on board." His heart pounded in his ears, nausea building at the thought.

"Listen to me. This connection was made only three days ago. From what I've been told, she just found out yesterday—after that gunfight you mentioned. The facts are, another agency is coming into play and will take over the whole operation.

"A lot of people want DeLuca's head. We weren't the only ones affected by his work. It seems he's been in business for years, and because of Macy, they now have a name, a face, and several other nuances that she was able to construct when she gave her report. She'll be pulled out."

He reminded himself to breathe while the words sank in. She needed to be as far away as possible. If DeLuca discovered her involvement ... Kane shuddered to think about what would happen.

"Are you certain she'll be pulled?"

"That's the information I received."

"Why did they call you?"

"Let's just say I have a vested interest in his capture, and several people have been made aware." Jon's chuckled.

The chuckle made Kane smile. Jon had more connections and money than he knew what to do with, and yet, he never used either. He said using people as puppets for personal gain proved a person lacked a certain moral fiber. But now, considering what he'd gone through, it seemed Jon was willing to take the help and information offered.

"If I felt you could do a better job, I would've put you in the middle of the search when I found out. But the truth is, the men and women they have are excellent at what they're trained to do. I'd be lying if I said I didn't want you back here for my protection as well, though. As long as DeLuca is free, I have a shroud covering me. I can't trust my own eyes."

Kane exhaled, closing his eyes, attempting to calm his body. "You know, she'll assume one of us got her kicked off."

"I came to the same conclusion."

"She said I could give you her number, that she'd like to talk with you."

"Maybe after she calms down. Perhaps in a couple of days."

Kane scoffed. "So, you're going to let me handle all of this myself?"

"Yes. Consider it part of the job."

"You realize I might not be able to hold her off?" Kane chuckled. A woman scorned wasn't something he wanted to deal with. But with Macy, he would take just about anything she dished out.

"I understand. If you can't calm her, bring her here. Call me first, but bring her here."

"Sounds like a plan."

"Oh, and Kane. Please don't tell her what happened."

"I wouldn't tell anyone what they did. That's your story, not mine."

"Thanks."

The call ended, and he headed for Collin's apartment. Knowing Macy would be safe and away from DeLuca gave him a sense of peace. At least he didn't have to worry anymore tonight about her safety.

Driving back to Jon's home, Kane realized how detached he'd become from his own life. Five years had passed since he'd lived in his own place. To work for Jon, he'd moved into in the upstairs suite to provide around-the-clock protection.

But, at the time, it had only been him and two others, one for the gate and one for the nighttime hours. Now that Jon had an entire force working to protect him, did he still need to live with Jon full time? Kane needed his own space and wanted his own home. That would be a discussion for after he went back full time.

Collin was sitting at the bar when he came in.

"So, what made you take off?"

"Just checking on something."

"That's it? You don't plan to tell me what's going on?"

He shrugged. "Nothing I can talk about."

"Fine. I'm going out tonight. A group is headed to the new club on Tenth."

"Again? Do you go out every night when you're home?" He frowned.

Collin chuckled. "I'll try to be quiet when I come in."

"I'll be fine." He tossed his keys on the bar and headed for his room.

Within minutes, he heard Collin leave. He made his way back to the kitchen for a snack and turned on the TV. He sank into the comfort of the leather couch, remote in hand. Might as well make the best of the evening. With the news he'd just received and Macy on his mind, he didn't see himself falling asleep tonight.

15

Banging brought Kane out of his stupor. He stood, unlatched the lock, and swung the door open to find Macy glaring at him.

"What are—?"

"Don't. Don't say a word." She pushed past him.

"How?"

"I said, quiet." Her voice trembled, but she had no problems projecting. "Did you do it?"

"Do what?" He closed the door and latched it.

"Why are you acting like you don't know? You're a terrible liar."

"Look, I found out some things after Jon called me, after I spoke with you."

She met his gaze, but he could barely see her blue eyes in the dark apartment. The TV was the only light, casting shadows as it dimmed then brightened.

"Was it Jon, then?"

"What do you think he did?" He shoved his hands in his pockets.

She stood feet from him, practically seething. "Got me kicked off! That was my job, my decision. They didn't even ask

—they just said I was done, and that was it. Even my boss didn't have an answer. He said it came from somewhere higher than he knew."

"From what Jon told me, it had nothing to do with you, him, or me." He softened his voice, hoping to calm her. "He was simply informed about the situation. Apparently, several people who know him understood he wanted to be kept in the loop. He received a call. It wasn't his decision."

"So, people just tell him stuff? National security stuff? Just like that?" She approached him this time.

He could finally see her face. She must have come straight here after being dropped from the case. But how did she know where he lived?

"Yes. And I'm not allowed to tell you why or what he does or anything. But, he did say he wanted to see you, maybe after you calm down."

He smiled, but she only turned and walked away.

"How did you know where I live?"

"What?" She turned, then paced, resting her elbow on her arm while she fingered her bottom lip.

"How did you know where I live? No one knows. It's only under my brother's name."

"Yeah, so?" She shrugged and continued to pace.

Taking a chance, he came up behind her and blocked her path as she turned. "Macy ... How did you know?"

She narrowed her eyes and paused, keeping her distance from him. "I got the address from a friend and considered writing you a letter. I figured your brother would be able to get it to you." She cut past him toward the door and gripped the knob.

"Hey, wait." He pushed a shoulder against the door. "While you're here, let's talk."

"I almost got blown up today, and then I got removed from my detail. I'm not in the mood to talk."

"So, you just wanted someone to yell at?" He smiled down at her.

"Well, it seemed logical. I figured you recognized someone and decided to stick your nose in."

"I have a feeling you're trying to make me mad." He frowned.

She avoided eye contact once again. "Look, I believe you, okay? I'd like to go home now."

She waited, but he didn't move.

"Would you feel better going to the park to talk?"

"It's almost two in the morning."

"So?"

She finally looked up at him with red-rimmed weary eyes. Noting the cuts across her cheeks and forehead, he frowned as he gently fingered her cheek.

"Did you get checked out?"

"I'm fine." She stepped back.

He sighed and slid his hand in his pocket, leaning back into the door. Her arms were crossed, and judging by the weariness of her shoulders, she needed rest.

"How about I drive you home?"

"No, I can drive. *If* you'll get out of the way." Her hands moved to her hips.

"Okay, I'll follow you."

"Why?"

"I just want to make sure you get there all right."

"Kane, stop." She frowned. "You're acting like I need a babysitter or someone to hold my hand. I'm good."

"You don't get it, do you?" He licked his lips, ready to spill his guts when fear gripped him again.

The fear of her walking away, even after he told her how much he cared for her and worried about her, held him back. Just like the first time he saw her in the park. Shaking his head, he grabbed the knob and opened the door for her.

She blinked and looked him over before stepping toward the opening.

"Since you don't have plans tomorrow, how about lunch?" He

moved into the open doorway before she could run away from him.

"Why would you want to do that? Don't you see? I'm—I'm a mess." She ducked her head and darted past him to the stairwell, wiping her face as she hurried off.

He closed his door and took off toward the balcony, taking the fire escape. He reached the ground as she walked up to her car.

"Macy." He rounded the car.

She spun on her heels, her hands fisted in front of her.

"I didn't mean to scare you. You just took off, and I wanted to talk to you."

She huffed and lowered her hands. "Just stop, okay?"

"Not happening." He moved close but kept his hands in his pockets. "Macy, I'm not going anywhere, and you're not going to push me away. I know you want to, but I'll still be here when the dust settles. What you don't understand is that I *want* to help you. It's not because I don't think you can handle it, but because I want to be here for you.

"At the hospital, I was stupid and didn't listen. Collin told me you wanted to see me, but I didn't think he understood. The worst two days of your life, and you wanted to see me? A reminder of those two days? I figured he didn't get it." Kane cleared his throat, attempting to rein in his ramblings.

He tugged on her sleeve at the elbow. "Macy, you got me through that last day." He leaned against the car and took a breath. "I knew it was the last day. Whatever information they wanted from Jon, I told him only to give it if I was dead. They knew he was hanging on to it because of me."

Kane cleared his throat again. Her fingers wrapped gently around his forearm. He finally caught her intense gaze.

"Those cuts weren't new. They opened them up every so often. But, they were more intent that time, and I think they were hoping I would pass out, make Jon think I was dead." He nervously chuckled as her jaw clenched. "Or maybe let me just bleed out to get what they needed."

"You don't have to tell me."

"Yes, I do." He narrowed his eyes as he moved closer, wiped the tears from her cheek with his free hand, then gripped her other arm. "I saw your face, through that hole in the wall telling me to wait, to hang on until you got back. I saw you leave." His grip tightened, his face burned.

He looked away for a minute. "I saw that guard take you. I tried to unlock the latch, but the nail was too big. Nothing worked, I heard you a few times, but I couldn't protect you."

He swallowed as she squeezed his arms, his gaze jumping back to hers.

"When you got out, I knew, I knew you would get help, and all I had to do was wait, just like you asked me to."

She leaned toward him, her eyes focused on his.

"Then, I saw you with your brother, I guess." He felt his face heat. "I didn't know, but I figured I'd better distance myself." Looking down at her, he swallowed, moving his hands to her waist. "I really messed it all up, didn't I?"

Her gaze shifted downward, and he smiled. When his lips brushed hers, he felt her stiffen. He hovered, just above her face.

"I'm sorry, I thought you wanted—"

"It's okay. I, I didn't think I would."

She closed her eyes, then pulled him in, her arms wrapping around his neck. He held her while her body trembled, hoping the tremors weren't somehow because of him.

"Tell me what's wrong," he whispered.

"I don't know. I told you, I'm a mess." She sighed and squeezed his neck tighter.

"Are you talking with anyone?"

"Not yet."

He wanted so badly to carry her up to the apartment and settle her on the couch, wrap her in his arms. But based on all her reactions, she wouldn't want that.

"I should go."

"You want me to drive you home?"

"No, it's okay." She let go, sliding her hands from his chest slowly to his waist.

He stiffened.

"I'm sorry, you okay?" Her eyes filled with concern.

"I'm good." He leaned down and kissed her forehead. "Better than I've been in a long time." He hugged her close, content to stand there and hold her all night if she'd let him. "I am going to follow you home, though."

She tensed, but he kept his grip.

"Just let me, it'll help me to sleep." Who was he kidding? There was nothing that could help him sleep tonight.

She pulled away.

He frowned, still gripping her arms.

"I don't want ... I mean, I don't want you to think you owe me anything."

"What?" His voice must have sounded sterner than he intended based on the flinch and her furrowed brow. "Macy, this isn't because I feel like I owe you, it's because I—" He swallowed and decided to sidestep the feelings that overwhelmed him. "It's because I care a great deal about you.

"You gave me hope, you made me see things I've never considered before, and I'd be crazy to walk away from a beautiful, strong woman like you."

He smiled, but she frowned.

"What now?"

"Nothing." She reached to open her car door.

He stepped in front of her again and received a deep sigh for his efforts.

"Now look, I don't give compliments often, so when I do, you should know this—I never lie." Threading his fingers through hers, he pulled her close.

Her eyes stayed focused on his chest.

"Macy, I thought you were beautiful, inside and out, from

the moment I saw you." He kissed her forehead again, then leaned down to the side of her face. "The haircut just proved how strong you are, how amazing you are. Please believe me."

This time her body didn't stiffen or flinch when he leaned down, kissing her cheek. Macy turned into him, and her eyes met his, offering another kiss. He took it, holding back as much as he could. She gripped his hands tightly and pushed into him. Then, she pulled away just as quickly, leaving him to catch his breath. He smiled, seeing her catch her breath too. Her brows knit together.

"Is something wrong?"

She frowned. "I don't understand what was different, and I —" She released his hands and covered her face. "I just don't know what's wrong with me."

"Nothing. Based on that? Nothing is wrong."

He grinned big. She sighed, releasing his hands and giving him a smirk.

"Kane." She bit back a smile.

He moved in again, clutching her shoulders. "I like to see you smile. It makes my day."

She rubbed her hands through her short hair.

"It looks really good on you, you know."

"I still can't get used to it." She frowned. "My hair was all the way down my back, and I—it's been hard for me to adjust."

He stepped in and hugged her. "One day, you'll wake up, and it will be long again, and everything else will fade away."

"You think that'll happen to you?" Her soft voice made him smile.

"Nah, I'll have to carry my scars around. I don't have much of a choice."

"Yes, you do." She leaned back to look up at him, her baby blue eyes shining bright.

He grinned. "And what do you suggest?"

"You said you had considered things you wouldn't normally

consider. Were you talking about faith?" She raised her eyebrows.

"I, well, I have looked into some of it. I've been reading, but I haven't changed my mind."

She smiled. "You will."

"And what makes you so sure?" His gaze dropped from her eyes and focused on her lips, lips he wanted to kiss.

"I think you need God a lot more than you're willing to admit right now, but you think He can't help."

"Macy?"

"Yes?"

"Of all the things I'm thinking right now, needing God isn't one of them."

"It should be Kane." She caught his chin to get his attention. His gaze found hers.

"Dealing with what you've been through, I have no doubts how strong you are, physically and mentally. But to move on, to be able to allow others in, you'll need a power greater than yourself." She leaned her head into him, sliding her hands around his sides to his back and squeezing him tight.

He closed his eyes and held her. She quickly shut him down, but for him, this was more comfort than he'd ever known.

"I'm going home."

"I'm following you."

She only nodded and let go. He opened her door for her and jogged to his car. As he pulled out of the lot, he smiled while she waited for him.

The ten-minute drive felt like an hour. The need for her in his arms ate into him, even though he'd just held her, just kissed her. All this seemed too much, and suddenly, he realized he felt more and more for this amazing woman.

They pulled into a residential area, and immediately, police lights caught his attention. Now what?

16

Macy pulled to the side of the road in front of a partially standing, smoldering building. Parking behind her, Kane got out and jogged to her side.

She approached an officer standing at the scene. "What happened?"

"Do you live here, ma'am?"

"Yes. I mean, I did." Her eyes widened as she observed her decimated home.

"We responded to a call a few hours ago. Seems some sort of blast took out four townhomes."

Her jaw dropped. "Was anyone hurt?"

"No. The bomb was planted in an empty home, and only one of the tenants next to it was here. She escaped with minor injuries."

"Bomb?" She covered her mouth.

Kane placed his hand on her back, steadying her.

"Ma'am, what building did you live in?"

"401."

"I'll need your information. The officer in charge tried to contact you, but the line was out of order."

Nodding, she clenched her hands together. "There's a reason for that."

She wrote down her cell number and name, explaining that with her job, she rarely gave out any personal information.

"I'll have the officer in charge call you in the morning to discuss what happened."

She nodded and walked back to the car, Kane's hand still on her back. Macy leaned into him.

"Oh no, my dad!" Yanking her cell phone free, she punched in the number. "Dad? I need you to do something for me." She leaned against the hood of the car, her face pale.

"Just listen, pack a bag. I'm calling Jasper, and he'll come get you. Go to a hotel for a few days, please, just listen. Go to a hotel, and I'll call you in the morning when I figure everything out."

He gripped her elbow as she nodded into the phone.

"Yes, I'm all right." She sighed. "No, I'm not alone, just please get ready." She hung up and dialed again. "Jasper? Get up, get a bag packed, and go get dad. You two need a hotel for a few days."

She straightened, her eyes closed, tears streaked down her face. "I understand how early it is. Please, just go now. I'll call in the morning when I get some answers."

A tremor ran through her as Macy ended the call. Kane pulled her in. She clutched his sides while he rubbed her back, holding her close as she cried.

Once she stopped shaking, he spoke quietly. "You need a hotel too."

"Yeah." Wiping her face, she pushed away and started for her car. "I'll talk to you later."

"Oh no, I'm going with you."

She ignored him, got in her car, and started it. He jogged to his car, pulling away quickly to catch up to her.

He followed her into the hotel parking lot. She grabbed two bags from the trunk, which he took from her. Then, he followed her into the lobby and up the elevator. Once inside the room, she sat on the edge of the bed, staring into nothing.

"Hey, lay down. You need to rest. Your dad and brother will be fine."

His breath hitched in his throat when she looked up, her tear-stained face and red-rimmed eyes took his breath away. All he wanted was to fix everything, take away this day. She didn't deserve any more pain in her life.

Macy set her gun and phone on the nightstand, rolled into the bed, and closed her eyes. He moved her bags out of the way, latched the door, and scooted a chair in front of it. Pulling down an extra blanket from the closet, he covered her already sleeping body, frowning at the cut on her forehead.

Situating himself at the door, he watched her sleep.

Would her belief in God protect her?

It seemed unreal, her entire life taken away again. Would she still have the same faith? Was God responsible for this?

He thought back to the stories about Paul, who he had been, and who he became. Paul had obviously been a hard man, determined to destroy anyone who didn't believe what he did. Then, to admit his wrongdoing to people who knew him best? It seemed an impossible feat.

From what he read, Paul had been tortured for his new-found faith, whipped and jailed, beaten several times. But, he kept believing and writing about Jesus. Kane had never had that much conviction about anything.

Leaning his head back, he thought of Jon's stories from the Bible and how people accomplished great things because of their faith. Could a person do more simply because of a God they believed in?

Actions always brought consequences. He understood cause and effect. But, all in all, were people in total control over what they did and who they became? Or did God help his believers do more, accomplish more in their lives?

His gaze once again fell on Macy, and his heart ached. Her home destroyed, everything she owned taken from her. She'd been removed from her position, one where she'd just saved a man from a bomb blast. She feared for her family. And now, she must be wondering how to fix everything, how to rebuild her life again.

When she mentioned being back at work, she simply blew off the two days she spent in prison with him. But he knew it wasn't that easy. There was no way she could simply write it off.

Her brow furrowed as she gripped the blanket tight before relaxing again. What did she think of at night? What did she do to get to sleep?

A fleeting thought hit him hard. Did she ever think of him the way he thought of her?

Hope sprang up again.

AS SUNLIGHT FILTERED through the blinds at the window, Kane forced his eyes open. Standing, he stretched his arms and legs, glancing at his watch. He'd only slept a couple of hours, fear gripping him every time he closed his eyes.

He filled the coffee maker, then paced around the room, stretching out his stiff neck and back. As he poured coffee in the paper cup, the blankets rustled. He stood at her side and kept still. She sat up quickly, grabbed her gun, and swung it around the room, finally honing in on him.

"Easy, Macy. It's just me."

She blinked several times, lowered the gun to the bed, and frowned, searched the room. Groaning, she fell back into the bed for a moment, only to spring back up.

"Wait, what are you doing here?"

"I sat in the chair last night, kept an eye on things."

"Why? No one knew I was here."

"I just wanted to make sure you were all right."

"Kane ..."

He held up his hand before she went off again about his need to protect her. He was much too tired to play games, and if he told her how he truly felt, she'd bolt.

"Don't, okay? You were exhausted, scared, and had just lost your home. Give me this one." He sighed. "I've got to make a phone call. I'll be outside for a bit. There's coffee, well, kinda like coffee if you want some. Shower, change, whatever." He waited for her to nod, unlatching the door and stepping into the hallway.

He paced the hallway, stopping to look out the window over the parking lot.

"Jon, I need some information."

"Good morning, Kane. You sound tired."

"Someone blew up Macy's house last night."

He heard an audible gasp and a crash. "Jon? What happened?"

"I-I just dropped my mug. It's fine. Um ... wait, are you sure it was blown up?"

"That's what the officer said when we pulled up."

"You were with her?"

"I followed her home. She was pretty upset last night. She seriously thought either you or I butted in."

"Oh, I'm sorry."

"Can you at least find out what they know? The police officer in charge is supposed to call her this morning sometime about what happened. But I doubt they'll give her specifics. I want to know if the bomb signature is the same as the one used on her employer last night."

Jon sighed. "I'll do what I can, but I'm not good at this."

"Whatever you can do, I'd really appreciate it."

"Give me some time this morning, and I'll call as soon as I get anything."

"Thanks." He blew out a breath and pocketed the phone, gripping the coffee cup and fearing what lay ahead.

If DeLuca knew about Santiago and knew where Macy lived, she was in grave danger. There was no way he could go back to work. Not until she was safe.

17

S tanding in the shower, the memories came flooding back. Macy tried to keep from screaming. The dirt floor, the pain, the smell of cigars, beer, and some disgusting cologne. She pushed them away, searching for something to cling to, but the only image that filled her mind was the remains of her home.

She leaned into the water's spray and cried. It wasn't anything fancy or big, but she'd loved living there. Her neighbors were older and friendly. Her home had all the comfort she needed when she'd been released from the hospital, and her father finally let her go home alone.

"God, what else? What else do You want?" she mumbled.

It felt as if she'd done something wrong, or He wanted something more of her. But she knew that wasn't true. It wasn't the first time God had used the pain in her life to help others, to ease the hurt of others.

But this time, things moved much faster than when she experienced the sudden loss of her mother, then her father's cancer diagnosis. Grief and heartache were commonplace in this world. This seemed different.

She dried off, ignoring the shortness of her hair as she dressed quickly, pulling on a pair of jogging pants and a T-shirt, the only clean clothes in her bag. Her vanity over her hair bothered her. Kane's scars would always be evident. A haircut should be the least of her worries.

Grabbing her phone from the nightstand, she called Zander. Surely he'd know something about the bombing.

"Zander, it's Macy. Call me back as soon as you get this." She frowned as she hung up.

He didn't allow calls to roll to voicemail.

Macy shoved her dirty clothes into her bag, and the phone rang. She blew out a breath and picked it up.

"Hey, I wondered if you heard about my place last night?" Silence greeted her. "Zander?"

"So lovely to hear your voice."

She nearly dropped the phone and fell to the floor, bile burning her throat. She tried to swallow. "W-what?"

"I am sure you will remember me. Because, my dear, I have not forgotten you." The hardness in DeLuca's tone heated her face. Her hand clenched into a fist.

"What did you do? Let me speak to Zander."

"I wish I could, but it seems he is not a very strong man."

She gasped for air. The door opened, and Kane rushed to her side, finding her hand. *Your phone*, she mouthed, and he handed it to her.

"Why did you go after him if I'm the one you want?"

She quickly texted the number for the special op's unit Zander used from time to time when doing international security.

01142

"Well, I still did not have much information on you."

Report.

She quickly typed in a response.

Zander Nichols has been kidnapped and possibly killed. Trace his phone.

"I needed more information, and it seemed Mr. Nichols had even more than what I needed."

"How did you find him? He's not an easy man to get to."

Kane gripped her hand. She squeezed his fingers, thankful he was there to hold her up.

"He was easier than you. It seems since your time at my home, you are more paranoid. Getting close was a challenge, and I am afraid I am in a time crunch."

"What do you mean, time crunch?" She steadied her breathing in an attempt to keep from hyperventilating.

Kane moved closer, pulling the phone away so he could listen.

"Oh, that is neither here nor there. But I want you to know, I blame you for the fire in my life."

"You should blame the men who brought me to you. Have you dealt with them?"

"They are of no concern. But you, I just want to repay you for what you did to my empire."

She started to shake. Tremors overtook her body.

"I will see you soon, Macy Packer."

The line died. She dropped the phone and ran to the bathroom. Hunching over the toilet, her stomach emptied, and she slid to the cold floor.

"Macy?"

"No, go away." Her voice ached. She reached up to flush the toilet and sank back to the floor, resting her head on her knees.

With the tremors in her body and the ringing in her ears, she didn't hear Kane enter, only felt the cold washcloth on the back of her neck. She pulled it around and wiped her face, gripping it hard as she lowered her head.

"Macy, come on." Kane's gentle voice sounded.

He took her hand, and with his help, she stood, allowing him to pull her out of the small space. Wrapping her up, she leaned against his chest and let him take her weight.

"I couldn't hear well. Who was on the phone?"

Unable to stop, her tears came out in sobs as she trembled. Her legs gave way. He picked her up and sat her in the chair next to the bed. Then, he knelt in front of her and held her while she cried. His arms encircling her, holding her against him calmed her quickly, even faster than last time. There was something about him, something that could still her mind and body.

"Who was on the phone?"

"It was him. DeLuca," she mumbled. "He has my boss."

She buried her face in his neck, closed her eyes, and breathed him in. The bombing. DeLuca had to be responsible for the bombing. Zander must have given up something about her.

Macy trembled again. Kane's arms gave her a squeeze. Her phone rang, and she stiffened. Kane grabbed it from the floor, handing it off to her.

"Packer." Her voice was almost done.

"Agent Packer, we were able to get a trace on the line. You'll want to see this."

"Is he alive?" she whispered.

"Barely, they just loaded him on a med flight. But, based on the scene, I'm not making any promises. He was ... unrecognizable."

Bile rose in her throat. She fought the urge to retch. "Send me the address. I'll be there as soon as I can." She ended the call. "I've got to go. They found Zander."

"I'm going with you."

Her phone dinged, and she looked down at the address and handed the phone to him.

"I need to get it together and get over there. I just—I just don't know if I can handle it." She wiped her face.

"Okay. Do you have other clothes?"

She shook her head.

"Finish getting ready. I'll check you out and drive you to get something to eat. Then we'll head there."

"I don't think they'll let you in."

"You'd be surprised." He grinned.

The darkness under his eyes and the strain on his face showed how little sleep he got, if any. She smiled as best she could. He kissed her forehead.

"You okay to stand?" His low growl echoed as he held out his hands.

Sighing, she took them and stood on shaky legs. Wrapping his arms around her waist, he pulled her in again.

"I thought I was supposed to be getting ready to go," she whispered.

"I just want to make sure you're okay."

"I'm fine now. I'm just not good with someone hovering." She put her hands on his chest to create some distance, but it did no good.

He had a firm hold on her, and the only thing she could do was to attempt to hide her grin at the impressive work he'd done with his body during the past couple of months.

"I'll try not to hover, but I'm not going anywhere either. Okay?"

She nodded, and he slowly released her, allowing her to step away and head for the sink.

In the mirror, she watched him leave and let out a breath. As terrible as this day had already become, at least he was here.

She grabbed her toothbrush and leaned over the sink. Kane filled her thoughts constantly. His green eyes had haunted her for six weeks. All she saw at night were his eyes through the hole in the wall.

But, after him finding her two days ago and the apparent misunderstanding about Jasper, it seemed like he was willing to do anything to make up for lost time. Including moving quickly into a more physical side of things, something she hadn't expected.

Of course, his eyes weren't his only attractive quality. His deep voice comforted her. His sandy brown hair and the trimmed shadow he wore was much better than the bushy beard he'd had when she first saw him. Tall, dark, and handsome, he was the quintessential prince charming her mother read to her about in childhood fairy tales.

His character also impressed her. She'd done nothing but push him away, and the fact she had obvious emotional issues would scare off pretty much any guy. But Kane persevered. She chastised herself for pushing him away so much.

In the early morning hours, his confession almost brought her to her knees. To hear what they did to him, to hear the anger in his voice when he mentioned seeing the man take her away to the room under the stairwell.

She leaned against the sink, gripping the counter and breathing deeply. Just the memory of that was enough to send her into a spiral. She should've gone back for Kane, released him right then. If she had, he wouldn't have experienced more torture. That decision had kept her awake for weeks. She had caused him that pain.

And now Zander's life hung in the balance because of her. He had to be okay.

The door opened. She jumped and spun around, hugging herself.

"You okay?" He started for her.

Macy quickly threw her supplies in the bag, zipped it, and grabbed her gun. "I'm good. Let's go." She sidestepped him, guilt hanging onto her.

He pulled the bag from her arm.

"I've got it, let's just go," she muttered.

Once in his car, Macy focused on the air from the vent, letting the cold air freeze her out and calm her nerves. He pulled into a drive-thru, and they ordered, even though the thought of eating nauseated her. The plain croissant and bottle of water seemed enough to settle her stomach yet allowed her to have a little energy.

They remained quiet during the drive and pulled up to a home with police cruisers and government SUV's surrounding it.

"You sure you want to go in there?" He gripped her fingers.

"Yeah, are you?" She finally made eye contact and squeezed his hand. "Please, just wait outside for me. I can't ask you to go in there."

"Let's just see what they say." He gave her a half-hearted smile, released his grip, and opened his door.

Taking a breath, she did the same, then climbed out as he came up next to her and shut her door.

18

"Agent Packer?" A man in full body armor approached her.

"Yes?"

"My boss needs to talk with you."

Macy nodded. She heard someone call Kane's name.

"Kane Bledsoe? What are you doing here?"

Turning, she saw another man in tactical gear shaking Kane's hand. She smirked as he gave her a full smile. Of course, he knew someone on the case.

Macy turned her attention back to the scene and cautiously stepped inside. Overturned furniture, smashed glass, and blood spatter. Her heart sank.

"Any word on how he's doing?"

"Not that I'm aware. In here, ma'am."

She nodded and continued through to a back room where a chair sat facing a wall. Blood covered the floor. She froze.

"Agent Packer? Macy Packer?"

Macy turned toward the voice. "Y-yes?"

"My name is Special Agent Gains. I was called in after your tactical force arrived."

She nodded and barely registered. Shaking the man's hand, her eyes still focused on the room.

"Maybe we should talk elsewhere."

He led her back to the main living area, where Kane stood by the door, arms crossed, wearing a stern look on his face.

"Agent Packer, can you explain what's going on here?"

She turned her attention back to the man in front of her, hugging herself. "I'm pretty sure this is related to the bombings from last night."

"Bombings? You mean there was another bombing besides the home assigned to Nichols's team?"

She nodded and stepped back, watching as Kane's buddy led him toward the hallway.

"No, you're not going back there." She faced him fully, glaring, and hoping he understood. Macy didn't want him to have any flashbacks, and that room would do it.

He clenched his jaw, then leaned against the wall behind her.

"I'm sorry, who are you? Who let him in?" Agent Gains's voice rose above the clatter.

"I'm Special Agent Kane Bledsoe. This involves me as well."

"What agency, Bledsoe?"

"That's classified." Kane's expression turned to stone.

"Hang on." Gaines pulled out his cell phone.

Macy nervously shifted from one leg to the other.

Kane's eyes met hers. "Macy?"

"Just please, don't go back there." She averted her eyes as nervous energy surged through her.

She had never reacted like this at a scene before, and the unprofessionalism bothered her. Kane stepped closer, enabling her to still a little before Gains got off his phone.

"Okay, it seems Agent Bledsoe has access here. So, tell me what's going on."

"Have you heard anything about Nichols?"

"No, I haven't been updated."

She sighed, gripping her arms.

"Who were you speaking with, Agent Packer, when you called the team?"

"L-Luis DeLuca."

Kane shifted, then paced.

"Okay, and he is?"

She stared at Gains. "You need to get in touch with the FBI. You obviously haven't been read in."

Gains frowned. "I'm in the FBI, Agent Packer."

"Then get your supervisor on the phone. If you don't know that name, I'm not speaking with you." Her composure returned, her brain finally clicking into gear.

"I can assure you—"

"No, you can't. Call your supervisor. There's no way you can know about the previous assignment I was on and not know DeLuca." She swallowed hard. Just saying his name caused her mouth to go dry and increased her breath rate.

"Excuse me, who's in charge here?" A man in a suit entered, an officer in tow.

"And who are you?" Gains appeared more than agitated with the extra people who'd just arrived at his crime scene.

"Special Agent Crow." The agent held up his badge and nodded toward Kane. "Bledsoe."

Kane had been right. She was indeed surprised.

"This case is mine. It was handed off before all the information was given." The agent's stern voice echoed.

"No way." Gains turned, his face red, his hands fisted.

"Call Burger. It should never have been handed off."

Gains left, yanking out his phone and storming through the front door.

"I want to talk to both of you, but not here. I just received word on Nichols. He's in critical condition. They're not that optimistic. I'm sorry."

Macy groaned and leaned over a minute, feeling Kane's hand on her shoulder. Once again, the indecision to call Zander last night as she should have, caused him pain at DeLuca's hand. She straightened.

"Let's head to the office. Bledsoe, I've heard some things."

The agent smiled and offered his hand. Kane shook it, then returned his hand to Macy's back.

"Don't believe everything you hear."

"It's a reliable source." The man's smile disappeared. Silence covered the room for a moment before Crow nodded and left.

At Kane's prodding, she followed, taking a deep breath as they walked outside in the fresh air.

"See you there." Crow got into his vehicle.

Kane pushed her along to his.

Once on the road, she glanced his direction.

"Yes?" His eyes never left the road.

"So, you seem to know a lot of people."

"I do."

She let the silence linger. "I feel better since whoever is handling this is someone you know. Do you trust him?"

The question sat for a minute before he answered. "Crow's a good agent, by the book and reliable."

"That sounds rehearsed."

He glanced her direction then turned back to the road, a smirk on his face. "I could name a few different agents I'd rather be the lead, but at least I know I can trust him."

They had a history, and it was clear he didn't want to discuss it.

"What was back there, Macy?"

She swallowed hard. "Do you trust me?"

"Yes."

"I know you wouldn't want to react with everyone there to see you." She took a breath. "It looked similar to the room we found you in." She could barely get the words out.

His jaw clenched, and his knuckles turned white as he drove. She tugged at his forearm until he finally released the steering wheel, allowing her to hold his hand.

"I'm sorry, Kane."

"What? Why? You're right. I wouldn't want to see it."

"No, not that." Her heart pounded as nausea overwhelmed her, churning her stomach.

"Then what?"

She released his hand and clasped hers together. Breathing methodically, her nausea finally passed.

"I should have come for you first. I shouldn't have left."

"Macy ..."

"No, just listen. I didn't even think, I was out of it after being in that room, and then I just didn't think. I could've gotten you out, I know there were some keys somewhere, he had to have one to open my cell. I should've gone for you first, released you, but I didn't. I'm so sorry." Closing her eyes, she wiped her face, and her head spun. The car jerked to a stop.

Kane appeared outside her door. He opened it and pulled her to him.

"No, I'm really sorry."

"I would've told you to leave."

"But, if I'd gotten you out, you wouldn't have had that last day."

"We never would have made it. One person could escape, but all of us?"

She pushed away from him. "You could've hidden in the back of the Jeep. They didn't check it at the gate."

"Macy, stop." His deep voice rose.

She looked up. He pulled her to the side and lifted her into his lap so he could sit on the seat.

"Look at me." He lifted at her chin until she found his eyes.

"You did what I asked you to do. I told you to get out. That's why I gave you the coordinates. You needed to escape alone. There were too many of us to get out without being caught. They would've just shot us down."

He gripped her hands tightly. "I was trying to open the lock, not for my sake, but because the thought of what he was doing to you—it killed me." He cleared his throat and closed his eyes a moment, leaning back into the seat. Opening them again, he caught her gaze. "Don't second guess yourself. You did the right thing. You called in the cavalry, and we all got out."

"But you, what they did to you."

"What they did doesn't matter now. It was something I'd have to deal with no matter what, even without that last day." He released her hands and wiped her face, leaning his forehead to hers. "Macy, don't do this. You saved all of us, don't you see that? Stop trying to make it into something it's not."

Wrapping her arms around his neck, she leaned into him. Zander's room flashed in her mind, then the sight of Kane in his own room that day surfaced. Her tremors started, and she stiffened.

"What makes you do that, Macy? Talk to me."

His whispered words tore at her. She couldn't answer. Instead, she focused on taking long, deep breaths.

Once the tremors passed, he angled to catch her gaze. "Just tell me. Am I doing something wrong?"

"Of course not." She sighed. "It's happened since I got back. I can't control it, and they seem to be getting worse."

"But, it happens a lot when I'm around."

"It's not you." She drew in her bottom lip and took a breath. "You actually help." His green eyes tugged on her heart. "They usually take a long time to go away fully. But, since yesterday, whenever you hold me, they go away faster." She released his neck and gripped his hands.

A smile lit up his face.

Tracing her hand along his cheek, feeling the stubble under her fingers, she returned his smile. "Thanks for being here, Kane. I'm not sure I would've made it past that phone call this morning," she whispered.

Her hand dropped to his chest, and she felt his heartbeat pounding.

"I'm worried about you, Macy." He swallowed hard. "He's targeting you, and I'm afraid you won't like where this is headed."

"Where what's headed?"

His narrowed eyes and clenched jaw proved he knew more than he was telling.

"They'll put you in protective custody."

"What?"

His hands slid to her waist, and she sat back, processing his words. She flinched and pulled away, then jumped from the car.

"Macy?" He caught her hand.

She yanked it back, her breaths uneven and labored.

"Macy, slow down, you'll pass out."

She closed her eyes, reaching out to him. Unwilling to be held, but she still needed to feel his closeness. After a few moments of breathing long, slow breaths, her body eased.

"Better?"

She nodded as the fear faded. Her heartbeat returned to normal.

"I'm sorry. But you going into custody is a fact I can't stop."

Sadness washed over her when she saw his red face, his furrowed brows.

"Tell me what happened. Did I do something?"

"I think—it's when you held my waist." She closed her eyes, the memory pulling her back as her attacker gripped her waist, squeezing her and moving his hands to her bare skin.

A shudder moved through her as Kane threaded his fingers with hers, holding her steady.

"That's where my hands were the first time I tried to kiss you, Mace."

She nodded and shut her eyes. Everything clicked.

"You need to talk to me. I don't want to frighten you."

She opened her eyes. "I will, just not right now. We really need to go." She tried to pull away, but he held her firm.

"Macy, I'm serious. You need to talk to me, so I don't do anything that messes this up."

He wrapped her up in a hug, and she leaned in.

"I want this to work. Please tell me you want this to work

too." He moved his head down to her ear, whispering as he held her.

"Kane, you're moving fast here. You don't know me that well."

"I know you well enough, and I'm sorry, I'll slow down. I'm not asking for a promise here." He sighed, sending goosebumps over her skin. "I just want to know I'm not wrong."

"You're not."

"I sense a 'but' coming on."

His low growl made her smile. "No, no but. I just don't want you in the middle of this."

He stepped back, frowning at her.

"He's coming after me. I don't want you in the crossfire. So, maybe after we leave the FBI office, you should keep your distance. Kane—"

She didn't get to finish as he walked away, his stony expression returning.

"Please, I don't want you to get hurt."

"Don't treat me like that. I'm not incompetent just because of what happened back there." His voice rose, practically yelling.

Her mouth dropped, and her face turned red hot. "You think it's because of that?" Her voice heated as well. "Stop and think for a second. Have I mentioned what happened to you other than to ask if you've healed?" She waited as he crossed his arms and glared at her. "Do you really think that's what this is about?"

His silence made her clench her jaw. She threw her hands up and got back in the car, slamming the door and waiting for him to get in. After several minutes, he slid in, started the car, and drove in silence.

She propped her chin on her hand and stared out the window. The scenery, the drive, nothing registered. Why was it okay to need to be there for her, but she wasn't allowed to care enough about him? She didn't want to navigate this nightmare alone, but she sure didn't want to risk his life in the process.

God, please, just give me the words to help him understand.

19

Inside the FBI office, they found Crow waiting at the front desk. He looked between them both and frowned when Macy glared back.

"Follow me." He led them past the metal detectors and to the elevators.

Keeping her distance from both men, Macy leaned against the back wall, gripping her arms. With Crow being a friend to Kane, she figured her asking him to back off wouldn't amount to much anyway. But she had to voice her opinion, hoping he'd at least consider it.

Crow led them into a small room and asked her to sit at the table. She noticed Kane took a seat to the side immediately without being asked.

"So, I need to know what's going on and who you were talking to."

"Someone blew up my townhouse last night."

He wrote in his notebook. "And you think it's related to the bombing of Carlos Santiago?"

"That's what I want to know. After securing my brother and father, I got a hotel room. I didn't make contact with Zander until this morning. I guess I was so out of it ..." She rubbed her hand through her short, ugly hair, feeling her gut churn again.

"What happened when you called?"

She snapped out of her remorse. "It went to voicemail. I left a message, and then his phone called me back."

"So, it wasn't him?"

"No." She cleared her throat. "I spoke, but no one answered. When I spoke again, DeLuca answered."

"And you're certain it was him?"

"Yes."

"How certain?"

"I met with the man several times in two days. Trust me. It was him." She sat back, crossing her arms.

Crow looked over at Kane.

"Don't do that. You can take my word for it. Wouldn't you remember the man who kept you locked in a prison and physically beat you for two days?" She sneered at Agent Crow as she gripped her arms, nervous energy building up. Her leg started to bounce.

"What did he say?"

She cleared her throat, then took a deep breath. "He said Zander was easier to get to. Apparently, he made me paranoid and harder to grab. Being in a time crunch, he said, he needed my information fast. Zander gave up a lot on me. Then, DeLuca blamed me for destroying his business."

"So basically, he called you out as a target."

"Yes, but did you hear the part about a time crunch? He has other plans."

Crow only nodded. "We've been tracking him. He's in the states, but not here."

"Then, how did he have Zander's phone?"

"That's why I asked."

"It was him." Her voice rose through her teeth, and she forced herself to stay seated. But if he asked her again, she wasn't sure she could keep from decking the guy.

"Then, our intel is bad. Excuse me for a moment."

Crow stood and left the room, leaving her sitting with her back to Kane.

"Mace, I'm sorry about Zander."

She ignored him, not in the mood to be placated.

"Macy ..."

"Don't. I don't have anything to say right now, so just stop." She glanced over her shoulder, only catching a glimpse of him sitting against the wall.

A few more minutes of silence ticked by before Crow returned.

"We found some footage of him leaving Nichols's house right before the tactical team arrived. How did you know to call them?"

"It was basic protocol for our team. If one member is in trouble, we call in the unit. Zander didn't like agents working alone to try and combat those kinds of issues. We usually only use the team for international situations, but they are always there for back up."

"Where were you?"

"Puking my guts up in a hotel room." She glared at the man again. It was unbelievable that even with the proof she'd been right about DeLuca, he still treated her as if she were incompetent.

"My boss wants a word. If you'll follow me. And Kane, I want to speak with you before you leave."

She stood and ignored Kane as they left the room, unable even to look him in the eye as frustration over the situation overwhelmed her.

MACY SAT outside a large office with two men guarding her.

"No, sir, I took care of that earlier today." The woman at the desk beamed, her friendly voice echoed throughout the quiet room. "Yes, sir." She hung up and stood. "You can go in now."

Macy followed the woman inside the large office.

A man behind a large desk stood when they entered. "Thanks, Carla. I appreciate your quick work with those emails." He nodded as the door closed behind Macy. "Agent Packer, please have a seat."

She nodded and sat, suddenly very aware that she was in her workout attire and speaking with a senior member of the FBI.

The man stood and came around to her side of the desk, reaching out to shake her hand. "My name is Senior Special Agent Burger."

She nodded and shook his hand. He sat down next to her, turning his chair to face her. "I understand you've been in contact with Luis DeLuca?"

"Yes, sir."

"We have reason to believe that although your life is now in danger, he might have other targets as well."

"Do you have any information on him?"

"Very little, I'm afraid."

"Does he know who he has when people are delivered to him?"

The agent kept his face emotionless, no flinch or reaction, but the moments of silence spoke volumes. "Why do you ask?"

"First, I'm wondering how he knew who my supervisor was when he admitted he didn't have all my information, including both my first and last name. His commentary on the time crunch also makes me wonder if he knew who he had when I showed up. The men he already held hostage, I mean." She narrowed her eyes, watching his move back and forth, searching.

"I don't know exactly who Jon is, but I know he's an important person. I just wonder why no one is reading me in on this. I worked for the secret service for several years before moving to a private agency. My abilities and my clearance keep me in the loop for government operations if I'm ever needed."

"I've read your background, and as impressive as it is, you're not here as a hired agent. You're here as someone we now need to protect. And because of the questions you asked, I have to wonder, if you knew Jon was an important figure, why have you not looked into him?"

"I've been a little busy, sir." She clenched her jaw. "If he wanted me to know, he would've contacted me. But I think all of us who returned from that place have been a little busy." She stood and moved to the window, pacing as she turned back to the chairs.

SSA Burger stood.

"Sir, my brother and father—they're still waiting on me to tell them what to do."

"We can offer protection, once we get a plan in place."

She frowned. That seemed ominous. Either they had several plans or no plans, and since he wasn't sharing, she was concerned.

"This situation was taken over by the FBI because it is fast becoming a national security issue. We'd like to get a handle on it before another agency jumps in."

"Homeland?"

He nodded. "So, we're in the process of devising a plan to move to the offensive."

"You want to use me as bait?" Her tone turned flat as that possibility came to mind. Logically, it was the best way to make a move instead of sitting around, waiting for DeLuca to act. But the thought terrified her.

"Perhaps bait is the wrong word. We're assessing the best way to keep you from being a distraction to any other targets DeLuca might have."

"Wait, you want to put me in custody with Jon?"

He shrugged. "That's one possibility."

She frowned again, moving back to the window and crossing her arms over her chest. "I don't want to put Jon in danger."

"He has a steady protection detail. It would be hard for anyone to get to him."

"But you can't wait forever. DeLuca will strike, and it would be better to anticipate the action instead of trying to make up for it."

"You have a point." Burger stood watching her, his hands in his pockets.

She leaned against the windowsill, eyeing the man who seemed to do an excellent job at keeping his mouth shut when it came to interviewing and assessing. It annoyed her. A knock interrupted the lingering silence.

"Yes?" Burger turned.

The same woman from earlier entered and whispered something in Burger's ear. He nodded as he looked to the door. Kane came in along with Crow. Burger smiled, shook Kane's hand, and the two returned greetings as if they were old friends.

Annoyed as she was with the situation, she couldn't help but admire how nice Kane looked in his jeans and T-shirt. He didn't need all that weight he kept mentioning he'd lost.

Stifling the urge to smile, she turned back to the window. Exhausted, her brain shut down. She stood alone, the only one not involved in the situation even though it surrounded her.

"I haven't had a chance to talk with Jon yet, but I'll give him a call. I'm sure he'll have some ideas," Kane said.

She turned to face them.

"Agent Packer, you now have Special Agent Crow on your detail until we figure out the best plan. Bledsoe will keep me apprised of the situation as well. Call your brother and father, have them come here and give my name. I'll be expecting their arrival."

Her gaze narrowed and shifted between the three men. She frowned. Ignoring their stares, she hurried past them to the door. Agent Crow opened it for her, and she left the room feeling heat creep up her neck.

"Macy, where are you going?"

She spun to face Kane before getting on the elevator. "I need to go shopping. I have no clothing except a few things in my bag downstairs." Turning on her heel, she entered the open elevator.

Before she and Crow reached their floor, his phone rang.

"Crow." He glanced her way and nodded. "Bledsoe says your bag is in his car."

She groaned and leaned against the elevator wall.

"Let's wait in the lobby. Besides, you know you can't get out. Just make a list, and we'll get everything for you." He escorted her out of the elevator.

Within seconds, the hair on her neck stood on end, and the feeling of being watched came over her. Glancing around the large lobby, she searched the faces and came up empty. But someone was watching. She could feel it.

20

"Mace?"

Macy jumped when Kane stepped in front of her. "What's wrong?"

"Nothing." She huffed and straightened.

Crow followed close behind. He escorted her down the steps to his sedan in front of the building and opened her door.

"A word?"

She heard Kane's voice as the door shut. Great, now what interference did he have planned? She sighed, attempting to ease her irritation while Kane spoke to the man who'd be guarding her.

She was curious, though. Had Kane worked for the FBI? What other agencies had he worked for? All she saw was a military man.

A knock on her door startled her. Kane stood outside with her bag. She opened the door, but instead of passing her the bag, he took her hand and assisted her out, then shut her door.

"Macy, don't be mad at me."

"I don't want to talk about it right now. I'm too tired and—"

She suddenly saw a distinct profile up against the agency's

front window—a man dressed in a blue jumpsuit with a long brush, washing the windows.

"Mace? What is it?"

She ignored Kane's question, focused in on the man. It couldn't be. She moved closer to Kane, narrowing her eyes and watching as the reflection of the mid-morning sun bounced off the window, lighting the man's face. Her body shook as his features became clear.

"Macy?" Kane's voice cracked. He gently gripped her upper arms.

"The man washing the window, it's, I think it's him." Her voice trembled, and she struggled to get the words out.

"Crow, stand here." Kane squeezed her upper arms as Crow took his place, shielding her.

"What do you see?" Crow's voice cut through.

Macy leaned against the car, hugging herself and shaking. "There's a man. I think I recognize him. It's not DeLuca." She swallowed hard, then straightened, noticing Kane had disappeared. "Where did Kane go?"

Crow's chuckle surprised her. "You don't know much about him, huh?"

"I know enough that if he gets to him, and no one is there to stop him, Kane might kill the guy." She looked up to see Crow's frown.

He pulled out his phone, speaking to someone inside the building about the situation. "They'll be watching. Once he makes contact, a few agents will step in."

She kept her eyes focused, ignoring Crow, searching for Kane. Suddenly, he came from behind the man, pushed him up against the window. She moved toward the building, but Crow blocked her.

"Let me get the all-clear first, Packer. Okay?" He held his hands up in front of him. Obviously, Kane had told him to take it easy on her when it came to getting too close.

A moment later, Kane rushed down the steps to her, his neck and cheeks red.

"What do you think?"

"It looks like him. I only saw him a few times, though. You want to ID him?"

Fear faded, and anger boiled as she pushed between the two men. The suspect had his head down while she climbed the steps. When he finally looked up, bile rose in her throat. Her attacker stood feet from her. His beard couldn't hide his face— the man who'd beat and tried to rape her stared right through her.

She lunged forward, gripped his throat, and slammed him against the glass.

"Macy." Kane's low voice boomed.

"Are you here, working with him?" She had her free hand against the glass, holding the man firmly and working her fingers around his throat. "Answer me."

As she glared at him, he finally nodded.

"You'll tell these guys everything, or you'll deal with me alone. They won't be able to save you," she whispered. Macy released her grip, and the officers took him away.

Leaning her hands against the glass, she took a few breaths, begging God to give her the strength to walk away. Right now, her whole body wanted to shut down.

"Macy, let's go."

Kane's voice broke her fury, and she straightened, working on releasing her irritation. She took the steps down to the car. Kane caught her hand.

"Give me a minute, Crow."

Macy paused and closed her eyes. She heard the car door open. An instant later, Kane pulled her close. Breathing him in, she rested her head against his chest. A few tremors moved through her body, ending as quickly as they'd started while he held her.

"You'll be going to Jon's house. I'll see you there."

She shook her head. "I shouldn't be there."

"Why?"

He stepped back, nudging her chin until she opened her eyes and looked up at him.

"You'll be too distracted." She managed a small smile.

"Not when I'm on duty. I can be professional." He grinned, squeezing her back into him and dropping a kiss on her head.

She pushed away and heard him grunt. "I need to go. And you need to become professional."

He frowned and opened her car door for her. Gripping his arm, she gazed into those green eyes before sliding into the seat.

She pulled out her phone and texted her brother.

> Get to the FBI. The director there is expecting you.

What's going on, Macy?

> The FBI will put you in protective custody.

What about you?

> I can't get into it, Jas, I'm sorry.

Sure, sorry. Not cool, sis, I'm not cool with this.

She released a breath at his reply, his comments so very Jasper she didn't even have to worry that it might not be him texting her back. After what happened to Zander, her heart felt as if it were in her throat. She hated that her brother and father were stuck in the middle. At least her brother understood, to an extent, her job and responsibilities. But her father, it would only make his worry increase.

I'm under protection too, so tell dad not to worry. Everything will be fine.

If it were fine, we wouldn't need protection, Mace.

Just cut me some slack. This isn't my idea of fun either. It's been a rough couple of days.

Dad said you weren't alone. Who's there?

She paused, not sure if she should let her brother know or not. Sighing, she texted him back.

Kane.

The guy we pulled out? The one you wanted to see but couldn't talk to?

Yeah.

I'd like to hear about that.

Nope, no more texting or calling. I'll get a new number and call you. Don't talk to anyone but the FBI, Jas, I'm serious.

Got it. Be careful, sis.

Always.

She handed Crow her phone, knowing she couldn't use it anymore.

As they drove, silence filled the cabin, her mind and her heart raced. Dealing with her attacker in the middle of this. She hadn't expected to see him.

"So, who exactly was that guy?"

She looked over at Crow, wondering how much he knew.

"I've read your report."

"I wasn't aware that was for anyone to see," she muttered and swallowed hard.

She had included everything she could in an attempt to describe every man she came in contact with, hoping it would lead to more arrests down the road. The things she included in the report were personal, and the fact he read it flustered her.

"Not everyone, just me, and of course, SSA Burger, once we took over your previous case and decided to use Santiago as leverage for DeLuca."

"So, you've known about DeLuca for a while?"

"Long enough. He's a bad man. He's killed too many Americans to be left to his own. He needs to be stopped."

The comment came out harsh. This case could be personal to him as well.

"That man—I don't know his name— was a guard. He promised to get me out." She cleared her throat and focused on the road ahead. No need to go into detail if Crow had read the report.

"Just so you know, I would've let you strangle him."

She turned her gaze to Crow. An uneasiness washed over her.

"What about Kane? Would you let him?"

"No. It's not his place, no matter how close you two are." His jaw clenched as he turned his focus back to the road.

For some reason, his comment unnerved her. Not that he would let her, but that she had been that close to taking the man's life. Killing had always been a downside of the job for her, for most who served. It's not that they wanted to kill, but that they wanted to survive and protect their employer. That was the job.

Even with what the guard did to her, to kill him in cold blood? That wasn't who she was. With a huff, she leaned her head into the seat.

God, forgive me for my anger. It's not my justice, but Yours I should be after. I'll let You handle it if You could just give me a little peace. Protect my family, please.

MACY'S EYES widened when they pulled up to Jon's estate. At the gatehouse, steel bars and guards met them with cameras surrounding the perimeter, and a K-9 unit waited to search the car.

The home itself appeared much smaller than she expected. If Jon really could influence people so well, she expected a castle behind the gate. Instead, the large home looked comfortable, not kingly. A guard opened her door, and she slid out, her eyes searching the grounds.

"That didn't take long."

She moved her gaze to the doorway to see Kane coming out in a suit minus the tie. It looked pretty good on him, and she smiled before she could rein it in. At least she kept her jaw from dropping.

"Let's get inside." Kane gave her a wink. He motioned her and Crow up the steps.

Jon waited in the living area. Two guards were visible behind him, but her eyes immediately focused on Jon's smile.

"Macy, it's so good to see you."

She smiled, holding back her tears. Jon looked almost the same, minus the darkness on his face. He hadn't gained any weight, and it hit her hard.

"You too, Jon." She grabbed his hands, then dropped them for a hug.

He returned her hug. "How are you?" His voice trembled slightly.

"I've been better. Today wasn't a good day. But then again, I've had worse." She swallowed.

He nodded and didn't appear surprised. She figured Kane had passed on everything that had happened.

"You need some rest. I had someone prepare a guest suite for you."

"We need to talk." She squeezed his hand.

"Yes, we do. But after you rest." He smiled again, guiding her to the stairwell where Kane waited. "Rest first, and we'll talk later."

She ascended the stairs with Kane behind her.

21

At the landing, Macy waited. Kane passed her, then opened the first door on her right, following her inside. As she turned, his hands took hold of hers.

"You okay, Macy?" He squeezed her fingers, holding them tight.

Looking up into his green eyes, she smiled. "I'm okay. Just worried about Jasper and my dad and being here with Jon. You didn't tell me Jon wasn't doing well."

"He is, just in his own way."

She nodded as he released one hand to trace her jaw, brushing his thumb against her cheek.

"This is professional behavior, huh?" She grinned.

He frowned. "It's not, but considering the circumstances, this is about as far from you as I'm going to be able to get. I don't like this. I don't like DeLuca being here and targeting you."

"I'm not your objective, Jon is. Don't forget that."

"You both are." His green eyes searched hers, and his lips parted as if he wanted to speak, but he clamped them shut again.

Taking a step back, Kane released her hand, shoving both of his into his pockets. "Macy, I know there's a lot going on here, and I'm usually pretty good at reading people. But, you're stumping me." He rubbed the back of his neck, then raked his hand through his sandy hair. "I don't know what you're thinking, and to be honest, I don't like it."

She grinned at his annoyance. Seemed she wasn't the only one unnerved by this whole situation. He wasn't as calm and cool as he conveyed.

"Why are you smiling?" He frowned at her.

"It's just interesting to see you react like this. You seem to always be in control. I guess I'm glad I'm not the only one at odds here."

"So, what does that mean?" His frown turned to a smirk.

Crossing her arms, she watched as his eyes roamed her face, his hands shoved deep in his pockets.

"I'm thankful you're here. God seems to have a timetable that I don't quite agree with, but we're here. I just wish you wouldn't worry so much about me and at least see things from my point of view."

"Which is?"

She enjoyed hearing his low growl. Smiling again, she continued, "If the situation were reversed, if he was after you and I tried to help, what would you do?"

He frowned again. His jaw clenched.

"Exactly, you'd try and stop me, right?"

"It's different."

"Why?"

"It's just different."

"Because I'm a woman, right? You've been forcing this issue the whole time, acting as if it's okay to want to try and protect me, but I'm not allowed to protect you."

He opened his mouth to speak, but she put her hand up and stepped up to him.

"And don't even think about bringing up your injuries again as if that's the reason. Because if you do, this," she pointed between them, "isn't going to work. If I can look past your injuries, then why can't you look past thinking I can't help you simply because I'm a woman?"

Gently gripping her shoulders, he pulled her in and kissed her hard. Her hands on his chest, she breathed him in as his lips pressed into hers. Finally, he eased back, and her face heated when she looked up into his green eyes.

"What—what are you doing" Her breath stalled in her throat.

"Well, seeing how you admitted to wanting this to work, I just felt the need to show you how happy I am." He grinned, moving his hands gently down to rest them on her lower back. "Trust me when I say it's not because you're a woman. I can't believe you aren't getting it when we seem to be on the same page." He leaned closer.

"I care about you, and obviously, you care enough about me to want me to stand down. I'm sorry I didn't see it earlier. Like I said, you're hard to read." He chuckled.

She smiled, looking up into his eyes, losing herself.

"Look, you being in danger is hard for me to deal with, and I'm sorry I went off about my injuries. Seems like that's a sore spot for me."

"I get it, Kane. I really do. Honestly, besides hating the fact they put you through it, I haven't given your scars much thought." Macy focused on his chest, running her fingers down and around to his stomach. She pushed her hands around his sides under his jacket, enjoying his strong body being against hers.

"But, like I said, you need to focus on Jon. He's your objective. Me being here will be a distraction." She sighed and pulled away, looking up at him and taking his hands. "I don't want anything to happen to you or Jon because I'm here."

"Well, as long as you can refrain from doing that again, it would help," he muttered.

She noticed the catch in his voice, his face serious.

"I'm sorry. I should've remembered the last time. I forgot it bothers you."

"It's not a bother." He threaded his fingers with hers, squeezing until she made eye contact again. "It's hard to ignore you when you're doing that," he whispered. "Let's just try to keep from running into each other while I'm on duty."

"I thought you were always on duty." She pushed and pulled against his hands, feeling lighthearted for the first time today.

"Since Jon hired more men, I've got from midnight till nine in the morning off."

"Oh, okay. So, I'll be asleep, and so will you."

"I'll try and keep my distance. I don't want to push you too hard. But, my room is right next door and—"

"Wait, next door?"

He nodded. "Jon had it set up before I got here."

She rolled her eyes and tried to release his hands.

"Hey, I want you close, but this will be a challenge. Let's just work on other things until this is all over." He held on, not letting her go.

"You should go. You're on duty."

She tried for a smile, hoping he wouldn't take it the wrong way. But if he was next door as they stayed under the same roof for no telling how long, some ground rules would have to come into play.

"I'll talk to you later."

He nodded, his eyes dropping to her lips. With a sigh, he kissed the top of her head. "See you, Macy."

"Bye." She followed him to the door, shut and locked it, then proceeded to collapse on the bed, groaning into the pillow.

God, You have got to be kidding me.

The emotions overtaking her at the moment left her reeling.

Losing her home, her job, and seeing her attacker in person made her feel like throwing in the towel. Now, having to go into protection herself, with Kane leading the charge—it was too much to deal with.

She kicked off her shoes, pulled the comforter up over her shoulders, and burrowed herself into the bed, ignoring the light and closing her eyes as sleep called out to her.

If everything went right after she woke, she'd have Jon convinced she should stay elsewhere, and Kane would be best if he stayed with Jon. As mad as Kane would be, it might help with the tension and keep things friendly and platonic instead of the physical side they teetered toward.

With a sigh, she attempted to push away the feeling of his body holding hers, pushing up against her, the feeling of his lips pressing into hers. A shudder moved through her, and she curled up again. As much as she felt they needed to slow down, she hadn't had that kind of contact in a long time, that closeness. And she craved it.

God, ease my impulses and help Kane ease his as well. This is going to be a difficult road to manage, Lord. Give me strength too. Sighing, she gave in once again, attempting to let sleep overcome her and give her mind and body some rest.

A QUIET TAPPING WOKE HER. Stretching out, Macy quickly sat up, allowing her eyes to adjust to the bright light over her head.

"Macy?" Kane's voice came through the door.

She smiled.

"Macy? Wake up. I don't want to have to unlock the door."

She slid from the bed, flattening out her hair, and straightening her shirt. She unlocked the door and eased it open.

"You slept?"

Kane leaned against the door frame, and his smile nearly bowled her over.

"Yes. Can I help you?"

He only grinned bigger as she gripped the doorknob.

"Kane, what is it?"

"Jon is having an early dinner at four. He wanted me to see if you wanted to come down and eat. And I have the things you ordered from Crow."

With a nod, she took the sacks. "Dinner sounds great. What time is it?" She looked around the room but didn't see a clock on the nightstand.

"It's almost three."

"Okay, I'll be down after I shower and clean up."

She smiled up at him as his green eyes followed her.

"Anything else?"

"Yeah, but I'm on duty." He winked and straightened, his hands still shoved into his pockets. "I'll see you in a bit."

Macy nodded, and he moved from the doorway. Her heart fluttered inside her chest as she pushed the door closed and locked it. With a huff, she leaned against the door for a moment, wondering how she would be able to handle him when he looked at her that way with that big grin.

She unpacked her new clothes, tearing off labels and tags, then picked out an outfit to wear to dinner. Mindlessly wandering into the bathroom, her jaw dropped at the marble tile, claw foot bathtub, and massive shower. This suite had all the luxury of a five-star hotel.

After taking her time in the shower, she dried and dressed, then sat in the high back chair at the vanity in the bathroom. She reluctantly studied herself in the mirror

A stylist had come to the hospital to do what she could to even out Macy's hair. And then, she refused to look at herself. Once she made it to her father's home, she waited three weeks to take a glimpse of her hair. She'd been disappointed, hoping and praying the extra vitamins and home remedies would make her hair grow faster. But, of course, it didn't.

Frowning, she studied her left side. The hair growth almost covered the scars from the stitches. She assumed the cut had come when Jay struck her, knocking her out.

She pulled the front down with a comb and brushed it to the

side. It still wasn't long enough to do much with, but it needed to be combed. At least that proved it had grown.

Sighing, she picked up her makeup and did what she could to hide the dark circles under her eyes. The two cuts from the bombing had thick scabs. Ignoring them, she applied some eye makeup and lip gloss, still frowning at the reflection. Leaning back and closing her eyes, she prayed.

Vanity had gotten the best of her, and the devil had a good time using it against her. She'd become depressed over the past month, hating to look at herself and not allowing herself to enjoy life.

Her family, friends, and coworkers had mentioned it, but dismissing them was easy enough. However, now, as she sat alone, seeing what everyone else saw, she understood how far she'd allowed herself to fall.

Feeling a new resolve, she opened her eyes and attempted to see herself through Kane's eyes. If he saw someone beautiful, why couldn't she? Her prayers were answered as the promises of God filled her heart.

She'd been made in His image, the way He wanted her to be. If He'd created her to look a certain way, hair or no hair shouldn't matter. This just happened to be one time in her life when her hair would be short. Kane was right. One day she would wake up, and it would be long again.

Smiling, she stood and slipped on her boat shoes and walked to the door. Taking a deep breath, she stepped into the hallway.

22

Macy descended the staircase and heard Jon's voice.
"I take it you rested well?"

She met him at the bottom and smiled at his happy demeanor. "Yes. Jon, I can't thank you enough for all of this. I almost feel like I shouldn't be here."

"No, no time for discussion right now. Let's talk after we eat." He offered his arm.

She took it, noticing how thin he was. "Jon, how are you doing, really?"

"I'm getting better. I know I must still look frail, but I'm working on eating a better diet and working out as well. I will admit sleep is hard to come by."

"I think that's a problem for all of us."

She smiled as he looked over at her. Jon had a small stature, only an inch or two taller than her. But the gauntness of his face and frame worried her.

"I've been praying for you, Jon."

The comment must have taken him back because he paused on their way to the dining room.

He sighed. "I'll be honest, Macy, my faith is struggling. It's not that I don't believe, but it's hard to look at the situation and not wonder why. Why God allowed such an evil man to be in business for so long? Why He would allow Kane and me to suffer ..."

She cut in front of him, holding his arm as she looked into his gaunt face. "I can't answer that. And I don't know what he did to you, and I don't need to know. I just don't want you to give up on God's plan.

"The pain and trials we endure are for good, eventually. Even if that good is simply a life lived for heaven."

She squeezed his arm, and he gave her a thin smile.

"Besides, I can think of one good thing, even if it's a small thing."

"What's that?" His voice wavered.

Macy took a breath. "I got to meet you. You helped me those two days, and I'll never forget it. If it weren't for you putting my shoulder back in, I'd have never been able to escape."

She looked down, gripping his arm. "I—I needed the leverage to be able to kick, and if my shoulder had still been out, I'm not sure I could've done that."

He placed his hand over hers.

"I know that will never make up for what they did to you, and I don't expect it to." She swallowed as she met his gaze and tried to smile. "But I want you to understand that you gave me life."

He nodded, tears filling his eyes. She wiped her face and released his arm. He stepped back in front of her, hands in his pockets, and she followed.

"By the way, Jon, I get the feeling you're not a medic."

He chuckled and glanced back at her.

"No, no, I'm not a medic. I did study a lot in school. I was in med school at one time. Kane just thought it would be better if I posed as a medic. He didn't want any questions asked."

"Makes sense."

They walked into a large dining area where Kane and Agent Crow sat at a long table, waiting.

Jon motioned to the table.

"What makes sense?" Kane focused on her, a smile playing on his lips.

Macy sat down. "Nothing. Jon and I were just having a chat."

Jon seated himself to her left and nodded.

"I think there's more to it than that. Jon?"

"You pry too much, Kane. What are you so worried about?"

She leaned into the table, Kane's green gaze on her. He finally conceded, moving to the chair opposite her, next to Jon.

"Have a seat, Danny. More eyes are watching than they know what to do."

Agent Crow looked around. Two other agents stood in the dining room as well. Macy assumed several others stood guard outside the home. Reluctantly and with a grunt, Crow moved toward her and sat on her right.

A woman brought the food out, placing dishes in front of each person before leaving and returning with drinks.

Macy bowed her head and said a special prayer over Jon, who needed the comfort and peace he struggled to find. When she looked up, no one else had eaten yet. Once Jon picked up his fork, Kane did too, smiling when he made eye contact with her.

The dinner seemed very formal, and as much as she wanted to speak to Jon, she decided to wait until someone else started the conversation. They were several minutes into the wonderfully cooked meal when Jon finally spoke.

"Macy, tell me about yourself. Did you grow up around here?"

She frowned. Jon had barely touched his plate, and she wondered if he ate at all.

"No, I didn't grow up here. We lived in a small town in Tennessee during my childhood and moved here when I was sixteen."

"From small-town Tennessee to the city in Virginia. That must have been a bit of a shock." Jon picked at his food.

"Yes, it was. We moved here because my mother had just passed away, and my father was diagnosed with cancer. This was the closest treatment center. And, with no family in Tennessee, my father thought it best to move everyone instead of him traveling here on his own."

"I'm so sorry, Macy. What kind of cancer?" Jon's voice dropped. He wiped his mouth with his napkin.

"Colon cancer. He spent a few years in treatment and has been in remission since."

"That's amazing. May I ask what happened to your mother?"

She paused for a moment, her fork hovering above her plate. "She was hit by a car."

Even after all these years, the emotional toll of her mother's death was a sore she couldn't let heal. She could reminisce and think about her mother and be fine. But when asked about her, the topic was too difficult to discuss. Macy cleared her throat and took a drink of water.

"Where did you grow up, Jon?" Resting her fork, she put her hands in her lap and noticed his plate was almost empty. She smiled.

"I grew up here, went to school here. I've led a rather boring life."

A snort came from across the table. Kane smirked down at his plate.

"You think my life isn't boring, do you?"

She couldn't tell if Jon's tone had Kane pegged or if he was just joking.

"Jon, only you see your life as boring. Normal people see your travels, your insights, your abilities as something much more, intriguing."

"Perhaps you're right. But I'm not interested in speaking about details." Jon stood and left the room.

Kane followed.

"I was told to keep my comments slim when speaking with him." Crow shrugged his shoulders.

"Okay, so what does he do?" She frowned.

Crow's mouth dropped open. "You don't recognize him? His name? Nothing?"

She shook her head.

"That's Jon Warrick. He's the founder and CEO of two different companies that work here and overseas. He's one of the smartest men alive. He's considered national security since he's designed and created computer programs that run our defense systems."

She sat back to think for a moment. The name Warrick did ring a bell, but his face wasn't someone she recognized.

"So, you had no idea, huh?" Agent Crow looked amused.

"No, I didn't. I didn't have any reason to dig either." She frowned at him and stood. Setting her napkin next to her plate, she left the dining room with a huff.

23

Walking through the house, Macy took note of where each corridor led. The main hallway wove through two sitting rooms, a large living area with a huge flat-screen TV, a music room with a piano, and ended at the dining room she'd just left.

Ending up at the staircase and the small entryway and foyer, she noticed another small kitchen on her side of the home as well as a small living area with a TV.

"Lost yet?"

She spun around. Kane stood next to the wall, his hands, once again, in his pockets.

"Just exploring. Is Jon all right? I didn't mean to pry."

"He's fine."

"He said we could talk after dinner."

Kane shook his head. "Not right now. He needs some downtime." His expression showed concern for his friend.

"It can wait." She went back to the small living area and stopped at the large picture window that centered the room. It only took minutes to feel Kane behind her.

"What did you want to talk to Jon about?"

"Why do you want to know?" She smirked

He sighed. "Why do you always answer a question with a question? Why can't you just be straight-forward?"

"Did you ever stop to think that maybe you're a little nosy?" She faced him, arms crossed, and leaned against the windowsill. A smirk formed on her lips.

"Maybe, but when it comes to Jon, it's my job." He mirrored her, crossing his arms and looking down at her.

She watched him for a moment. He wouldn't like where the conversation would lead.

"Does he know how much danger he's in? Especially with me here?"

"Don't go there." His voice dropped.

"He deserves to know. I don't want to put anyone in danger who doesn't have to be, mainly, you and Jon. And if he doesn't know, he needs to be told."

Her jaw stiffened as Kane paced a few steps, his stone face returning.

"Macy, when I told him the situation, he asked me to bring you here. I didn't suggest it. It was his call, and the FBI agreed. Having the two main targets in one place with enhanced security was the best idea."

He turned back to face her. Pushing his hand through his hair, he frowned. "Did you really think I would allow him to do this without giving him the details about the danger?"

She shrugged. "I don't know. You seem to jump in and take over things, and I think you forget we don't know each other that well. I can easily see you holding things back to keep someone from being in danger or worried. You have that protective gene that wants to fix things and keep people from hurting or being hurt."

She watched as he paced a few steps in front of her again.

"Tell me I'm wrong."

He paused in front of her for a moment. "You're not wrong, but I wouldn't lie. And I sure wouldn't place Jon in any more danger than necessary. This is the safest place for both of you. You've seen the setup he has here. I know a few of the men outside, and they're the best. I'd hire them if I needed protection."

He moved next to her, staring out the window. His leg pushed up against hers. "I want you here where you're safe, and I can breathe."

His lowered voice sent a chill through her as she looked away, finding a focal point in the room and concentrating on it. How did he convey so much through one little sentence? There was more there than she'd experienced with any other man in her life.

The serious boyfriends, who found her work too nerve-wracking. And the one man who'd all but promised her a future but backed out because her work sent her away for a month straight. He bailed when she didn't choose him over her job. Even with all his promises of love, he never communicated such affection.

"We don't know much about each other, do we?"

"No." Yet she was already grouping him in with men she'd dated.

"Maybe, that's not such a bad thing?" He chuckled.

She glanced back up. Hope dwelled in his eyes, as well as worry.

"I'm sorry about your mom, Macy."

She nodded, stood, and his arm came around her stomach instantly. Although she intended on staying to talk with him, she'd walked away so many times he felt the need to stop her.

With a sigh, she held his arm and turned to face him, leaning in so prying ears couldn't hear. "I wasn't going to walk away." She knew at least Crow would be close by, if not others. "I'm sorry you always seem to think that's my plan."

"I'll work on that, promise. As far as our past, I want you to know, I'm not all that concerned with who you were or what you've done, Kane." She gripped the edges of his sport coat, putting her focus on his chest again and refraining from leaning into him.

"I'm much more concerned about who you are now and what you want for your future."

Hazarding a glance upward, she melted, seeing his green eyes wide, a smile on his lips.

"But, I'm willing to share if you are— if the past is something you want to talk about."

"I'm pretty one-sided on that one." He chuckled as he gripped the belt loop on her jeans. "As much as I want to know about you, I definitely don't want to tell you about my past." His smile disappeared as his gaze slipped from her eyes to her lips.

She pulled away, stepping back to a safe distance where he had to drop his hand.

"Then, I guess that's a conversation for another time." Tucking her hands into her back pockets, she turned. "I assume Jon has a workout room somewhere in this place?"

"Yeah, I'll let Crow know where it is."

She sighed and headed back to the staircase leading to her room.

After changing and grabbing her phone, she stretched out. The tension in her neck and shoulders had only worsened, and with the close conversation with Kane on her mind, she needed a workout.

Running had become her go-to after she returned and healed enough to start working out. But since outdoor running wouldn't be safe, she hoped Jon had a treadmill.

She opened her door. Crow leaned against the wall, waiting on her. He wore running shorts and a T-shirt.

"I guess you're planning a workout too?"

"Yes, and just so you're aware, this is my room in case your boyfriend isn't around to help you with something." He pointed to a door.

Macy narrowed her eyes at the comment. "Let's just go."

She frowned as Crow led the way down the stairwell and

through another hallway off the small kitchen on their side of the estate.

"By the way, my boss called and said your brother and father are safely tucked away for the next five days. If we don't have a break by then, we might have to find other means."

"Okay, so, you believe they'll be safe where they are?" The thought of DeLuca getting to them ate at her.

"They'll be safe. Let's just hope we get to DeLuca before we have to move them." Crow led her down another hallway at the back of the house with floor to ceiling windows showing off a serene garden, water features, and beautiful blooming flowers. It soon opened up to a large room with a lot of equipment, including a weight bench, Nautilus equipment, and treadmills.

Macy stepped on a treadmill facing a window. She started it up and turned on her music, drowning out the noise from Crow using one of the machines.

Setting a good pace, she closed her eyes and let the motion of her feet hitting the machine turn into a rhythm that matched the music flowing from her headphones. The rhythm took over, and her body moved on cruise control as the chaos of her life faded into the back of her mind.

24

Kane did his rounds, feeling useless because he flinched every time another bodyguard crossed his shadow. He wasn't used to working nighttime hours, and having three other people around the house to bump into wasn't helpful. A discussion with Jon in the morning might be needed to find a better use of everyone's time.

At 11:55, he headed back to his wing, gliding quietly through each corridor and double-checking the rooms. Hearing a muffled sound, he silently hastened to the small kitchen on his wing. Macy stood in front of the open fridge.

"Midnight snack?"

She turned quickly, her hand on the small of her back before she paused, taking a quick breath.

"Do you want to get shot?"

"I could ask you the same thing."

"Look, I turned on the light over the sink, so any one of the ten guards wandering around this place would see me."

"It does seem like a traffic jam around here." He chuckled.

She closed the door, holding a bottle of water.

"Okay, since I'm officially off the clock now, I'll show you my secret stash. But don't tell Crow or he'll raid it and blame it on someone else." He winked at her, trying his best to keep from admiring the view of her capris and tank top.

He reached up to the cabinet above the fridge. She shuffled to the side so he could pull down his hidden snack food.

She looked over the box. "How old is this?" Her nose wrinkled.

"I stashed it as soon as I got here."

He grinned again as she dug through, pulling out some pretzels while he settled for a bag of chips. "I bet we can find a movie on. Jon has pretty much every channel imaginable."

Leaning against the counter, her mouth pulled to the side while she considered his request.

"It's just a movie. I'll be on my best behavior." He lowered his voice and smiled.

She always gave him a grin when he spoke just above a whisper. It confused him. He thought maybe he'd just imagined it. But even earlier, he hadn't realized his voice had lowered until she smiled. He wouldn't think she'd want any reminder of those two days, but when he thought about it, his voice barely rose above a stern whisper back then.

"I guess—if you think you can behave."

"Promise." He followed her to the living area and found the remotes.

Pulling up the guide and flipping through channels, he skipped past the movies they definitely couldn't watch together and tried to find something that would be easy to enjoy.

Settling on a comedy, he noticed her grin at the selection and joined her on the couch.

She put a pillow between them and leaned into it. Propping his legs on the coffee table, he tried to get comfortable, but no such luck. He glanced over, watching her laugh, smiling at the sound. How could she smile, laugh, find humor when her world crumbled around her?

He stood and moved to the kitchen. Grabbing a bottle of water, he leaned up against the bar to watch her.

She smiled and laughed as she curled up on the couch.

It didn't make sense to him. Her home had been destroyed by a man who was chasing after her, her family moved into protective custody, and now, she was custody as well.

"Hey, if you don't want to watch this, we can find something else." She smiled at him.

His heart rate jumped.

"No, it's okay." Moving back to the couch, he undid his sleeves and rolled them up, unbuttoned his collar, and sighed.

After shifting and moving a moment, he glanced over to see her intently watching him, her blue eyes shining in the glow of the screen.

"Have you decided yet?"

"Decided what?" He huffed and rolled over to face her.

"What it is you want to say?" She had her head propped up on her hand as she leaned against the pillow that separated them.

He smiled and took a breath. "How are you doing this?"

"Doing what?"

"Not to bring it all up, but with everything that's happened, how can you sit here and watch a movie, smiling and laughing like nothing's wrong?"

His smile faded as she leaned back against the couch. Her jaw clenched, and her happy demeanor vanished.

"I guess there are a few reasons. For starters, I'm choosing to enjoy this time." She faced him again, her eyes scanning his face. "It all starts with a decision. The first one I make is usually to ask for strength and peace about everything. I can't deal with it on my own."

"Strength and peace?" He tried to keep from sounding so condescending.

"Kane," she shifted and pulled her legs from under her body

and tucked them next to her, leaning toward him. "Have you ever had a friend or family member or someone in your life who made things easier when you were with them? Or you found yourself stronger and braver just because you knew they were there and had your back?"

He nodded as he watched her play with the corner of the pillow.

"It's really not any different. Except when I ask for strength and peace, it's a thousand times more than what any friend can give me." She glanced up, a small smile on her face.

"I just don't see how you can have peace about any of this." He cleared his throat.

Her grin grew, and she threaded her fingers through his. Having her hold his hand gave him comfort, a lifeline that grounded him. Emotionally, he was spent. Wanting to be with her, but being chained to his job and feeling the need to protect Jon too. It made things more difficult than he'd ever experienced. Her touch eased his breath, and his body relaxed.

"I know that Jon is having trouble too. I just, I can't answer the why questions because I don't have those answers." Her focus changed to their hands. She moved her thumb across his knuckles.

"So, he doesn't have peace then?"

She shrugged. "I don't know. I don't think so."

"What makes it different for you?"

He watched as she placed her other hand on his, tracing the line of his fingers. He swallowed at the feeling.

"Kane, I didn't go through what you two did. There's no way I can compare what I'm dealing with to what you two endured. I'm really sorry you both went through that."

"Since Jon's a Christian, why did he have to go through it?"

"Christians aren't exempt from pain." She glanced up and smiled. "We live in the same world and deal with the same issues everyone else does. We just try and handle it differently. We fail a lot, but we try."

She lost him again. None of it made any sense.

"So then, what's the draw? Why bother if it's not going to change anything in the long run?"

"Well, it does. It changes everything. First off, just like I said a couple of months ago, I believe in a place worse than the one we were in and a place of perfection. I would rather be in perfection." Her focus returned to their intertwined hands. "Also, to have peace after what happened—it's not an easy thing to do. But, if I ask God to take the pain, then actually let Him take it and not dwell on it, He does."

"Just like that?"

She shrugged. "Well, it would be if I let Him take it. It's really easy to get sucked in, allow the anger and sadness and depression to take over and wallow in it." She paused, licking her lips. "But, yeah, if I just let it all go, my life is instantly better. Paul called it the peace that surpasses all understanding." She smiled and looked up at him.

"Peace, huh?"

"And love. The Bible says you can't fully love someone if you don't know God."

"I don't believe that." He shook his head and frowned. He had loved a few women, even considered marrying one.

"You can love, but what happens when it gets hard? Relationships are hard. Fighting, arguing, temptation, trying to make concessions, giving up a little bit of power. What happens when all those things hit? When you want to walk away?"

"I don't know. They've never come back." He grinned.

She frowned at him.

"Sorry."

"It's okay."

He shrugged. "I get that part. It is hard, and sometimes it's just easier to leave when it comes to relationships. I guess that makes sense. But that still doesn't change the fact that we had to go through everything we did. I mean, where's the line? God allows this man to torture people for information and money? Why does He allow him to live?"

He swallowed the rage that pulsed through as he spoke of the man responsible for his pain, hours of pain, every day for weeks before Macy arrived. Sitting up, he released her hand and leaned against his knees.

"Look—" she dispensed with the pillow and sat up next to him "—nothing I say will make up for what happened to you. God allows men to make their own choices. He won't force anyone to follow Him. It's a choice." She stood and paced a few steps.

"Kane, I just want you to know that if it weren't for you and Jon, I wouldn't have made it out alive. That's a fact. I know it doesn't make up for what you had to deal with, but having you there allowed me to find a way out." She propped her hands on her hips as she shifted nervously.

He stood and led her toward the tall pub table in the corner of the room, offered her a chair, and moved the other seat in front of her. Hopefully, the corner would provide more privacy from the three or four guards who now roamed the inside of the home.

"You're much stronger than that. I have no doubts you could've made it out."

"I don't think you understand."

"Then tell me." He rubbed the top of her knee, fighting every urge to hold her.

"If I do, you'll only get mad and upset, and I don't want that." Her voice dropped as she rubbed her bare arms.

"No, I won't."

Her expression showed her doubts.

He grinned. "Okay, I'll try my best."

Leaning against the table, she held her head for a minute. "From the second I got there, you kept telling me to find a way out. I was already on it, but there was nothing I could do, especially after Jay almost beat me to death."

He flinched, sitting up slightly and clamping his mouth shut.

"I didn't have any arm strength, and my back was so busted up from my fall that I couldn't bend or twist at all. I knew I might be able to run a short burst or kick maybe, but ..." she paused and took a breath. "Kane, when that guard had me cornered, I was trying to blow him off."

"I remember." The words came through his jaw. He suddenly saw where her story was leading, and he didn't think he could handle it.

"I heard your voice saying find a way. He pushed me against the wall and had his hands under my shirt, squeezing my waist."

He stood quickly to move, but her hand shot out and grabbed his arm.

"I wanted to do the same thing, Kane. In fact, I would've tried to kick him down, kill him, whatever. But I'm pretty sure I would've failed. He either would've killed me there, or I would've had to wait until the next morning for the men who brought me in to kill me. You can ask anyone who knows me—accepting that offer wasn't in my playbook.

"I always told myself I'd rather die than deal with that situation." She moved into his space.

Kane tried to steady his breathing, calm his body.

"But, because you supported me, talked to me, encouraged me, I went along with it. I wanted to save you and Jon and the others. I wanted to get out alive too, but it was no longer about me."

"So, because of me, you allowed yourself to be taken and almost—almost raped?" His voice came out harsher than he anticipated. But the frustration of the situation had sunk in, and he felt sick to his stomach that she credited him that way.

"That's not what I'm saying." She squeezed his arm before she let go.

Feeling as if her understanding of the situation came from a different dimension, he turned, took a few steps away from her.

Macy was next to him in an instant. "I'm just trying to get

you to see another side of things, okay?" Her whisper barely held as her eyes started glossing over. "It will never make up for what happened to you, but if you hadn't been there to help me, I wouldn't be here. You gave me the strength to take that risk, one I'd already written off long ago. I—" Tears streamed down her face, and she took off for the stairwell toward her room.

25

Kane turned off the TV, sank onto the couch, and tried to find a thread to pull this all together. He'd encouraged her to do whatever she could to escape. He knew the risk involved, allowing the guard that close. But, he had to admit to himself, when they first brought her into his cell, besides the shock and anger that moved through him, he saw a chance at escape.

Little did he know how much those conversations would end up meaning to him, and obviously, to her as well.

Sighing, he grabbed the snacks, put them in their hiding spot, and eased up the stairwell. He paused at her door, wanting to apologize and hating the fact she became so upset at him. She'd just relived a terrible experience, and he blew her off. Maybe he just wasn't cut out for this kind of relationship.

Facing the door, he leaned his head against it for a minute, trying to decide if he should knock or not. Before he could come up with an answer, the door opened, and she pulled him inside.

"Macy, I'm—"

"Just hang on, okay? I'm sorry I brought it all up. I shouldn't have. I guess I just thought it might help you understand, but it's too personal." She wiped her face and paced.

He caught her arm, slid his hand to hers. "I do get it."

She looked up at him for a moment, and he saw the war going on in her eyes. There had to be more to the story she'd held back from him. There was only one reason that guard had taken her back there, and although she escaped, he couldn't imagine her fear.

"I just need you to understand. You can't change what happened. You may never understand it either, but there's always a purpose behind the trials we face. It's your choice how you respond to it. You can get bitter, mad, and depressed, or you can find a way to use it. Find at least one thing good." She bit her lip

He pulled her in, needing her in his arms. She pushed back after a moment, still holding his sides as she gazed up at him.

"My mom was killed by a hit-and-run in a small town where everyone knew everyone. No one ever came forward, and her killer was never caught. It's been the hardest thing for me to deal with. But, after dad got diagnosed with cancer, we moved. I hated that town and everyone in it for covering it up. I was so certain someone knew and just didn't want to tell." She shook her head and took a breath.

"So, when we moved, I made some new friends. Dad was clear and in remission. Then, right after college, one of my friends lost her mother to cancer. I was there to talk with her and help her through it." She focused on him again.

"Every day, I wish my mother was here and that she hadn't been killed. But, when we moved, my dad got help. I found friends who are still very much in my life today, and I've been able to help more than one friend deal with grief because I lived through it. That's the way I choose to look at my trials. God helps me with that."

He wiped her cheek and finally began to see what she'd intended to say all along. She looked through her life with a different filter, one he had no idea how to use. He traced her jaw to her neck, then pulled her in, kissed the top of her head.

Closing his eyes, he rubbed her back and felt her arms finally wrap around him. She had become his comfort, and he felt a nagging in his heart. Macy's faith was very important to her, and he began to understand why. Her life had one trial after another, and yet, because of her faith, she found a way to not only deal with it, but flourish.

"You need sleep." He sighed. "I can't believe you're even awake."

She squeezed him tighter, and he smiled, reveling in the feeling of her wanting him to stay.

"You're the one who has to work, Kane."

She started to pull away, but he stopped her, resting his head against hers.

"I'm glad you talked to me, Mace. I guess I'm just surprised you were even listening to me back then."

She pushed back to look at him, and he smiled at her amazing eyes.

"I don't think you get it."

"I do, I told you. Your face is what I see when I close my eyes. I remember every word, everything you said." He traced her jaw, just needing to touch her. "I'm slowly forgetting the pain." He swallowed and wrapped his arm back around her. "I haven't had a nightmare since seeing you that night."

She smiled up at him. Kane's heart stalled. His eyes moved to her lips, and she immediately leaned into him, burying her head in his chest. He smiled and blew out a breath, gripping her tightly. She was getting too good at shutting him down.

"I think I need to go," his whispered words barely came out at the catch in his throat.

"Yeah." She looked up with that smile.

"Why do you smile when my voice gets low?"

"I do?" Her grin went up a notch.

He squeezed her upper arms, enjoying her playful tone.

"I guess I just like it."

Moving quickly, he kissed her lips, taking his time. Her hands on his chest gripped his shirt until they slipped around his neck. On tiptoe, she pulled him down for a moment before lowering herself. He stepped back, catching her eyes, holding his stance inches from her face.

"Maybe we shouldn't do that so much," she whispered.

Her wide eyes looked into his. He smiled as her lips curled upward. They were both breathing heavily, and he caught her drift. It took great restraint to keep from moving in for more.

"Yeah, I do need to go." He watched her, just waiting for her to change his mind, but she didn't. Moving his hands down her arms and gripping her hands, he took a step back. "So, what now, Macy?"

"You go to your room and sleep."

"That's not likely." He grinned as she chuckled.

"Then, go back to the weight room." Her playful tone returned.

"Okay, then what?"

"Then, maybe tomorrow, someone will have caught DeLuca, and this whole thing will be over."

"Then?" He smiled as she rolled her eyes.

"I don't know. I guess we'll have to see what God has planned."

He sighed, wanting more. He wanted her with him all the time. The feelings he had were much too strong for barely knowing the woman. But he knew enough, and he loved her.

"Kane?"

"Yeah, I'm going. Get some sleep." He winked and moved quickly to the door before he did or said something stupid.

Entering his room, he sank to the foot of the bed, holding his head and feeling dizzy as the thought entered his mind. How could he love her? Usually, at this point, the only thing he felt had to do with the physical side of things, her attractiveness.

Suddenly, a thought hit him, and he groaned, covering his

face with his hands. He'd never dated a Christian woman before and hadn't thought of the morals she might have compared to his own. Physical stuff would be off the table. Anything more than what they were doing now would be off-limits. That wasn't something he was used to.

Embarrassment flooded him as he stripped off his work clothes, changed, and headed for the gym. No wonder she shut him down so easily and quickly moved him out of the room. He didn't even think about her side of things when it came to her faith.

Stepping on the treadmill and setting a quick pace, his mind rolled. What if she decided he wasn't someone she could be with because of his past relationships? Living together and sleeping together before marriage wouldn't be something she'd approve of, and he'd done both.

All those years in the military, moving around and finding a place to visit with friends, usually involved some kind of romantic entanglement. But, as he thought back on his many trysts, he couldn't even picture one face, remember one name. He shook his head, feeling sick at the life he'd lived. All those women he'd been with, told them he loved them, then left. How could he claim to love at all after what he'd done?

Her words from earlier hit him. She had clearly stated that his past wasn't as important as his future and who he was now. He kicked up the incline and breathed heavily as her words weighed on him.

After ten minutes of practically sprinting up hill, he decreased the incline and slowed down. He got off and leaned over to catch his breath. The same feelings still rose inside him. He loved her, very much. Maybe even more now that he thought about it. Yeah, the physical stuff was something he wanted, but she'd become more important than that to him.

Sitting on the weight bench, he closed his eyes and eased the tightness building inside him. How could his past really not matter to her? Admittedly, he was curious about her past, but then again, if she'd done something he disapproved of, it wouldn't change how he felt about her now. But she didn't do the kinds of things he'd done. His time in the military, the people he'd killed, women, children, and men.

Although, his life had changed during the past few years. The importance of working for Jon changed his stance on bar scenes and clubs, women, and frivolity in general. His age might also be a factor. But those were all things he knew she would disapprove of. So, where did that leave him?

With a towel draped over his head, her words echoed, but he couldn't believe them. If she really knew who he was, what he'd done, she could never love him. In his life, all the women he'd dated and the few he let close enough to love, the thought of losing Macy sickened him, and he ached. But he could never live a lie with her next to him. He had to come clean and tell her the kind of man he really was.

Wiping his face, he felt his body shake. He needed to get to his room before he collapsed from exhaustion and the shroud that now hung over him. Telling her would be the hardest thing he'd ever done, but he needed her to know before this went any further.

He hurried back to his room and showered before he collapsed in his bed. Nausea worked through his body as he tried to think of a way to tell her how little he deserved her. His phone rang minutes later as he rolled to the bedside and yanked it free.

"Bledsoe."

"Kane."

He straightened. "Bart?"

"We need to talk."

Taking a breath, he cleared his throat. "Okay. What do we need to talk about?"

"He's here."

"Who?"

"The man who held us captive. I know it."

"How do you know that?"

Bart's huff echoed. "I've got contacts too. I'm in Virginia. A friend has kept me apprised. I hoped you'd do the same, but since you didn't, I had to get other help."

"Look, I got your message and your number." He stood. "But I can't talk about it. I will say DeLuca's got a lot of people looking for him, and I think it's best if we let them do their job."

"Are you kidding me? You trust anyone else to take this guy out? What if they mess up?"

His jaw clenched. "I want him too. You have no idea. But we're not in Mexico. There are rules here and—"

"Rules?" A gritty chuckle echoed. "There are no rules here, man. Not when it comes to him."

"Bart."

"I've got a line, and I'm following it. I just figured out of all those guys we were with, you'd be the one who would want him worse than me."

"Just stop." He paced, doing his best to ease his voice. "I'll meet you, and we can go over what you have, okay?"

Silence resounded.

"Bart?"

"Fine."

He let out a breath. "Meet me at my brother's, 1459 Baylor Street. I'll meet you out front."

"Be there in twenty," Bart mumbled before the call ended.

Tossing the phone on the bed, he quickly dressed and shoved his holster back on. He snatched his keys and phone, rushed from the room and to the front door.

"You out?"

"I'm off till nine." He nodded to one of the guards and slid into his truck. "I'll be back by then."

Bart leaned against his car when Kane pulled to the curb.

"Took you long enough."

Kane frowned and motioned for Bart to follow. In silence, they climbed the stairs, and he unlocked the door.

Flipping the switch for the lights, he ushered Bart inside and shut the door.

"Tell me what you know."

"Maybe you should share." Bart glared.

He shook his head and settled against the bar. "Look, I don't know anything except that there's a task force already on it. This is a federal case now. He's on U.S. soil, and these people are good at their jobs."

"We're better. We should be in on this."

"You know personal assets never work. They don't want him dead. They want him alive so they can fish out his network. He's no good to us dead."

Bart huffed. "Not so sure about that."

"Just tell me what you know."

Bart paced a moment, his arms stiff. A red tinge crept up his neck. "I was given some breadcrumbs, just enough to get me here. I have an idea where he is and the group he's working with."

"What group?"

"Some local gang. A friend of mine says without proof, they can't just go in and take care of the situation. They want to prosecute." Bart's hollow stare met his. "But they don't understand who he is and what he's done. I don't need proof."

He nodded. "Your friend, you don't trust him to take care of it?"

"She's intel, not on the ground. She wouldn't tell me all of it, just enough to get me here. I do know they have a mole. Someone has been giving up bits and pieces, and that's the trail they're following. I've been poking around since yesterday. Someone with a lot of money and a lot of fear has moved in. Even the police say it's quiet."

"You have more than one friend."

Bart nodded and continued to pace. "Good friends, friends who know things were bad."

"So, you're going after him?" Collin stood at the door of his bedroom, fists clenched and glaring.

Kane spun, surprised to see Collin. "I thought you were gone."

"Got back this morning." Collin's stare shifted to Bart. "I get it was bad. I saw it was bad. But going in alone will either spook him back into hiding or get you killed." He stepped into the room and crossed his arms. "Is that what you want? To know this maniac is out there and back in hiding because you messed up?"

"I won't mess up."

"You've already been poking around. There's no telling how much you've already messed up."

"Enough." Kane stepped between the two men. "Bart, I'm not letting you go out there alone. But you have to make me a deal."

Bart scoffed. "I don't need to make a deal."

Stepping into Bart's space, he stared down the man who spent weeks with him in that cell, helping to bind his wounds. "You think I don't want him more? He's after her now."

"She's here?" Bart's eyes went wide.

"I want him more than you can imagine. But if we go, and we find him, we call it in. A visual from us is more than enough proof for the feds to come in and take care of it."

Bart nodded.

Kane turned to Collin. "You stay here."

"Not a chance."

"If something does go bad, it'll ruin your career." He frowned. "I'm not letting that happen."

"I'm going." Collin stepped forward. "You're not putting yourself back there again. Not if I can help it."

Shaking his head, Kane brushed past his brother to his bedroom and packed his extra equipment.

As long as he was back by nine, things would be fine. Jon's house was on lockdown, and no one would be able to get in. Macy would be safe.

"God, keep her safe," he mumbled as he lifted the duffel bag over his shoulder and headed through the living room. "Let's go."

26

Parked outside an old house on an abandoned street, Kane used his night vision goggles to peer into the residence a few lots down.

Vines and branches covered the outside, barely making it noticeable that a house stood within the brush. Two SUVs were parked up the street from the house, and empty lots littered the street.

"She told me the mole gave them a little info at a time, trying to keep himself from going to prison. The last thing he mentioned was DeLuca's need for men. He needed to hire out help, people with connections, and who weren't afraid to do what needed to be done."

"Still doesn't explain how you got here," Collin mumbled from the back seat.

"The SUVs. They don't fit. Regular gangs don't drive those kinds of cars—it draws attention. They have to be getting money from someone to have that kind of vehicle. This place, there's no one around, no homes. It's all abandoned." Kane lowered the goggles and handed them to Bart. "I'm guessing you have more than one contact in the police?"

"I grew up here." Bart shrugged. "But I moved to the east coast last year. I still know a lot of people."

"So, what's the plan?"

Kane tried to find a way to keep them both in check. Bart would go off if DeLuca really were in there, and Collin would start a fight just to keep everyone away.

"Did you ever see DeLuca?"

Kane's eyes flitted to the rearview mirror, Collin watching him from the back seat.

"Nope. Just pictures."

"I did."

Kane looked over at Bart, who shifted in the seat.

"He came in a few times.

Silence filled the cab as Kane pushed away the memories, the pain, the desperation from being taken captive. But now, DeLuca was on U.S. soil. And Bart had a point—they weren't looking for a case, they just wanted him caught.

"I'm going to take a closer look. You two sit tight."

Sliding from the truck, Kane pulled his bag from the back seat and secured it to his shoulders. As he turned, Bart and Collin stood waiting.

"We're going," Collin murmured.

"I don't know about him, but you sure aren't enough to stop me," Bart smirked.

Collin huffed.

"Fine. Just remember our deal. He's there, we call it in."

Both men nodded. Kane brushed past them and headed into the darkness.

Edging up to the hidden house, he squatted down at a fallen tree. So far, there had been no movement in or around the area. Was Bart wrong?

"At your 1 o'clock," Bart whispered from beside him.

Moonlight seeped through the trees. A glint made him freeze. Rifle slung across his chest, a man was walking around.

The guard paused and looked around a moment before

walking the perimeter. They'd been parked outside the house for at least an hour, and no one had come out. Why secure the area now?

After the man moved out of sight, Kane motioned Collin forward.

"Get out and watch the road. I have a feeling something's up," he whispered.

Collin nodded and slunk back into the shadows.

Motioning to Bart, he followed to the edge of the trees and snuck around the back of the house. The back was cleared, no trees or bushes blocked the creamy stucco that stood out in the moonlight.

The guard from earlier stood outside the door, smoking a cigarette.

Hunkering down, Kane waited as Bart edged closer. The stealthy sniper was impossible to see when clouds covered the only light.

Frowning, he shook his head. Bart better keep his focus, stay in control. If DeLuca was in that house, Kane was much too far away to prevent Bart from acting out.

A sharp bird call made him turn. Collin had seen something. Dim lights seeped through the trees, and a large truck came rambling up the road.

Pulling out the goggles, he searched the overgrown lot but didn't see Bart.

Stifling a groan, he turned to the truck. Sliding down from the seat, a large man shifted the hat on his head before strolling to the back of the rig. A series of clunks and metal rollers echoed in the air.

"Oh no," he whispered.

DeLuca stoically marched to the house, a detail of twenty men behind him. His chin raised and jaw set, DeLuca greeted the guard before the door opened, and he went in with a handful of men. The rest stayed in the darkness, pulling out cigarettes and talking loudly.

With at least fifteen men to combat, they were more than outnumbered and outgunned.

Where was Bart?

"We need to go." Collin's whisper barely sounded behind him

He nodded. "Bart," he whispered.

Collin grumbled behind him.

"Wait here."

Sliding the rifle to his back, he pulled himself on his belly and found the same trail Bart had taken, the grass bent and flattened from his weight. He did his best to ease his way across the lot without being seen.

A tug on his boot made him tense. Looking under his arm, he saw the back of Bart's foot as he returned on the same path.

Sucking in a breath, Kane looked up at the men, now only twenty yards away. A few were pacing the area, smoking their cigarettes, completely oblivious.

Shifting, he slowly made his way back to where Collin and now Bart, waited.

Leaning against the fallen log, Kane blew out a breath.

"Out of shape, old man?"

He frowned at Collin's grin.

"Let's get going." Bart took off back toward the truck.

Kane jumped up to follow. "In a hurry?"

"You said call it in, so make the call," Bart mumbled.

As they hit the road, a loud explosion rocked the street. He turned to see fire blasting in the air.

"What did you do?"

Bart stood, staring at the fire. His hollow features lit up. "Just making sure everyone knows where he's at."

With a groan, Kane unlatched his bag and slid into the seat, throwing the bag in the back as Collin and Bart got in. Before he could start his engine, gunfire erupted, and a group of men ran toward them.

"You should've had a longer timer," Kane muttered. He shoved the truck in drive and spun from the street.

"If you weren't so slow getting back—"

"Shut up, Bart."

Flying through the street, Kane tried to make the highway, but the men caught up. The large semi barreled toward them, its headlights blinding Kane as he tried to keep the truck on the road.

"Hang on!"

The hit from behind made them fishtail. He slammed on the brakes enough to stop the spin, his truck running backward while the semi bore down on them.

Bart shifted out the window, firing on the semi and taking out the lights.

"Get in! I'm turning here!"

He yanked the wheel to the left. The truck careened into the street, and the semi attempted to follow. Shifting into gear, he floored the accelerator and left the stalled-out semi behind, bullets ricocheting around the truck.

"Give me my phone."

Collin handed him the phone, and he dialed Crow.

"Kane?"

"We need backup. Now."

"Where are you?"

Kane turned his head in time to see the headlights just before the impact. His mind shut down, his body eased as darkness crept in.

27

Macy woke feeling rested. Knowing her family and Kane were safe had allowed her some much-needed sleep.

After dressing quickly, she took the steps down to the kitchen to find an empty room. With a frown, she strolled through the corridors and rooms, still seeing no one.

Her heart dropped.

Something was wrong.

Dashing back up the stairs, she banged on Kane's door.

"Kane?"

The knob turned, and she stepped inside to see his bed slept in, but no one inside. Rushing to Crow's room, she found the same thing.

"Jon," she muttered.

Sprinting down the steps, she paused at a knock at the door.

She pulled her weapon from the small of her back and approached the door as another knock sounded. Macy peered through the side window. A large figure stood on the stoop.

A shiver moved down her spine.

Macy ran down the hallway, yanked out her phone, and tried to call 911. But there was no signal, and her cellphone simply cut off.

Turning down a back hallway, she heard the breach at the front door. Darting from room to room, she looked for Jon. The sound of his voice gave her hope. She turned a corner and aimed her gun.

A man dressed in black stood between her and Jon, his back to her. He turned and fired a shot that went over her head. She fired two into his chest. Jon's face went white. She rushed into the room and grabbed him.

"Come on. We need to get out of here. Where's your safe room?"

"My room."

"Let's go."

She let him lead until the next corridor. Pushing him behind her, she slowly crept down the hallway, gun ready.

"Door on the right," Jon whispered.

They shifted to the right side of the hallway. As she opened the door, shots rang out from behind them. Shoving Jon inside, she quickly bolted the door and followed him into what looked like a closet.

"Can you call out?"

"Yes. I have a secure line inside."

"You're sure? Once we go in, we'll be stuck."

"Positive."

They entered the space and slammed the heavy metal door behind them. The locks automatically engaged, but Macy shoved a large hammer bolt in place anyway.

"We need help. Now. Where's Kane? Where's Crow?"

The banging on the door was barely audible, but it proved just how driven the men were at getting to them. How did DeLuca find them so fast?

"I don't know, I— I have no idea." Jon scrubbed a hand down his face and held the phone. "This is Jon Warrick, and we need immediate assistance at my residence. Yes, the FBI, now."

Jon's voice was calm, but she could hear the hysteria just below the surface.

He hung up and paced the room. "They're sending everyone. I talked with SSA Burger personally. He was already on his way, Crow never answered his phone call, neither did Kane."

"You don't know where he is? He didn't tell you anything?"

"No."

Her worry amplified while she paced. Where was Kane?

"Macy, you're bleeding." Jon's eyes widened.

Blood trailed down her arm and dripped off her hand. With the adrenaline pumping through her body, she never felt the shot.

Jon took off his outer shirt and ripped it apart, then tied it skillfully around the wound. "You should sit, prop your arm up until it stops bleeding."

"No, not yet. Not until our backup arrives."

The banging on the door grew louder, and she knew the intruders were close to breaching the room.

"Can you monitor the front gate from here? See where our help is?"

Jon sat at a small desk and clicked through a computer program. A color image of the front gate pulled up. The gates were locked in place with no one around.

"Where is everyone? What happened?" she muttered, looking over Jon's shoulder.

A large crash sounded. She turned to see a bend in the door.

"Jon, we need an escape route, I'm not sure the FBI will make it in time."

"There's not one. That door is supposed to handle anything the military can throw at it."

"Maybe, but all at once?" She frowned.

Jon started hyperventilating, gripping the edge of his desk.

"Jon, Jon look at me," she ordered and pushed herself into his line of sight. "We'll be okay. We'll be fine."

"I—I can't go back there. I can't," he muttered.

Her gaze moved back to the screen. An SUV was ramming the gate.

"Look, the FBI is here."

Macy started clearing a metal cabinet. Pulling out stacks of paperwork and heavy boxes, she threw them on the floor.

"What are you doing?"

"Buying some time."

After emptying it, she pushed and pulled until the cabinet crashed to the floor.

"Help me move it."

Jon helped her push the cabinet toward the door. Metal scraping the concrete made her head pound. She felt her heart pulsing through the cloth tied around her arm.

Once at the door, she grabbed a few boxes. "Okay, let's get it up. We'll use the boxes to lift it and block the door."

A glance at the monitor showed the FBI now climbing over the fences, but she wasn't taking any chances.

Grunting and straining, she and Jon managed to lift the heavy cabinet, and she pushed the boxes beneath it as the noise of gunfire sounded through the beaten door. Jon stepped back and took an extension cord from the wall. He used it as a rope to pull the cabinet upright while Macy pushed.

With the cabinet in place, the sounds of gunfire echoed, and she realized they had cut through the door, at least in one place.

"Are the locks good?"

Jon moved to the monitor and switched screens. "So far."

Needing to move, she stacked large boxes against the cabinet, knowing full well it wouldn't be enough if the men really wanted to get through.

The cabinet shook slightly. Macy and Jon both pushed their weight against it.

"FBI, don't move!"

The shouts preceded a barrage of gunfire. She held her ears as the noise filled the room.

"Mr. Warrick? Ms. Packer?" SSA Burger's voice carried through the metal door. Macy sighed, her body slid to the floor.

"We're here. Macy needs medical attention." Jon collapsed next to her. "Now," he breathed out heavily, "How do we move the cabinet?"

She laughed out loud and flung her arms around his shoulders. They clung to each other in tears.

28

After a cursory exam and some stitches, Macy collapsed in a new bed in a new safe house provided by the FBI. Her brother and father were there with her. Jon had been moved to another location of his choosing.

She still didn't know the breakdown of what happened, and they had yet to find Crow or Kane. Worry plagued her.

When she settled down for the evening, Kane's absence resounded in her mind. Nothing would pull him away, not without telling her. At least, she wanted to believe he wouldn't leave her. *Where was he?*

Jon promised he'd find out and make sure she was informed. But worry washed over her, and she knew sleep wouldn't come. Rolling from the bed, she paced.

The hostage situation she survived was horrific, but she had at least been there to save Jon, Kane, and the others. But who was going to save Kane this time? And what about Crow?

DeLuca was still out there and seemed to have no trouble finding her and Jon. Her optimism faded quickly.

"Lord, please protect Kane. Send him safely back to me, please," she whispered.

29

K ane's eyes snapped open.

Where was he? More important, who was watching? Faint streaks of light fell through the window of the whitewashed hospital room. His left side throbbed. A crumpled form leaned on the bed from a nearby chair, her upper body resting next to his hand.

Moving his fingers, he traced hers to wake her up. Macy rose quickly. Her eyes focused on his, and she smiled.

"Hey. You're awake." She gripped his hand tightly.

He could see streaks on her cheeks from dried tears.

"How's Collin? Bart?" He grimaced. The burn in his throat ached.

"Collin is in for surgery to set his collar bone. His room is down the hallway. Bart's already been discharged. You feel okay?"

Kane smiled and attempted to pull her to him, but his arm didn't work. He sat back with a groan. Bandages covered his shoulder and side. His upper body was bare, and he felt a frown forming.

"It's mostly superficial. The doctor says there's some slight muscle damage but nothing that needs surgery. You got lucky.

Bart told me how bad the crash was once he woke up." Her voice caught.

He pulled the sheet to cover his chest. The last thing he wanted was for Macy to see his scars, remind her of what they'd gone through.

"A few cracked ribs, bruising, a concussion," she trailed off.

"Come here, Mace." He motioned with his right arm.

She went around the bed, crumpling in tears next to him as he hugged her.

"I'm so glad you're okay, Macy. I'm sorry, I'm sorry I left and ..."

"Stop it. I'm not mad you left, okay? Just stop." She traced his cheek, then buried her face in his neck. "Bart told me what happened. I just—I'm glad you're safe now."

Fighting the emotions threatening to overwhelm him, he swallowed hard and held her close with his good arm. His body ached. He wanted to wrap her up and never let her go, but his mind pushed at the thought.

"Macy, I—I don't know what to say. I want you here, and I want to be with you, but ..."

She pulled back, wiping her eyes. "But what?"

"I've been thinking about what you deserve, and what I can give. I don't think I'm enough. I mean, I'm not good enough—"

"Don't do this. We can talk about everything later, after you heal."

He opened his mouth to speak, but red seeped through her sleeve. "What's that?"

He pulled at the sleeve, and she winced.

"What happened?"

She groaned and sat up, wiping her face. "It can wait until you're healed."

"No, no, it can't. What happened?" He looked behind her and scanned the room. "Where's Crow?"

Her jaw clenched a moment before she answered. "Crow's gone, I don't know where. We were attacked early this morning.

The men, they scattered. A few turned up dead. The FBI is looking for the rest."

His jaw dropped. He tried to get closer, wanting to see the extent of the damage.

"Stop it, Kane, I'm fine. It's just a scratch."

"You mean, everyone bolted? How'd they get in?"

"I don't really know." She shrugged and wiped her face. "They won't fill me in. I haven't seen Jon since I was taken to the hospital. He's staying somewhere else, I guess." She swallowed hard. Her shoulders drooped.

"Let me get out of here. We need to get you set up—"

"You can't leave. I'll be fine." She stood and glared at him, her arms crossed, face flushed. "Or do you just want me to leave?"

"I don't want you to leave, not until your protection gets here."

"My protection detail is outside." She shook her head and walked around the bed to where she'd been sitting. "I had to practically force my way here, and you wake up and don't want me here." She gathered her purse and jacket with a huff.

"I'll let you have some time to get your head on, Kane. I know you've been through a lot, but I've already told you how I feel about your past. If you can't get over it, don't use it as an excuse not to get close to me, okay?"

"Mace—"

She stormed out, letting the door slam.

He sat back with a wince. Nausea flooded him, and his mind started to spin. Macy needed protection, and he didn't trust anyone but himself to do it.

The door slammed open again. Jon entered with a frown on his face.

"What did you say to her?"

"I don't want to talk about it." He groaned, wiping his face with his hand.

"She's devastated. She's been here all day long waiting for you to wake."

"What happened? I know Burger probably informed you what's going on."

"Kane."

"Jon." His voice rose, making him grimace. "Tell me what happened. Did they catch him? Where's Crow?"

"No." Jon shook his head. "And as far as everything else, I'm not sure what's going on. Burger has been quiet about it and won't give me much. Several of my men are unaccounted for, which makes me nervous." He paced, his arms crossed against his body. "At least Lillian wasn't there. She would've been injured, or worse," he mumbled.

Straining to sit up, Kane watched his friend pace around the room. "Jon?"

Red bathed the smirk on Jon's face.

"The nurse? What's going on with you two? And why didn't you tell me?"

Jon shrugged and held his hands behind his back. "After the breach, things just happened, and I found myself worried about her safety. It's amazing how much can change about your life when you start worrying about someone else instead of focusing on yourself."

"I'm happy for you, Jon. You deserve it." He managed a smile.

Jon's gaze drifted to the cuts. "You deserve it too, Kane. Stop pushing her away and listen to her. She cares for you very much."

"I need to get out of here." He sighed and leaned back, pulled the blanket back up over his chest. "You and Macy need protection, and I don't trust anyone but myself to do it." Straining against exhaustion, he finally found the call button, ignoring Jon's stare.

"Can I help you?"

"I need to see the doctor."

"He'll be with you shortly."

He leaned back and huffed, closing his eyes.

"Where do they have her, Jon? Is she safe?"

"She'll be safe. But I want you to think this through. If you can't offer her what she needs, are you sure you should be the one protecting her?"

He sighed and allowed grogginess to overcome him.

PACING THE APARTMENT, Macy blew out a deep breath.

The morning started with a sitrep from Zander's boss about his condition. Although better, he was still critical. But of course, being in protection, she couldn't visit him.

After day seven with no contact, no plan, she was done waiting.

"I need to talk to your boss." She glared at the armed man sitting next to the door.

"Why?"

"This isn't going to catch him."

The man shrugged. "Not my call."

"That's why I want to talk to your boss."

He frowned and pulled his phone from his pocket, placed a call, and explained her request.

"Yes sir, here." He handed the phone over.

"SSA Burger?"

"Yes, Ms. Packer. What can I do for you?"

"What's the plan? How much longer am I going to have to stay here?"

He sighed heavily. "You know how this works. It's a waiting game."

"You mean, you're waiting on him to find me, or you have an actual trail to track him down?"

The silence lingered.

"We think we have a line on DeLuca. Give us time to work, Ms. Packer."

The call ended. She tossed the phone to the guard and walked away. "Thanks."

Macy sank onto the window seat, curled into a ball, and watched as the sun sank in the sky. Kane had made a few efforts to call and talk, but the conversations never lasted long. Mostly because she would get upset when once more, he'd comment on how unworthy he was and how he would destroy a relationship with her.

Hugging her knees, she held back her tears. Kane had been the only man she felt she truly loved, and yet, he had no idea what love was, even though he'd been adamant about how much he loved her.

Not seeing him since the day he woke in the hospital was killing her, knowing he was alone with no comfort. But she couldn't take it anymore. She wanted to jump off the pedestal he'd placed her on and forget how much she cared about him.

A knock sounded on her door. She jumped. Her guard stood and motioned her to stay back. After looking through the peephole, he opened the door.

"Jon, what a great surprise." She pulled him inside and hugged him.

Almost a week had passed since she'd seen him, and although he was still quite thin, he had a calmness about him.

"I hope I'm not intruding." Jon gave her a timid smile and shoved his hands into his pockets.

"Of course not. As you can see, I don't have much going on."

Her father entered from his room. Macy introduced them, and the two shook hands.

"I've heard a lot about you. Thank you for helping my daughter."

"She did all the work." Jon smiled

Her father nodded and strolled toward the kitchen.

She motioned Jon to the couch. "There's something different about you. Want to share?"

Jon's face reddened. "I—I'm seeing someone."

Macy's mouth dropped open. "In the middle of all of this, who could you have possibly been able to see?"

"Lillian, my nurse. I've been working with her since we got back, and after the breach, I just, we realize how important we were to each other."

Her happiness waned. She wanted to be pleased for her friend, but it was a shot to her heart.

"She's amazing." He finally sat down, leaning on his knees with a sigh. "Macy, have you spoken to Kane recently?"

"Not in a few days. I, well, I'm not taking his calls right now." She clenched her jaw and swallowed hard, forcing back a wave of emotions.

"I'm so sorry everything is disrupted. I've tried to speak with him, but he doesn't seem interested in talking to me."

"Yeah, that seems to be the case lately." She tucked her legs up underneath her. "Is he, I mean, has he been released?"

"Yes, three days ago. He's staying with me, insisting the men need his help in guarding me. I asked why he didn't come here, but he didn't answer."

Her face heated. "I thought things would change once he was discharged and feeling better, but obviously, he's holding on to something ..." she trailed off, trying to keep her tears back.

"I want to help you two. Tell me what to do." Concern and worry etched his features.

"You can't fix this. I can't fix this. Honestly, I don't even think Kane can fix this. He's confused and hurt— two things that make him shut down. I just pray. That's all I can tell you to do."

"I know you love him. I can see it."

She sighed. "He doesn't know what love means. Otherwise, he wouldn't push me away like this."

Jon frowned.

"By the way, how did you find out where I am? They haven't given me any ideas about where you are."

"I guess I have connections." Jon winked, then stood. "But don't worry about me, I'll be fine. I'll be praying for you and for Kane. Between DeLuca being free and this situation, I'm worried he won't be able to handle life until one or the other gives."

"Thank you for coming by." She swallowed hard, followed him to the door. "Take care, Jon."

He squeezed her hand and left.

30

K ane went to physical therapy to get his shoulder evaluated. He wore a tank top, allowing the tech to check his stitches without revealing his scars, keeping any questions at bay. His shoulder finally worked after a week of pain every time he moved. But with DeLuca still out there, he needed to be back in shape, back to work and healed, ready to go.

"Give me a week, man. I think we can have you up to par by then. You'll have to go slow, easy with those sore ribs."

"Sounds good." Kane nodded to the physical therapist and began his workout.

He grimaced at every extension in his shoulder, every rotation, welcoming the reprieve. The pain of not having Macy with him during the day, the fact she wouldn't even talk to him on the phone anymore, killed him, made him more than miserable.

The burning in his shoulder seemed to compensate, overtaking his despondency, and he found it ... necessary. If he was ever going to move past this, he needed the pain to push her away.

He did another few reps and stopped for a water break, resting his arms on his legs. Her face surfaced, and he did his best to control his anger and frustration. He'd never had feelings like the ones he felt for her.

Hope, that stupid thing that caused all of this, killed him. He'd hoped to be enough, want her enough, and be good enough, but the hope was wrong. He wasn't enough of anything for her.

Squelching his desire to hit something, he put the anger toward his workout and grunted. The sting of his shoulder kept him pressing on, moving forward to a future he didn't understand. A future without Macy and with DeLuca hanging over both their heads, waiting to strike.

STANDING inside SSA Burger's office, Macy frowned while she paced. It was Sunday. The meeting came almost two weeks after Kane's accident. During those two weeks of being held in one safe house after another, her mood deteriorated. Nothing made her happy anymore.

She feigned happiness during talks with Jon, but she still ignored Kane's sporadic calls. Her father had tried to calm her nerves, but he didn't understand, couldn't comprehend the darkness falling over her.

DeLuca was a force who had quickly found her last time. Impending dread filled her heart. He'd do it again. Only this time, the FBI wouldn't be there to protect her. Or Kane.

Her dreams and nightmares had worsened, and so had the tremors. But now, she didn't have Kane there to calm them. No one else could understand and help her. She blew out a big breath. When had she become so weak?

"Can I get you anything?"

She looked up and forced a smile to the nice woman who was apparently Burger's secretary. "No, thank you."

"SSA Burger will be here shortly."

She nodded as the woman sashayed to the door and opened it. Burger walked in.

"Sorry about your wait, Miss Packer."

Her jaw dropped when Jon and Kane entered the room behind SSA Burger.

"Wh— what's going on?"

"Macy, have a seat." Jon motioned to a chair.

She crossed her arms and refused to sit.

Kane's eyes stared right through her. She forced her gaze to remain on SSA Burger.

"I take it you've devised a plan?"

"Yes, we've discussed at length a plan to flush DeLuca out of hiding."

"Because that's worked so well in the past," she mumbled. Memories of her brush with death and the bomb blast that cost her job stole her breath.

"Macy ..."

She glared at Kane as his voice trailed off. His gaze locked with hers.

"Ms. Packer, we think we have a good lock on DeLuca. We have someone inside who's been able to make contact. I think our plan is good enough to trap him for good."

"Crow." She narrowed her eyes as SSA Burger's brows rose. "I'm former Secret Service. I have a working understanding of threat assessments and what it takes to design a protection detail. You wouldn't put something together for someone like DeLuca. He's too dangerous to risk losing to." She frowned. Being the bait was back on the table, and she didn't like it, not one bit.

"I was just read in, Macy, and I think it's a good plan. But I would like to hear what you have to say." Jon patted the chair beside him.

She sat, taking the folder from his hands.

"We think DeLuca is more interested in revenge than information at this point," Burger said. "If we position you where he can get to you, we'll be there to trap him."

She read through the scheme. The FBI felt secure enough to

offer her up as leverage. "You do realize fifteen men were guarding Jon's property when we were attacked? That means DeLuca has at least double the men. Thirty to forty men is a hard team to trap."

"Some of Jon's men were his. DeLuca found a weakness in the group and exploited it." Burger frowned. His face reddened.

She focused on the folder in her hand. The plan centered around an armored vehicle motorcade. Crow would dish the information out and help DeLuca plan an attack, an attack they could counteract. She leaned back in the chair and sighed.

"Mace?" Kane's voice hit her heart.

"It's good." She swallowed the lump lodged in her throat, allowing her eyes to flit toward his for only a second—long enough to notice the pain etched on his face.

He obviously hadn't slept in a while. Dark circles shadowed his eyes, and he was more worried than she'd ever seen him.

"It is good, Ms. Packer. But it won't work if you don't agree to it. I can't force you, and I need you to take into consideration—."

"I know exactly what could happen. I know the statistics and the odds." She stood and paced the room.

"Give us a sec, Marty," Kane said.

She paused at the window and looked out. Footfalls crossed the room, then the door opened, then shut. Kane's reflection appeared, and she hugged herself.

"What do you want, Mace?"

Closing her eyes, she took a breath. "I want this over."

He stepped beside her and leaned back against the window. She did her best to avoid his gaze as she stared out at the buildings.

"You look tired, Macy."

"Really?" She scoffed. "Have you looked in the mirror?" She finally faced him but kept her distance.

"Part of the job." He shrugged.

She frowned. "What do you think?"

"It's good." He sighed and shoved his hands in his pockets. "But we both know DeLuca is smart. In order for him to work for so long without anyone finding him, he's too sharp to simply trust what Crow says."

"But I don't want to sit around and wait anymore," she mumbled.

He wrapped his arms around her before she could stop him. Unable to resist, she clung to him, buried her face in his chest, breathed in the smell of his cologne. She'd missed him.

"Why don't you want to talk to me anymore?" he whispered.

She closed her eyes. "I can't stand to hear you say you don't deserve me or how bad you've been or the things—"

"Mace, I want the best for you. You don't understand."

She groaned and pushed away from him. Wiping her face, she took a few steps back.

"This! This is why." Her voice wavered as she crossed her arms, clenched her jaw. "Tell Burger he can do whatever he wants. I need this to end, and I need to get back to my life."

His mouth set in a hard line as he nodded, then turned to leave.

She turned to the window and wiped her face, a wave of unease settled over her. For so long, the feeling of peace seemed to rain down on her from God, like He was right there with her through all the trials and heartache. But now, she felt more than alone. Emptiness overwhelmed her.

Leaning her head against the cool glass, she whispered, "What now, God?"

31

"If everyone sticks with the plan and doesn't do anything crazy," Burger honed in on Kane, "this will work."

Attempting to hold his irritation in, Kane nodded and controlled his voice. "She's willing, but I'm not so sure. You do realize the stakes here, right?"

Burger nodded with a grim frown. "I do. If we miss him this time, he'll disappear forever and end up a ghost again, free to reform his business."

"Not just that. Macy. She's been through the wringer with this, Marty. I'm not willing to let her go through with this when we both know how tricky keeping her safe will be."

Burger nodded. Jon paced the hallway.

"Jon? What do you think?"

Jon's unease worried Kane. As an outright genius, Jon had never acted distracted when confronted with a strategic situation. But now, his demeanor seemed more than a little reluctant.

"I don't like any of it. My emotional reaction is to find another way." Jon scowled at him. "We both know what that man is capable of. Letting Macy out like a lamb to the slaughter isn't something I'm willing to accept. But, knowing DeLuca is free, roaming around and searching for weaknesses—I'm not willing to accept that, either." His focus turned to Burger. "Are you sure there's no other way?"

"Mr. Warwick, if there is, you would be the one to see it. This man has perfected the art of underground. He has a lot of money, and we never could catch up with him, much less freeze his assets. Nothing is in his name, and if it weren't for Ms. Packer, we wouldn't even have what we've got. With the intel she gave us, we still don't have anything on him. Enigma doesn't even begin to describe it."

Kane clenched his jaw and paced a moment, trying to keep his head on straight instead of feeling her arms around him and the smell of her next to him. He turned to Burger.

"What about me?"

"What about you?" Burger narrowed his focus.

"You could put me in that car, make me the decoy."

"Kane ..." Jon shook his head

"You know he'll be watching, but we can make a switch somewhere, rearrange the cars or switch the plates. It's not a new idea, Marty. I've done it before."

Burger leaned back against the wall, his arms crossed. "That would put our inside man in a bad position. If DeLuca suspects for one second that we're up to something, that we suspect anything, Crow would be the next one under DeLuca's thumb."

"How do you know he isn't already?" He glared at Burger.

Burger's focus never wavered. "I trust him. Do you?"

"I could never see him as a traitor, no, but I'm not so sure he wouldn't do whatever's necessary to save his hide."

"That's comforting." Jon's frown deepened.

"We'll run it. That's all I can give you, Kane. If it doesn't work in trial, I won't commit to it."

"Just give it a chance. It'll work."

The lump in his throat lessened as Burger walked away. If he could make this thing work, he could keep DeLuca away from Macy. And right now, that's all that mattered.

"You sure about this?" Jon stepped in front of him, concern and worry etched in the lines of his face.

He nodded. "More than anything."

"She won't let you—"

"Then she won't need to be told." His gaze narrowed until Jon got the hint and nodded. "You better go in there. She doesn't seem to want to talk to me right now."

"She does—that's the thing. If you'd just let your past go, she'd gladly be there to talk with you, be with you."

"Jon ..."

"No! I'm getting this out now."

Kane sighed and turned to leave, but Jon's arm shot out and grabbed his. In five years, Jon had never made physical contact, anything even close to it. The closest Kane had ever been to him was when he'd guided him during events. Jon had never acted this way.

"You need to let this go. You need to realize the guilt you're holding on to has nothing to do with her and everything to do with you. Realize, Kane, that you're about to let the most important thing God has ever placed in your life go because you can't recognize her love for what it is."

"What it is? She has no idea ..."

"She doesn't need to, and she could care less. Love is pure. It's forgiving, unrelenting, and patient. There's a whole chapter dedicated to it in the Bible. That's what she has for you, because that's what God has for you." He sucked in a deep breath. "If only you'd see it."

"Jon, I appreciate the sentiment, but right now, all I care about is getting Macy as far away from DeLuca as I can and putting DeLuca away for life. And I need you to promise me something."

Jon's eyes narrowed. He crossed his arms. "What?"

"If this works, and DeLuca takes me instead, promise me you'll watch over her, keep her protected. Everything I have goes to her. Promise me."

Jon's face went red as he nodded.

"Good. Go tell her we're on, and her detail can get her back to the safe house." He headed to the elevators. He couldn't handle seeing her again, having her pull away from him. He huffed out a breath, rubbing his forehead as the elevator descended.

"This has to work. I have to fix this. She deserves more than being tied to a protection detail and spending the rest of her life in fear," he mumbled.

HEAD POUNDING, Macy walked through the safe house, ignoring the two guards who were on night patrol. After two weeks, she should be more accustomed to the situation. Suddenly, she had a new respect and perspective for the people she'd protected during her years working secret service and private detail.

Her father was handling the situation better than she expected, making light of their confinement and enjoying game nights of cards or dominos almost every evening after dinner.

Of course, he was unaware of her situation's extent.

Macy sat on the couch, gripping her Bible to her chest. She needed to read, to study, to find some nugget of truth or promise to help her get through this. But seeing Kane, allowing him to hold her and comfort her and then pushing him away, had left a hole in her heart. The unfairness of life weighed on her, and for the first time in forever, she was fed up.

She sat the Bible on the couch cushion and grabbed the packet Burger sent for her to study. It contained a copy of the plan to lure DeLuca.

The four-vehicle team would allow DeLuca to have a visual of her entering the armored car, and then they'd head for the next location, supposedly a new safe house in the middle of nowhere.

If everything went as planned, Crow would suggest they attack at one of two pre-planned locations, since he'd be giving up the new safe house location. If successful, DeLuca would lead his men into an ambush, and the FBI would take them over before a breach occurred.

She sighed. Unfortunately, she knew they wouldn't be that lucky. DeLuca was too smart, and he wouldn't fall for any of Crow's ideas. Crow was risking a lot getting so close. Knowing DeLuca would be leery of his advice, it could easily blow up in his face.

Even armored cars weren't indestructible, and if DeLuca had as much money and pull as she assumed he did, they were looking at much more than thirty men armed with M16s and a few bombs.

Shoulder and even mortar launchers would be her guess, enough to take out as many vehicles as possible at once. She felt sick, risking the lives of so many men, including Kane.

Nausea threatened her as a tremor swept through her. Closing the folder, she pushed her hair from her face and wondered if Kane had already made plans without her—plans to keep her out of harm's way. She shivered. He'd do anything to keep her from DeLuca, even if that meant trading himself.

Lord, please let me be wrong.

If anything happened to Kane, guilt would trap her. She groaned and snatched the TV remote from the armrest. It would be a long night.

32

Burger managed to get everything moved into a nearby empty warehouse so the drivers could practice the switch without anyone observing. Kane had already scouted the best place for the switch to occur, but the drivers were far from the military trained specialists he was accustomed to.

"Look, we'll have multiple attack points and need to be aware, even as we switch." He motioned the men over to the playboard, a visual aide to help the lesser experienced understand their job.

Pointing at the bridge where they'd gradually increase speed, and his car would overtake hers, he motioned to one of the drivers. "You're the lead advance vehicle. You must be ready for a front attack. Let me know the second you notice anything disruptive at all."

He then turned to the other. "You'll be the CAT in back. When we're attacked, you move in and take them out or provide cover. Macy and I will be in separate vehicles in the middle, and I need to be apprised at all times. Our Exfil is here." He pointed to a slope a half click away that led to an abandoned gas station.

"If we're attacked at this point or the curve right after the bridge and things go south, we meet up here. Keep your eyes open at all times, and make sure you communicate everything. DeLuca is a pro, and he's hired pros. We know how they work based on how well they took over Jon's compound."

He frowned as the video feed he'd reviewed played through his mind. "These guys won't give up, so we must be at the top of our game. Yes, we have back up, and yes, if everything goes as planned, we should be able to drive straight through with only a few gunshots. But chances are, DeLuca won't let us go so easily. If he actually attacks where we have planned, I'll be shocked."

He sighed and rubbed the back of his neck. There were a few other points of attack, but none as appealing as the bridge and the blind curve. With the FBI lying in wait, hopefully, they'd keep this thing from blowing up in their faces. But the switch needed to be his focus right now. If they couldn't get everything smooth, Burger would never approve it, and Macy would be at risk.

"Let's give it a try. I'll be watching. Keep talking. I'd rather hear about something that wouldn't explode than you not mention it and end up blowing yourself up."

The chuckles made him frown. Keeping things lighthearted might be the way some of the men worked, but not him. This was serious business. His life and Macy's were on the line, and he needed this to be perfect.

"This has to work," he muttered as the cars started their engines.

MACY STOOD in the FBI lobby. Her stomach leaped up to her throat, and she tried to swallow. Telling her father goodbye this morning had killed her. It was her idea to keep him in the dark, and Burger didn't object. She knew her father would be adamant about not letting her be bait, but even as scared as she was, she needed all of this to end.

"I won't be afraid," she mumbled as she tried to recite the Lord's prayer in her mind.

"Mace?"

Kane's voice echoed in her head. She closed her eyes. Taking a deep breath, she turned and crossed her arms.

He looked better today, calmer. She frowned.

"And just what do you have planned?"

"What makes you think I have something planned?" His eyebrows arched as he took in a breath.

Yep, he was up to something. "I know you too well, Kane." She stepped in front of him, letting anger fuel her words, keeping fear from taking over. "If you've already planned a switch or a fake, let me be clear, I'm not for it. Burger wants it to go a certain way, and I agree. Any deviation from the plan could result in a mistake neither of us could live with."

"It'll be fine. Promise." He reached for her.

"Just make sure you follow the plan." She backed away, her body shaking. She tried to hide her tremor and created some distance.

Burger sauntered up and nodded with a grim frown, obviously the situation weighing on him as well.

"Ms. Packer, you'll be in the middle car and Kane in the back. Let's get this show on the road. And no mistakes. Got it?" His gaze drifted from the men and few women in front of him before landing on Macy. "You're still good?"

"As long as the plan hasn't changed."

His gaze narrowed, and her heart fell. She knew it.

"We're all set." Burger walked away before she could question him.

"Get this on." Kane pushed a vest into her arms.

She snatched the vest and pulled it on, then retrieved her sidearm. Checking the rounds, she took the offered clip and shoved it into the back of her pants before returning her Sig to its holster.

"See you on the other side, Mace."

Swallowing hard, she made eye contact. Those amazing green eyes seemed brighter today than they had in the past few weeks. Not trusting her voice, she nodded and slipped past him, brushing his arm and trying to ignore the stir of attraction.

The vehicles were lined up just inside the garage, visible enough to anyone who might be watching. She took her spot in the vehicle, seeing Kane enter the SUV behind her. He winked.

Once inside, she sat in the middle, where she would ask her protectee to sit if she were on duty. Leaning on her knees, she tried to focus. Two men crawled in on each side of her, and the vehicle started.

"You good?"

"Not my first time. Let's get this over with."

The vehicles moved out of the garage, each one armor-plated and ready for action. She scanned for the typical threats provided by urban areas: roadblocks, gridlock, and detours.

Kane's voice periodically came through the radio as the lead car gave a step-by-step account of everything he saw on the side or in the road. She shook her head and tried to contain her smile. Kane had these guys trained well.

As they neared the bridge, she tensed up and reached for her gun. This was one of the ambush sites, and she frowned as the vehicle behind her suddenly moved to the front, smoothly and without hesitation. Kane.

That had been his plan—for DeLuca to attack the wrong vehicle and him to be taken hostage, if necessary. Her jaw clenched. She refocused on the drive and the possible attack.

As they rounded a sharp curve, her anxiety crept up. The bridge and the curve were the ambush sites they had prepared for. So, what now?

The motorcade entered the freeway. They traveled a few miles, the radio strangely silent. After the next onramp, a large semi pulled alongside them.

"Watch it ..." she murmured.

The two lead vehicles appeared unaware as the semi crept closer to Kane's SUV.

"Radio in. This is it!"

Just as she yelled, the semi rear-ended Kane's car, simultaneously slamming their vehicle into the median. They flipped and rolled.

Gripping her seatbelt's shoulder strap, she tried to keep from crashing into the men or the seat in front of her. She failed, and pain centered over her left eye. Metal crushing metal echoed as they rolled and finally bounced to a stop.

She held her head to ease the pounding. Kane. She had to get to Kane. Working aimlessly at the seatbelt, she finally freed the latch.

"You need to go, run ..." a fading voice from her left echoed as she wiped the blood from her eye.

Dizzy and disoriented, she pulled herself over a mangled man before reaching the door. Macy checked the man's pulse and swallowed hard. Bile filled her throat—another man lost to DeLuca.

Kicking at the door, she cracked it open enough to see men gripping Kane's arms, dragging him, unconscious, to the back of the truck. They heaved him inside.

"No," she murmured and pulled her weapon free.

The men climbed in the back of the semi while she pushed and shoved against the SUV's frame. She had to get free in order to attack. Otherwise, they would both be in trouble. With a groan, she finally opened the door enough to crawl out.

Falling to her knees, she aimed her gun. But the truck was already gone. Taking Kane with it.

"Macy!"

Turning, she squinted to see a form running toward her. She aimed her weapon, and the man slid to a stop, his hands raised.

"It's me. Drop it."

Crow.

"What—what are you doing? Why did they take Kane?" She slowly lowered her weapon, uncertain of his intent.

"I tried to tell him DeLuca would do anything to get to you." He stepped forward and grabbed her arm, helping her stand. "The switch worked. But, when they didn't see you, they took him."

"Why didn't the FBI stop them?" She pulled away and fell into the SUV behind her.

"They weren't ready for the attack here. I swear, Macy, I had no idea this was the plan. DeLuca told me the bridge."

Sirens echoed in the air—the FBI backup that was supposed to stop the entire thing and capture DeLuca. Too late. She held her head and looked up at Crow's red face, his shirt torn and bloody. Was it fake?

"If you betrayed him—"

"I know Kane better than you. I'd rather die."

His grim voice made her anger boil.

She motioned to his shirt. "Was that good enough to convince them?"

"It's not all fake. They were going to take me out anyway. They just have terrible aim." He gripped his side, pulling his hand away to show real blood saturating through his shirt.

Macy shook her head and groaned at her mistake. "Let's go."

"Where?"

She pushed him off and steadied herself.

"You need a doctor and stitches. We're not going anywhere."

"DeLuca has Kane again. I'm not letting him down. We need to go." Macy fell forward, slamming her palms and knee to the ground. She winced from the heat of the road and the burning of glass.

"I already called Burger. I know where they're going, and Burger is getting a team together."

She looked up to see him kneeling next to her.

"If you're wrong ..."

"I'm not. One of his men shot me. I'm dead. They won't

change up the plan worried about me coming back." The grim line across his face deepened.

Macy was still unconvinced.

"Come on. I'll help you get cleaned up and your head working, then we'll get to Burger and the men."

She allowed him to ease her up. Disoriented and injured, there was no way she could navigate this without help.

Lord, give Kane protection until we get there. Please, Lord. You have to save him.

33

The pressure on Kane's chest lessened. He rolled to his side and coughed, an attempt to get his lungs moving again. The acrid taste of blood filled his mouth. He spat.

"You are awake."

Kane squeezed his eyes shut. *DeLuca.* His plan worked. Macy was safe.

Pushing up from his side, he straightened and opened his eyes. A man sat in front of him, rugged and dirty, gripping his hands tightly. Looking him over, Kane could tell this man wasn't used to a life on the run, a life filled with sleepless nights and uncomfortable bearings. DeLuca had grown weak.

"You look tired, DeLuca," he muttered.

"No, not tired. Angry. Where is she?"

Kane shrugged and spat out some more blood. Instead of a dirt floor, he sat on concrete, filled with dust and debris. He groaned and straightened, leaning back against the cold wall.

"Just who is it you're after?"

DeLuca's laugh was dry and forced. He was a desperate man, and that made him dangerous. But DeLuca had no idea how desperate Kane was to keep Macy safe.

"You are playing a dangerous game, Mr. Bledsoe." DeLuca

stood and paced. "You know, I enjoyed watching your stay at my home. You were strong, and to witness you shrivel into the measly, weak and bleeding man you became made me confident about my job there."

"But we're not there anymore," Kane growled.

"No, no, we are not. However, that does not change things. I am still very passionate about getting what I want, and I know you have it. You and Ms. Packer, you have grown close, have you not?"

Kane shook his head. "She doesn't like me very much, hardly talks to me. Your intel is mistaken."

"It is not exactly intel."

DeLuca took a folder from a man standing next to the door holding a rifle across his body.

He tossed the folder on the floor. Pictures scattered around Kane's feet. There was a shot of him visiting Macy at the scene of the bombing, holding her arm as she ushered him down the driveway. A picture of them standing outside the FBI office, her eyes closed as she leaned up against him, and he held her. His heart pounded harder.

"That was before," Kane muttered.

"Humph." DeLuca used his foot to push the pictures around, finally pulling out the one he wanted Kane to see.

Standing at the window in Marty's office, a keyhole photo showed him holding her right before she pushed him away. *Was the mole in Burger's office?* Not good. Hopefully, DeLuca still didn't know about Crow.

"Did your mole tell you what happened right after that?" He looked up with a grin.

DeLuca shook his head.

"She shoved me off and yelled at me to leave." Kane chuckled. "Trust me, you've got the wrong bait."

DeLuca's stare was almost as good as the glare of Kane's boot camp drill instructor. "She will come for you."

"How can you be so certain?"

DeLuca only chuckled before he left, slamming the door behind him. As if on cue, another door opened. Four men entered, intently making a path straight for him.

Kane waited until the first was close before he leaped with a throat punch and kick to the groin. The first man went down. Kane landed a right hook on the next guy's jaw, then jabbed his elbow into the man's ear. He fell, but a searing pain sliced through Kane's back.

Turning with a yell, he snatched the knife and broke the attacker's arm as he twisted and ducked under, avoiding another strike by the fourth man. Shoving the wounded man, he knocked both down before a surge made him fall. His body quaked as the voltage of a stun gun paralyzed him.

"Get some pictures and send them in."

"Not yet."

A fist slammed his face, followed by a kick to his gut. Kane groaned as he tried to pull his knees to his chest. A boot came at his face, and he closed his eyes, unable to defend the hit. His mind shut down, and the pain suddenly vanished.

"YOU WHAT?" Macy jumped up from the hospital bed, barely able to keep herself upright as Burger grabbed her arm.

"Easy."

"Don't tell me easy. Crow was supposed to be your inside man, your trusted inside man." She barely contained the anger in her voice, glaring past Burger to Crow.

"You calling me a liar?" Crow stepped forward.

She tried in vain to sidestep Burger and get to him.

"I'm saying this whole thing seems off, and you're right in the middle of it. You told me you knew where they were keeping him." She pushed Burger's hand away for the second time.

"I do know where, but they've got it on lockdown. We can't just break in. You have no idea—"

"Don't tell me what I don't know."

"Look," Burger's loud voice echoed in her ears, "we need to sit down and work this out."

"You have no idea what they're doing to him in there. I do." She glared from one man to the other, fear rocking her. She stepped back and leaned against the bed. "You have no idea ..." Her voice trailed off as she strained against the tremors.

The doctor came in and huffed. "Ms. Packer, you need to get in bed."

"Discharge me now. Take out this IV, or I will." She took a deep breath, striving to appear in control while she fell apart inside.

The doctor called a nurse to remove the IV. "I'll get your papers ready."

"Thanks," she mumbled.

"Now, if we can sit down and talk calmly ..."

"She's not going to trust anything I say, for some reason." Crow glared at her. "Did Kane tell you I wasn't trustworthy or something?"

"No, he just seemed reserved about you. He's a good judge of character, so I'll trust his gut." She made her way to the small fold-out couch against the wall and bent to put her shoes on. Dizziness threatened to overwhelm her when she leaned over.

"It's not that." Crow groaned and knelt in front of her, wrestling the shoe from her grip. "We met in boot camp. I was younger than the others and a jerk. Then, after we were separated, we ended up together in an overseas ... situation. I was too eager to prove myself. I messed up, and Kane had to clean it all up for me."

He finished tying her shoes and sighed. "Look, trust wasn't the issue with us. It was my lack of responsibility back then. Since gaining over a decade of experience in the Marines and nearly another at the FBI, it's no longer an issue."

She leaned back, studying his face. Everything in her said he was telling the truth, his body language, the control of his voice. But, she really just didn't like him.

"Fine. But as far as this breach is concerned, I'm involved, understood?" Macy noticed the hesitancy of both men. She stood. "I know DeLuca better than both of you. I'm what he wants, and I'll do whatever it takes to get Kane back."

"Then let's go." Burger nodded.

Macy slowly followed the two men.

34

Pacing the large warehouse, Macy clenched her fists. She knew Burger and Crow were doing everything possible to plan the breach, but her patience was shrinking.

"This came for Ms. Packer." One of the men who'd been on the driving assignment strode toward her with a phone. Snatching it away, she powered on the phone and gasped at the image of Kane, bloody and beaten, lying on the floor, unconscious.

"No ..." A lump formed in her throat. She fought the urge to vomit. Closing her eyes, she steadied herself against the table's edge. A text notification pinged, forcing her to focus.

I am willing to exchange him for you. No FBI, no one else around, Ms. Packer. I am watching.

"He's watching?" Her gaze met Burger's.

Besides Crow, everyone who survived the motorcade was present, along with a few extra agents to fill in the gaps.

Crow took the phone. His face paled as he read the text.

"If he does have someone watching, and they see me, they'll

move." Crow handed the phone off to a tech to debug. "Make sure we aren't being traced."

"You have a mole." She turned to Burger.

"He's bluffing."

Shaking her head, Macy groaned at the pieces falling into place. "How did he get Jon and Kane in the first place?"

"The detail was tracked from here to Germany. They attacked the second Jon and Kane landed. It wasn't FBI jurisdiction."

"But you knew about it, right?" She frowned at Burger. "I mean, national security like Jon leaves the country, I'm sure you weren't the only agency aware. In Mexico, my detail was blown, the information about the senator and where we were leaving from leaked. No one knew that little detail about how we were leaving." She shook her head.

"We arrived by plane at the airport and had one waiting to take us home when we diverted. The FBI gave us the all-clear for the transport." She pointed a finger at Burger's chest. "You have a mole, SSA Burger. And they've been busy."

Burger's mouth tightened. He frowned. "Not in my building. DeLuca is just messing with us."

"I agree with Macy." Crow looked to her with a nod. "The fact that DeLuca found us at the Warrick residence has been bothering me. No one outside of us and the men already hired on duty knew. Someone has been listening in. It's your call, sir, but I'm concerned about my being here. If we lose the location on Kane, we may never be able to get him back."

"Let me make a call." Burger left the area.

Macy pressed a hand to her stomach.

"We'll get him back, Macy."

She only nodded at Crow, wiping her face as she sank into the chair.

KANE AWOKE, gasping for breath. With a groan, he held his stomach. Pain and breathlessness overwhelmed him.

"Wake up."

A gritty voice came from overhead, and he rolled to his knees. The taste of blood once again in his mouth, he spat and wiped his face. That shock had taken all his energy, and his eye was so swollen, he could only see out of one now.

"You get water."

The sound of a slam made him grimace. Looking up, he saw a bottle of water sitting on the floor next to the door. He slowly crawled to it, his entire body aching from being a punching bag. He collapsed against the wall, taking shallow, even breaths to ease the pain.

He drank what he could, not caring whether or not it was drugged.

Why was DeLuca keeping him alive? Better yet, how could he destroy DeLuca from the inside so he couldn't get to Macy?

The questions rolled around in his head as he leaned back against the cold, hard wall. His mind grew tired.

"IT'S BEING HANDLED." Burger returned, red-faced and obviously upset.

"You know who it is?"

Macy stood as he passed her, making his way to the table.

Burger shook his head. "No, but with the dates from the abductions and now this, we should be able to narrow it down. The good news is, they didn't know about Crow. Otherwise, the compound wouldn't still be crawling with his men."

She blew out. "We need eyes in there."

"Can't," Crow shook his head. "I noticed he has a protection grid against electronics. It's very high-tech for a man who has no ties here. I've never heard of him working within the U.S., and

I'm wondering how he got manpower, weapons, and equipment he has."

"The same way he got his mole. Money." She shrugged. "Besides, that mole has more than just information on senators and persons of interest. Whoever it is will have the names of who to go to for all those things you mentioned." She sighed and leaned against the table, looking over the blueprints. "I need to text DeLuca back. We need to get in there."

Crow frowned. "And you're willing to do that? Go in there blind?"

"I don't think I have a choice. If I can get to Kane, get him in a safe place, then you guys can come in hot. He's the only hostage, so if I go in, maybe I can keep us from being in the line of fire."

Burger leaned against the table, staring at her. "Going in hot on a man like this won't give us the name of the mole."

She glared. "I know you want that name, but capturing or killing DeLuca is more important in the long run. You'll get your answer, and you'll find your mole. But you may not ever get another chance at DeLuca. He's too dangerous to simply let him get away."

"He's not getting away ..."

"Just let me do this." She eyed Burger. "Give me the phone."

With a frown, Burger took the phone from the tech's hand.

"It's clean. I've blocked the GPS."

She nodded to the tech, then typed a reply to DeLuca.

> Name the place and time.
> I have no problems getting off the FBI's radar.

I am sure you will not. Five Hills Park, eight o'clock in the morning.

We will find you.

> If I don't see Kane, I won't be willing to come easily.

236

> You better bring him.

You are not in the position to negotiate, Ms. Packer.

Her anger boiled as she groaned.
Crow shook his head.
"I know, I know," she muttered.
Taking a deep breath, she texted back.

> You're not the most trustworthy man Señor.
> I'm only willing to give up myself if it allows Kane to go free.

Seconds went by before she finally received the reply:

I will consider your request.

"We need eyes in that compound, and we need to figure out a plan." Macy blew out a breath and faced Burger and Crow. "I want Kane taken care of and safe."

She stared at Burger, who nodded. Shoving the phone into Crow's hands, she made her way outside, needing some air and a chance to breathe.

Minutes later, Burger stepped out. "Jon wants to speak with you."

She took the phone from his hands.

"Macy? I've been worried sick. What's going on? Burger's been tightlipped about everything."

"He's got Kane, and I have no idea what to do." She paced as she spoke. "I told DeLuca I would meet up, but I'm not so sure he'll bring Kane along."

"Macy?"

She leaned against the wall, her emotions now in pieces at the thought of losing Kane. Sobs and shudders overwhelmed her body.

"Macy? Talk to me. Where are you, and how can I help?"

"We're—we're at some sort of warehouse. Burger set it up." She wiped her face. "He's got a mole, and we're doing what we can to keep things quiet."

"I'm headed that way. I'll have Burger give me the details. Macy, you've got to have faith here."

She groaned. "My faith is shaky. I just—things have been so bad, and now this. I don't think I can take much more."

"Macy, did you ever call the number I gave you? The therapist I wanted you to see?"

"No, I've been in custody. Things are just too busy right now."

"Let me talk to Burger. I'll be there as fast as I can."

"Okay."

"I'm praying, Macy. You should too."

"See you soon." She leaned against the wall, handed the phone to Burger, his voice fading as he headed back inside the building. Sliding down the wall, she wrapped her arms around her knees. "God, this isn't how it's supposed to go."

Her life flew more and more out of control, and she had no idea how to handle it anymore. All the times she talked about giving her fears and failures to God and moving on, she still couldn't let go of her anger about Kane's capture. It just wasn't fair. It wasn't right.

DeLuca was still alive, and now he had Kane, again. What could she do?

35

As Macy leaned against the building, several of the men filed out, jumped into their cars, and left the parking lot. "What's going on?"

Crow paused and looked down at her. "Burger wants to clear out for a bit, says you should stay and wait."

"Jon?"

He only nodded, climbed into an SUV with Burger, and left.

After only a few minutes, a large, dark sedan pulled up. Jon stepped out of the car, a case in hand.

"Come on, Macy. After talking to Burger, I think I have a plan." Jon reached for her hand.

Taking his hand, she stood and followed him inside. Jon pulled out his laptop.

"I think I can take care of the tech side of things. Burger mentioned they have a lock on the compound Kane is in, but the tech is keeping everyone in the dark."

Sitting next to him, she watched his hands fly over the keyboard. "Why did everyone leave?"

"I told them to. This borders between legal and me needing an attorney."

She smiled as Jon became completely ensconced in his work, his focus solely on the screen in front of him.

"I should be able to hack into the system and get a picture."

After a few more clicks, a set of images popped up. The breath stilled in her body. Pointing at the corner, Jon nodded and clicked on the image. There in black and white was Kane, lying on his back.

"No!" She covered her mouth. Even with the grainy image, she could tell he was badly hurt. He held his stomach, and his chest moved up and down with slow, haggard breaths. "He looks terrible."

"He's tough, Macy. He's been worse, and I'm certain he'll come through."

She could only nod, reminding herself to breathe.

"Now that we have eyes, we have options."

Tears traced down her cheeks as she studied the image. His face looked so swollen.

"Macy?"

She refocused on Jon.

"Macy, we have to get a plan in place. Now."

"I know." She cleared her throat. "I just, he looks so ... I don't think I can do this."

Jon's arm wrapped around her shoulders. She wiped her face. Her eyes focused on Kane.

"We *can* do this. You just need to breathe. God has Kane in the palm of His hand."

She pulled away and stood, fists clenched.

"We've got eyes. Now we need to get a plan together." Jon's voice echoed.

"Burger's on his way."

Focused completely on the computer, Jon sat back down.

"What're you doing now?"

"I'm securing a mirrored image of the video being shot, just in case we need it."

Jon was just as much the genius she'd heard. Even she hadn't thought that far ahead. All she could think of was Kane, injured and in the hands of that monster DeLuca.

Macy paced while Jon worked. Crow and the others slowly filed back into the warehouse.

She glanced up and noticed his eyes went wide and his jaw dropped.

"What, what are they doing?" She rushed around him to see.

Two men dragged Kane down a hallway and into another room. They latched Kane to a chair. Pain etched his face as she stood by, powerless to help.

"Jon." Macy swallowed hard against the bile building in her throat.

Jon stood and pulled her away.

She protested. "No, I have to see, I have to know ..."

"You can't. Neither of us can."

Crow suddenly rushed past them and stared at the screen. "He's just sitting there. I think someone is talking to him. Did you see DeLuca?"

Jon shook his head held Macy. She reined in her sobs, but the tears rushed down her face.

"We need to get started." Crow's voice echoed in the large warehouse.

Jon gave her a squeeze before he let her go and headed back to the computer.

She had to pull herself together. Kane needed her—not this emotionally crippled mess she'd become. Wiping her face, she took a few deep breaths while Jon and Crow studied the blueprints.

"Here, these are the interior rooms. This is where they're keeping him. DeLuca is too smart to hold him on an outside wall we could breach easily."

"So, where do I need to go to stay safe when I go in?" Macy squeezed between them.

Jon looked up from the computer. Crow and Burger stared.

"What? I'm going in. I'm the one he wants. If something goes wrong, I can keep him distracted while you breach."

"Macy, this is—"

"I won't sit here and do nothing." She gritted her teeth and marched up to Burger. "It's not up for debate. You don't let me on, I'll move in without you."

"Macy, Kane made us promise to keep you safe." Jon stood at her side. "Keep you from putting yourself in harm's way because of him."

"What?" Her gaze snapped to Jon. "There is no way I'm sitting out." She looked up at Crow. "You know what's at stake here."

Crow nodded. "I do, and I think you're right. You need to be there in case something goes wrong."

Nodding, she eased the pain working its way through her jaw. "Get it ready and read me in."

She waited until Burger and Jon both nodded before turning and heading to the far end of the building, needing some space.

"God, I ..." her voice trailed off, not knowing what to say. She believed God would deliver her one way or the other. After all, not all trials ended the way they were prayed for. It could just as easily be true she would meet her heavenly father before the night was over. "Be with Kane, help him to see You, and understand what Jon and I have been telling him for so long," she whispered.

Macy paced the length of the area, and her mind wandered as she tried to ease the pressure in her chest. She didn't doubt God. She just really didn't like the way things were heading, and she was fed up with the darkness edging into her life.

It was her turn to have light, her turn to have happiness. She had that in Kane. Then suddenly, it was gone. Kane's guilt had hit him hard. Part of her assumed that DeLuca would be captured, and then she and Kane could have enough conversations to help him understand, help him to see that her love wasn't contingent upon his past.

With a huff, she leaned against the wall, sliding down to rest on the ground. Her head ached, and her body was spent, but all she could think of was the picture of Kane, beaten and bloody and passed out on the floor.

Lord, please save him.

STIRRING in and out of consciousness, Kane took a steady breath and forced his eyes open. His shoulders ached, and the rope tight against his wrists burned where they'd tied him to the chair.

The bright lights hurt his head, so he closed his eyes, wincing at the pull in his side when he breathed. The memory of meeting Macy and their conversation after her first beating at the prison played through his mind.

'My name is Kane.'

'What? You didn't like Gruff?'

He'd managed a weak smile at her easy tone even then. She was so strong, so amazing. The fact she'd still been lucid, almost amused, using a nickname for him, even though she'd been in pain ...

But she was safe now. That's all that mattered. He'd gladly sacrifice himself over and over if it meant her safety.

Sacrifice. Jon mentioned that several times to him throughout their partnership. The sacrifice that God and Jesus willingly made for him.

'That should be something you understand.' Jon's comment seemed so odd then.

After all, it was his job, a paid job to protect. It had started in the Marines and then settled in his bones, his life. But the willingness to sacrifice, yes. He'd seen it, done it on the battlefield. Every single man he worked with would've done the same for him. It didn't seem so amazing.

Lord, why would You do it?

God saved those He knew, those He cared for. But God didn't know him.

'He created you for a purpose, Kane, and God loves you very much.' Jon's words echoed once again.

Why would God choose to save someone who didn't know Him? Even if God did create him, something he hadn't really thought about, why would He even try and save someone who didn't know Him?

'Jesus sacrificed for everyone. It's an offer He gives to everyone. You just have to accept it.' Jon's voice rattled around in his brain.

All of Jon's words, Macy's comments, swirled around his head, and he couldn't pick them out, not right now.

God, just keep Macy safe. I need her safe.

As he sat here, aching, a calmness settled over him. He had no fear of DeLuca. He could handle DeLuca. As long as Burger kept his promise and took care of Macy, as long as Jon kept her protected, nothing else mattered.

The door clattered, and he winced.

"Awake now?"

DeLuca's smooth accent turned his stomach.

"Fully awake. What do you want?" His right eye opened, and he ignored the pain pulsing through his swollen left one.

"I want Macy Packer," DeLuca seethed.

"Won't be an easy sell." He chuckled. "She's hard to get to, even if you do have a mole."

DeLuca frowned. "I am willing to go through the same punishment as last time to prove how serious I am."

"She's safe." His smile vanished, his jaw clenched. "That's all that matters."

"You think you are strong?" DeLuca leaned down to glare in his face.

"I'm not strong, just settled. I did what I came to do."

"And what is that?"

"Keep her safe. I'm here because I chose to be here. Nothing you do will change that."

DeLuca's fist slammed into his face. Kane moaned as his head bobbed. The sound of the door echoed in the room, and he tensed, waiting for the men to come back and continue the beating.

As he waited, he gingerly leaned his head back, opening his eye and looking up at a camera in the corner of the room. If Crow was alive and they knew where he was being held, they could be watching.

He gave a slight grin at the camera before he slowly drifted off again.

"DID YOU SEE THAT?" Jon stood.

Macy jogged back to the other end and peered at the screen.

Kane was slumped over in the same chair, same room as earlier.

"What?"

"He—he smiled. At the camera, he smiled."

Her spirits lifted for a moment. "He knows we're coming for him."

"Let's get this thing briefed."

She nodded agreement to Burger's plan, but her gaze riveted on the gritty black and white screen image of Kane's motionless body.

"We're coming, Kane. Hang on," she whispered.

The sound of boots on the floor approached from behind. Some men from the motorcade entered with her father and Jasper in tow.

"Jas?" she rushed into her brother's arms and gave him a tight hug. He pulled back and looked at her.

"What happened?"

Jasper's focus went to the cut on her face. She batted his hand away.

"Nothing, I'm fine."

"Fine?" Dad's voice sounded more than a little upset.

"Dad—"

"No, we need to talk." His mouth set in a hard line.

Her heart pounded. She glared at Jon, then Burger. This was their plan? To guilt her into staying because of her family? To have her father convince her otherwise?

"Yeah, we need to talk." She tugged her father to the other side of the building and motioned Jasper to follow.

"Dad, he has Kane."

Her father's eyes dulled. She glanced at Jasper for help.

"How did he get Kane?"

"It was a diversion." Macy paced. "We had a plan to lure him out, only Kane made a switch that I didn't know about."

"He took your place," Dad murmured.

"Look, we know where they're keeping him. I'm going to help with the breach."

Dad clamped his mouth shut and nodded.

"Be careful, sis." Jasper pulled her in, squeezing her tight. "This guy, I'm worried."

She held on, feeling some form of comfort, knowing her family was safe.

"I will," she muttered.

The sounds of cocking guns echoed in her ears. Several men bolted toward the doors.

"What's going on?" She rushed to the computer screens and noticed two men advancing on the building, weaving from building to the cars parked in front.

"Intercept," Burger spoke, sending a few men outside.

Staring at the screen, she recognized the build of one man and how he moved.

"Wait!"

Rushing outside, she pushed her way through the FBI men surrounding the area.

"Wait." She looked around but didn't see anyone. "Bart?"

A man stepped out in fatigues, his gun held tightly across his chest. That grin appeared, and she smiled back.

"Bart? How did—"

He chuckled and strolled toward her, ignoring the men with guns behind her.

"I haven't been able to get in contact with Kane. He told me he had something going on, and if I couldn't get in touch, that meant it went south."

She shook her head, but movement behind him caught her attention—another familiar face.

"Collin?"

He nodded and stepped forward, his arm still drawn up in a sling.

"He wouldn't let me go without bringing him." Bart frowned as she chuckled.

"Come on inside." She placed her hand in the crook of Bart's arm as the FBI let them pass.

With a smile, she led them to Burger.

"This is Bart. He helped us out of the compound. And this is Collin, Kane's brother."

Burger shook their hands and frowned. "How did you find us?"

Bart shrugged. "Followed her brother and father."

"I never thanked you." Jon stood and held out a trembling hand. "You saved us."

Bart clasped Jon's hand and shook his head. "You and Kane, you helped us out more than you know."

Memories seized her of those two days. The pain and fear washed over her. Tremors came, and she sank into a chair before her knees gave way.

"Macy?" Jon's gentle voice called to her. "Macy, I—"

She flinched. "Jon, just don't," she muttered, taking a deep breath.

"If you know where they're holding Kane, I want in on the rescue." Bart's words echoed as he got in Burger's face.

As much as she wanted to interfere, Macy knew her body wouldn't allow it. Besides, she'd barely convinced Burger to let her in. She knew he wouldn't be thrilled with Bart tagging along as well.

"I can offer more than what you have with these agents." Bart's tone sounded condescending.

"I understand your training. Kane has spoken highly of you. But this isn't a military operation."

"I don't want to be paid." Bart narrowed his eyes.

Burger blew out a sigh and glanced her way. She nodded, the trembling continued.

"Fine."

Burger stepped back to the map, and Bart followed.

"You okay?" Jasper knelt in front of her.

She nodded. "I just—need a minute."

He frowned, then stood next to her, with a protective hand on her shoulder.

36

The plan was laid out.

They loaded up after midnight. Burger informed Macy that she and Bart would enter, detain Kane in the building's center, the sturdiest area. Then, they'd breach and get them out.

Her father grabbed her tight. "God, be with the men and with Macy. Give her Your protection and bring her home to me."

She smiled and hugged him back. Then she hugged Jasper. "Keep Dad calm, please."

Jasper whispered back, "I'm not sure I can do that, Mace. Be careful."

"Always." She pulled away, heading to the waiting SUV.

CROUCHING DOWN IN A DITCH, Macy took a few deep breaths to calm her nerves. Bart crept close and nodded. The sentry trudged toward them on the road.

She held her breath, leaning into the dirt, closing her eyes. The sound of footfalls passing by them sent a shiver through her. Bart covered her body with his. Had Kane made him promise to protect her as well?

"Go."

Jon's voice sounded in her ear. Her eyes popped open as Bart's weight left her. She darted after him, then paused at the side door behind him.

"You have two minutes before the next sentry comes past. Hurry."

Bart produced a tool that opened the door in silence, and they crept into a hallway. Macy quietly closed the door behind her. The security system panel on the wall went to green, and she sighed. At least Jon had access, and, so far, it was working well.

"Go right. Hurry, men are heading your way."

She swallowed the taste of vomit lingering in her throat and dashed after Bart, following him down the hallway and taking a left like they'd planned.

The compound was a run-down sawmill. Debris and trash were strewn everywhere, and along with the vile smells of the building, she caught the faint odor of wood. Pushing against a wall, she paused when Bart turned with wide eyes.

He backed into her, his arm holding her against the wall. She clutched the rifle to her chest and forced her breathing to steady.

Conversation filled the passage as two men approached them. There was a slight indentation in the wall, just enough for one person. But with Bart's camouflage, she hoped they would go undetected.

He leaned harder into her, and she stilled.

"That's not what I heard. He's got some kind of bomb in there."

"There's no bomb. That's crazy. He's definitely strange, but crazy? Nah."

The voices faded as the men turned down the hallway to their left.

"That was close. Keep going. Follow them."

As they moved, the man's words echoed in her mind. A

bomb? Surely that wasn't DeLuca's play here. He thought Crow was dead, so he wouldn't be expecting anyone to come.

"Second door on the left."

Macy moved to the opposite side of the door. Bart nodded. Gripping the handle, she turned the knob as Bart pushed inside. She swung her gun around and cleared the left-hand side of the room.

Kane's crumpled body was still tied to the chair. Seeing him, she stifled the urge to yell. She collapsed at his feet, pulled out her knife, and cut through the ropes holding his legs and arms.

"Kane?" she whispered, looking over his beaten face.

"We need to get him out." Bart stood guard at the door.

"The plan was for Burger—"

"I know the plan, but it won't work. Burger makes a run on this building, and we'll all be dead."

She swallowed hard. "You think it's true about a bomb?"

Bart shrugged.

"Kane, Kane? You need to wake up."

She patted the right side of his face, then raised his chin. One green eye opened and focused on hers.

"Mace?"

She smiled as tears ran down her face. "We—we need to get out."

He shook his head. "No, I can't. Just go," he muttered and slumped forward.

As he all but fell out of his chair, Macy did her best to get him to his feet. Bart stepped in and shouldered Kane's weight.

She pulled out the burner phone Burger had given her and texted Jon's secure line.

There was talk of a bomb. We need to get out. We have Kane.

"I'm not sure it will be as easy," Jon's voice came through her com-link. "There's a group headed your way."

She glanced up at Bart. He nodded, and they sat Kane back

in the chair, leaning him up against the wall, keeping their weapons ready. If there was a team headed their way, they might be coming to gather Kane.

"Keep quiet."

She nodded at Jon's instructions, forcing her mind to focus.

The door creaked open a crack.

"Not yet. Boss says to give it some more time. He thinks they will show soon."

"Is he serious?"

Groans and curses came from the other side. The door shut.

She texted Jon.

Either DeLuca knows we're coming or he's already caught wind of something.

"We're in the clear. The video is streaming. They have no idea you're inside. Gather Kane. You have about a three-minute window to go out the same way you came in."

She huffed and helped Bart shoulder Kane's weight.

"Kane, you have to walk." She opened the door and looked down the hallway.

"Go now, left."

They staggered down the hallway as fast as Bart could get Kane to move. A groan escaped Kane when he stumbled.

"Quiet," Bart hissed.

Turning the corner, she backed up and pushed them out of the way. The man walking down the hallway didn't notice—his gaze focused on his phone.

"You have less than one minute to get through that next doorway, or security will spot you."

Taking a chance, she stepped out and saw the man shove a door closed.

"Now!" She motioned.

Macy opened the door to usher Bart through when a voice called out.

"Hey!"

"Go! get him out." She turned and ran down the corridor.

"Make the next right, Macy. It'll buy you some time."

She turned right, holding up her rifle and shifting to avoid the shot that embedded in the wall behind her. Firing, she ran down the hall, past the now dead man who'd fired on her.

"Macy! Macy, you have to turn back, you're going to corner yourself."

She blew out a breath and backtracked, shoving herself into a corner as bullets ricocheted around her.

"This is way too familiar," she muttered.

Macy pulled back, avoiding the clatter of bullets. Seeing a hallway to her left, she sprinted to a door on her right. Pushing inside, she quietly shut and locked the bolt in place. Looking around the room, she frowned. No cameras. Jon wouldn't be able to see or help her.

Footsteps rushed from the other side of the door. She stilled, waiting. The sound moved away. After a moment, she unlocked the door and poked her head out. With the corridor empty, she readied her rifle and pressed herself against the wall, creeping toward the outer hallway.

"No, don't! Please!"

Her pulse quickened. She froze. That voice. It couldn't be.

Rushing toward the shouts, she paused at the door.

"Macy? Get to the outer door. Now!"

Ignoring Jon's voice in her ear, she pulled out the com-link and leaned against the door to listen.

"Stop!"

Her heart pounding, she shouldered the door and aimed her rifle. She burst into the room and shot the man holding the gun. Her eyes widened. Zander sat in a chair, staring up at her, blood trailing from his lip.

"Z-Zander? But—how?"

"Macy? You're alive?"

Forcing her brain to work, she shut the door, dropped the

rifle, and rushed to him. Freeing his hands from the rope, she knelt and untied his ankles.

"I thought you were in the hospital. They said—they said you were in critical condition, that you probably wouldn't make it," she stammered.

"He told me you were dead."

She shook her head and stood, taking his arm. "The FBI is about to head inside." Scanning the ceiling, she frowned— another room without cameras.

How many hidden rooms were in this place?

"The FBI? How? Let's get going." Zander shouldered the rifle, strapping it across his chest. He moved to the door.

Pulling her handgun, she followed him into the hallway. "Why does he have you here?"

"Information," he murmured as he stalked to the next hallway.

"But then, who's in the hospital? What about your house? All that blood?" She shuddered as the image surfaced.

He shrugged, pushing her against the wall. "Your guess is as good as mine," he whispered.

The sound of footsteps echoed and disappeared.

"We need to go left, toward the outer hallway," she whispered.

Zander's jaw clenched. He shook his head. "Follow me."

With a frown, Macy followed her boss to the right. Zander cleared the rooms as they hustled down the corridor.

"Zander, we need to go this way." She pulled at his arm, pointing behind them.

In one move, Zander grabbed her gun, shoved it in his back waistband, and gripped her wrists. "You're coming with me."

Bile burned the back of her throat. Her knees stiffened. "Wh-what are you doing?"

"Saving one of us," he growled.

Yanking on her arms, she gathered her bearings and strained against him. "Zander?"

"Quiet," he muttered through gritted teeth.

When they rounded the corner, the sound of automatic rifle fire echoed. He shoved her into the wall. Plaster and debris flew around them.

"Knock it off, DeLuca! You won't get her alive if you don't control your men!"

She shoved at his body, her mind finally engaged. But it was too late. She screamed. Zander twisted her wrist, shoving her arm behind her back as he spun her around.

"Shut up!" he spat.

Using Macy as a shield, he held her up in front, the rifle aimed over her shoulder.

"Now, I bet you're ready to make a deal! Right, DeLuca?"

Tears streaming down her face, Macy's body shook as DeLuca's blurry form appeared behind the men.

"She's mine. You hurt her, and you deal with me."

DeLuca's gritty voice made her stomach churn.

"We both know what your plans are for her. What I want is my end of the deal. You've already proven yourself untrustworthy. I want what's mine."

"Or, I could kill you both right now."

Zander's chuckle pushed anger through her body.

"Why are you doing this? You were my boss, my friend. You got me out—"

"I didn't know the Marine unit was going to go in full force. I was told you were the target, and they would get you out. I had just enough time to call DeLuca and warn him. But apparently, that wasn't enough for him."

He twisted her arm tighter. Macy groaned.

"You know he'll kill us both," she muttered.

"Shut up!"

"You have only moments to live, Nichols."

"I want my money! I want the information promised me!"

"I'm not negotiating with a traitor!"

Macy closed her eyes and turned her head away from the rifle on her shoulder, waiting for it to go off and the return fire to hit.

"Now, DeLuca!"

Gunfire echoed. Macy opened her eyes and saw flashpoints down the hallway. Zander swung his rifle to the side. Macy spun from his grip, punched him in the sternum, and kicked out his knee.

Ripping her handgun from his waistband, she shoved him to the ground and rushed past him, ducking around the corner. Gunfire erupted once more, and she heard Jon's muffled voice as she searched for the com-link and shoved it back in her ear.

"Left, Macy, left!"

Glancing around the corner, she caught a glimpse of Zander's crumpled form on the ground before the gunfire forced her to move.

Following Jon's advice, she cut as fast as she could to her left, wincing at the pain slicing through her leg.

"The FBI is there, hang on."

Jutting into the hallway, she dove into a room, slammed the door, and rolled onto her back. With a groan, she stood and wedged the desk from the wall against the door, pushing the large bolt into place.

Her body shaking, Macy wiped her face and collapsed against the wall.

God, what ... what's going on? What now?

STIFLING A GROAN, Kane stood, moving closer to the screen to see Macy sitting against the wall, gripping her leg.

"Can't you get a better picture?" he mumbled to Jon.

"Kane, this is all we can do."

Jon grabbed his arm, but he pulled away.

"I need to get in there."

"You can't even see out of your left eye. You're injured, Kane. Let Burger do this."

He slammed his fist into the side of the van and collapsed back into his seat.

DeLuca was still alive, running through the hallway and centering on her location. The FBI team was fighting, but DeLuca's men held them back. Heat boiled through Kane's chest.

"I should've taken care of him before now," he muttered.

"And when would you have done that, Kane?"

He huffed at Jon's sarcastic tone.

"She can take care of herself, Burger and Crow are there. Bart has his weapon ready. They'll get her out."

His jaw clenched as he stood, turning to Jon. "I need to speak to her."

"Kane, I ..."

"Jon, please."

Jon handed over the headset.

37

Finishing the tourniquet on her leg, Macy leaned back against the wall. Zander's wild eyes and the look on his face flashed through her mind. How could he betray her? All of them? For money? Secrets?

She swallowed the tears. Sadness pressing on her chest, she did her best to stand.

"Macy, sit tight."

She stilled. Her eyes went wide, and her mouth dropped open. Scouring the ceiling, she found the camera to her left. Kane.

"Macy, I'm sorry. I didn't want you in there. I wanted you safe. Everyone was supposed to keep you back."

Once again, tears filled her eyes. The sound of someone removing the door from its hinges reverberated in the room. With a moan, she hobbled to another table and tried to move it. But it was bolted down.

"Macy, you need to rest. Bart is headed that way."

She pointed to the door and glared at the camera. If they could see the hallway, they'd see the men taking apart the door.

"Kane, I can't believe you," Macy muttered, shaking her head.

When they'd captured him, she could tell it wasn't just his face that was injured. His breathing was labored, and he probably had a concussion. Why didn't Jon make him go to the hospital?

She blew out her frustration. Probably the same reason no one could keep her away from the breach. She leaned a few slats of wood against the wall, balancing them and creating a hiding place.

"Macy, I love you. Please don't ... If you can, hold them off a little longer."

The sound of the worry and fear in his voice drove a knife into her stomach. She dropped the boards in her hand and wiped her face.

"I'm coming. I'll just—"

"No!" she shouted and looked up at the camera, shaking her head.

He couldn't hear her, but there was no way he could make it through alive if he tried to come inside.

The clatter of the door sounded, and she hurried to the hide she'd created, pulling her sidearm and taking a breath to ease her nerves.

Macy's set up allowed her to see through the slats just enough to count heads. Angled in the corner, she hoped the men would assume it was a stack of wood and nothing more.

As a diversion, she'd set up a few barricades, leaning tables and chairs to hopefully draw their attention from the corner and direct them into her line of sight.

Lord, please protect Kane and the other men, give me the strength to do what I need to in order to get away.

The prayer reminded her of the one she made in her prison. That prison still surrounded her as long as DeLuca was alive.

One, two, three, four heads made entry. Macy waited as long as she could. She had to attack first if she had any chance of holding them off, but she forced herself to be patient. To wait. She wanted DeLuca in view before she exposed herself.

One of the men glanced toward her position. She was out of time.

Bolting forward, she took out the first four quickly, then swung her gun toward the door and fired on anything that moved. Searing pain cut through her leg. She collapsed, a heavy weight pushed her down, stealing her breath.

"Finally! Hello, Ms. Packer."

The deep, throaty voice echoed in her head. Macy opened her eyes.

DeLuca sat sprawled on top of her. Only he didn't resemble the same man she remembered. Dirty, unshaven, and wild—this man was on the brink. His hand gripped the side of her neck, forcing her focused on him.

"You're going to lose." She grabbed at his shoulder with her right hand. Her left was wedged behind her back.

DeLuca pulled a knife from its sheath, grinning madly. He pushed the smooth surface against the side of her face.

"I've been waiting a long time for this. You will pay for what you did to me."

"I—I didn't do anything. You just got caught." Panic seized her voice.

The tip of the knife pushed into her throat at her jaw, and she felt the sting move down her neck.

"Why are you after me? I thought you blamed Zander?"

DeLuca gritted his teeth. "He got his payment in full. Now, it's your turn."

"What did he want so badly? Zander was a good agent." If she kept him talking, maybe it would be enough for them to find her, to get her left hand loose.

"He was like all the others. Greedy. Money and information. He wanted what was in your friend Jon's head. Disabling your government's computer system would be a high prize." DeLuca chuckled as he pressed the knife to the other side of her throat. "Even if I do lose, you won't be the same after today, Ms. Packer."

Using her wedged left hand, she unstrapped the knife at her lower back and worked her fingers around the handle. Shifting to her right, she tugged at his shoulder, hoping to distract him enough to make a move.

"Now, let's get to work, we have little time," he grunted.

Her eyes flitted to his as the knife appeared in her vision once more. When he raised his hand to strike, she used the last of her energy to roll. Her left hand freed, she shoved her knife into his side.

With a groan, Macy maneuvered her neck from his grip as he stumbled off of her. She braced for the impact, the shots she assumed would come from the few men left standing in the room.

But the room was empty. Silent, as DeLuca collapsed next to her, his breathing unsteady, gulping for air.

Was it over? She closed her eyes.

Suddenly, strong arms gently lifted her. "DeLuca ... where is he?"

"In custody." Bart's deep voice soothed her. "Trust me. No one is letting him out of their sight."

The feeling of cool night air washed over her as she sucked in a deep breath.

"Mace?" Kane's voice echoed in her mind, and she could smell his cologne close. "Don't give up, babe. I love you."

She tried to open her mouth to speak, but she was too tired. Her body relaxed, and she gave into the darkness.

DeLuca was there, pushing into her chest. The sting of the blade against her neck. She strained to fight him off as Zander's mad chuckle echoed in the night.

"No! No!"

A hand gripped hers, and she bolted upright. Kane.

"What?"

"Mace, it's me. You need to lie back."

Macy swallowed and focused on the room. A hospital. She eased back slowly and winced as pain knifed through her leg.

"You'll be fine, but you've got to rest."

The tremors started.

"Macy?"

Ignoring his voice, she curled into a ball as much as she could with a leg that didn't want to move. His arms wrapped around her. She melted into his chest, sobs wracking her body.

"Macy, calm down. I mean, what—"

He didn't understand. Things were so much worse now. Even he couldn't calm her body anymore.

Exhaustion overwhelmed her. She closed her eyes and breathed deeply, trying to memorize the calming smell of him as she drifted off.

As Macy relaxed against him, Kane frowned and gently settled her in the bed. He pulled the covers over her, frustration overwhelming him. He used to help with the tremors. She told him that. Just holding her would make them go away. But now, it didn't seem to do anything.

A soft knock made him turn, and Jon stepped in.

"Her father said she was resting."

"She woke for just a second, but she wouldn't talk and ..." he sat there, staring, unsure what to say.

"She's not doing well, Kane."

His gaze snapped to Jon. "What's going on?"

Jon's tired and weary face sagged as he sat down. "I've been talking to her over the past few weeks, trying to get her to speak with the therapist who helped me. She's holding on to so much."

A lump swelled in his throat. "I should've done more."

"This isn't about you."

He clenched his jaw at Jon's tone.

"She's been shouldering so much for so long, she just assumes the trials of her life can be turned to good, and then she'll be good. But that's not how it works. Did you know the death of her mother is still an unsolved case?"

He gripped her hand and ran his thumb across her smooth skin. "Yeah, she told me."

"Not to mention the way she escaped and ..."

"Wait, what did she say?" His gaze focused on Jon.

"She said if I hadn't helped put her shoulder back in, she wouldn't have been able to get out, to escape that room."

He swallowed hard. What that man had planned to do to her ate at him.

"Kane, she saved us."

"But she was almost—he almost got to her and she told me that she never would've done it if ..." He clenched his jaw.

"If what?"

"If we hadn't been there. If I hadn't pushed for her to get out, to find any way out. It's my fault. I almost got her raped, Jon." The words tasted bitter and he sat down next to her, her body curling into him.

"God was with her even then. He helped her escape."

"She didn't deserve it." He glared at Jon.

"No, she didn't. But it happened, and she's not dealing with it. Or with the threats on her life and body, her past. Her brain can only deal with so much at a time, and right now, she's on the brink." Jon let out a heavy sigh.

"What? What aren't you saying?"

Jon leaned forward. "While she was in lock-down, I tried to speak with her, but she always blew off my concerns. She's denying everything, pretending she's okay. Her faith is shaken and after you were taken ... She needs a lot of help, and I'm not sure she'll take it. Even now."

"What can I do?" he whispered.

"We need to get her help, convince her to get help."

Lord, You brought me out. Please help bring her to safety too. Bring her mind back so she can have peace.

"We can talk to her when she wakes up. Maybe we can all convince her ..." His voice trailed off as he watched her sleep.

That hope had sprung up again, and this time, he held on tight. He needed her much more than he ever imagined, and he had to find a way to convince her they had a future together.

<h1 style="text-align: center;">38</h1>

After over a week of living with her dad, Macy moved into an apartment next to Jasper, easing her father's worries over her need to be independent. She looked out the window and sighed.

Once released, she did her best to keep her emotional turmoil from showing. But between discovering Zander's involvement with DeLuca and the nightmares, the physical pain, she was running ragged.

Everyone around her constantly wanted to help or tried to convince her to see a therapist, pushing and prodding all the time—it was too much. And Kane was right in the middle.

He seemed changed after weeks of being apart. But her thoughts lingered on his comments about his past and the way he held her on a pedestal. Her heart hurt so badly when he pushed her away, and she couldn't go down the same road they'd already traveled.

Still, he called every day, offering rides to physical therapy or anything else she needed, but she kept him at arm's length. Her mind, her faith, it was all damaged and scarred, and she had no idea how to allow Kane in without it destroying what was left of her heart. Macy had to mend her relationship with God first. Focus on Him.

Sprawling on her couch, she stretched her legs. After her discharge from the hospital, she'd taken a leave of absence from work. Between her injuries, the situation with Kane, and her distracted mind, working wouldn't be safe for her or for whoever she was supposed to protect.

Macy wondered what she really wanted. She wanted a future, something much more than this. But right now, with her mind reeling, faith struggling, and her body healing, that was much too far away for her to attain.

A knock sounded on the door, and she flinched.

Approaching stealthily with her weapon drawn, she peered out the peephole. Jon. She holstered her gun and swung the door open. Her smile grew bigger as she saw Lillian with him.

"It's so good to see you." She hugged them both and sat down as Lillian beamed.

"We have news." Lillian held out her left hand.

"Oh?" Macy's eyes went wide. "You're, engaged?" As happy as she was for them both, she felt the twinge of jealousy and sadness.

"We have an engagement party next week. Would you please come?"

Incapable of speech, she nodded. Macy plastered on a smile and listened as Lillian and Jon discussed their romantic wedding plans. Her mind spun. Kane would be there too, so she might have to reconsider.

———

"You're getting married?" Kane's mouth dropped open as Jon's smile lit his entire face. He'd come back to the house after running errands to share some good news of his own and ended up getting blindsided by Jon's announcement. "I don't know what to say."

"Say you'll be my best man, Kane. I need you up there with me to hold me up."

"Oh no, I'm not good at that kind of stuff. You need to call your brother."

"I've already decided. You're my best man, and Trevor will do the speech. Deal?" Jon stuck out his hand, and Kane shook it. "I knew you'd agree."

He couldn't control his grin, his happiness for his friend. "When are you planning this thing?"

"End of the year. Lillian says she has to have at least four months to prepare. So, we'll do an engagement party next week, and in November, we'll get married."

"Wow, you have it all planned out, huh?" He chuckled at Jon's commentary.

"Well, I can't work without a plan."

"Yes, I know." He slapped his friend on the shoulder. Jon deserved all the happiness in the world, maybe even more after everything he'd been through.

"I have some good news too."

"Oh?" Jon's eyebrows rose.

"I spoke with the PI, and he's found the man responsible for the threats. The police arrested him this morning. That's what I was coming to tell you before your big announcement."

Jon's jaw dropped. "Who is he? Why was he threatening me?"

"He's just a man who feels insignificant. He fancies himself brilliant, and from what the lead detective told me, he just wanted to be noticed. He assumed you'd be able to relate to him, understand him in some way, so he started writing to you. When you didn't respond to his letters, he got mad."

"What letters?"

"It doesn't matter. What matters is the protection you have in place now. You're safe."

Jon's smile brightened even more as the weight visibly fell from his shoulders. "I've been praying for this since the attack on my home. I knew then I wanted to be with Lillian, but I wanted her safe. Now I feel like God's given me both. I have to call her." Jon waved, exited the apartment, dialing as he went.

THAT NIGHT, as Kane lay in bed, love and marriage moved quickly through his head. He loved Macy, longed to be with her. But right now, that was proving all too difficult.

Since her discharge from the hospital, she'd spent the past few weeks barely speaking to him when he called. He'd offered rides anywhere she needed, help with anything, only to be shot down.

Macy wasn't mean or harsh but made it sound like she already had things taken care of. She trusted God to protect her, not him. How could she trust a God she couldn't see when he was here in person? Every refusal of his help stabbed like a knife in his heart.

He sat up with a sigh, trying to ease the pounding in his chest. It had happened a few times since the compound, and he wondered if something in that place had messed with his body. His breath sped up, his mind reeling as a pressure he couldn't explain mounted in his chest. The first time it happened, he thought it was a heart attack. But after only a minute or two, he recovered quickly, as if nothing had happened.

Would the God who had helped Macy through her trials help him? Jon had encouraged him to ask. Kane looked up and sighed. *Okay, God, You have to give me something here.*

Kane had spoken to God several times since that day he'd been tied to the chair. It seemed almost natural as if he believed God had been there watching over him all his life. Praying for Macy had seemed the best thing to do. Now, it was him needing help, needing something to cling to, whether or not Macy was done with him.

He stood and paced, his brain whirling. Not that he blamed her. The way he'd treated her since his accident was much less than a man in love should have acted. She told him again and again, his past didn't matter to her, and he blew her off.

But his past still hung over him. He couldn't forget the things he'd done, couldn't ask God for forgiveness. He didn't deserve it. His stomach lurched as he sank in the chair.

39

At the engagement party, Kane kept on his detail, moving around the room, watching for anything out of the ordinary. As much as he pushed her to the back of his mind, in reality, he was searching for Macy.

It had been a long ten days, waiting for the party. He'd tried to talk to her on the phone. She'd only answered a few times, ignoring a lot of questions and being vague in every sense of the word.

He fought to keep his focus on protection. Even though the threats were resolved and the perpetrator found, he must remain vigilant. Another incident wouldn't happen while he was on duty. His shift ended at nine, something he'd argued with Jon over. But after fighting with him about even working tonight, he let it slide. As much as he was there for Jon because they were friends, he was still paid and needed to do his job.

Nodding to several people he recognized, Kane strode around the room before too many questions were asked about how he was healing from the wreck or the situation with DeLuca, neither of which he was eager to discuss.

"Kane?" Jon met him with a frown.

"What's wrong?"

"I told you, no working after nine. Two more guards have arrived, and I need you here as my friend, my family. Not as my protection."

"Is it nine already?" He smirked

Jon looked less than amused. "Where's Macy?"

His face heated at the question. "I don't know. I saw Jasper earlier."

"Didn't you ask?"

"Jon, it's a little uncomfortable right now."

He frowned as Jon cut through the crowd, making a beeline for Jasper.

Kane watched the interaction, hoping to read an answer for Macy's whereabouts. But all he saw was Jasper looking around, shaking his head.

At nine-thirty, Jon made his engagement announcement, and the room erupted in applause. He smiled and shook Jon's hand, then hugged Lillian.

He'd only been back in the house a week when Lillian wanted to meet with him for a private conversation without Jon. As unnerving as it was, she just wanted to find out more about Jon, what Kane thought Jon needed, and what would be best for him. He'd had doubts about Lillian more than once, but after that candid conversation, he was convinced she had only Jon's best interest at heart.

The night dragged on as he made small talk with the few men he knew from previous details, including SSA Burger and Crow. Bart was there as well, hanging on to a pretty blonde and wearing the biggest smile he'd ever seen.

As his eyes wandered across the ballroom, he caught sight of Macy's short hair weaving through the crowd. Excusing himself from the conversation, he darted through the obstacle course of people to catch up with her.

"Hey." He caught her elbow.

Wide-eyed, she feigned a small smile. "Oh, hi."

"I was hoping you'd show."

She scanned the room. "Yeah, I—I wasn't sure I'd come."

"How are you, Mace?" He shoved his hands into his pockets to keep from reaching for her.

She looked pretty amazing, the snug top showing off her toned arms and figure, her hair finally long enough for her to style as it was pushed back off her face.

"I'm good. Things are okay." The nervousness in her voice came through as she avoided his eyes at all costs.

"I've been worried about you." He gently took hold of her elbow, stepping in front of her, cutting off her view. "You're a hard person to get in touch with."

He frowned as her jaw clenched.

"Look, things are ... I'm still reeling."

"That's why I've been calling. I'm worried and want to help."

"Kane." Her bright blue eyes finally met his. "This isn't—" She shook her head. "I can't keep hoping for something that won't happen."

"We need to talk about that. And, since you won't take my calls, let's talk about it now."

"There's nothing to talk about." She shook her head as her eyes glossed over.

He fought the bile coating the back of his throat. "Are you— have you gone to see a therapist?"

"Look, Jon's got everyone thinking I need help." She sighed. "But I'm fine. I'm just fine."

He started to say more when she pulled from his grip.

"I see Jon. I've got to go." She darted through the crowd.

Blowing out a big breath, he made his way outside, feeling the breeze rush around him as he tried to calm himself. He'd hurt her time and time again, but right now, all he wanted to do was make it right. However, as much as he tried, she seemed done. The amazing, caring woman he'd known the past several months was gone, and it was his fault.

Minutes later, Macy strode across the parking lot. Jon had said she moved out of her father's home, but that's all he'd say.

Maybe if Kane figured out where she lived, he could at least find a way to talk to her that didn't involve the phone.

Sprinting to his truck, he backed out and sped through the intersection. She turned right, and he followed, but she disappeared. A sudden urgency rose in his chest as he drove and finally caught sight of her car again.

He chased her through the streets but lost her trail and ended up at the park where he'd found her the first time. He got out and walked along a pathway, attempting to clear his mind and ease the burden building inside him.

Guilt rose in his chest, and his head spun as he pushed tried to push it down. His actions as a Marine, as a single man, everything hit him at once. He barely made it to a bench before his knees gave way.

"God, are You there?" he whispered, holding his head in his hands. The big and the little things in his life gripped him. Awareness of his sin knocked the air from his lungs. "God, what do You want from me? You've seen my life, my hate, the evil things I've done. Why do You want me?"

Love.

As he leaned back against the bench, the word came through the fog, but he still didn't understand. Jon mentioned the chapter in the Bible about love and how selfless love truly is. He remembered Macy saying you couldn't really love without God because He is love. But, how could God love someone as messed up and scarred as him? He wasn't good enough, not by a long shot.

Something Jon had said years ago resounded in his mind. God didn't want him all fixed up and perfect—He wanted him scarred and messed up, sin and all.

"You would forgive me?" he muttered.

Sacrifice.

His pulse pounded in his head as he leaned over once more, attempting to make sense of the word rolling around in his mind.

Sacrifice was something he thought about at the compound, but now, the word took his breath.

A willing sacrifice—willing to give himself up for someone he loved. That's what he understood it was, just like what he did for Macy, what she did for him. But now, his sacrifice wasn't the point.

Paul had spoken of Jesus, a man who willingly gave up His life, sacrificed His life because of His love for His people. He died a terrible death, considered the worst one of the worst ways to die. Paul believed Jesus chose that death, allowed Himself to suffer, because of love.

It didn't matter if Kane had never known God before now, He still gave up His Son, and Jesus willingly went to that cross to die so that he could have a different life, a new life.

A new life. That sounded better than anything else he'd ever heard or thought about. He'd been so focused on how to fix his old life when the answer was right in front of him. He didn't need to fix his old life. He couldn't. But, he could embrace this new life.

"God, forgive me. I do feel the guilt of my life. I do believe You really do love me enough to forgive me. You allowed Your son to die for me so I can live with You. I need Your forgiveness and Your hope."

As he whispered the words, his body eased, the pounding ceased, and his breathing relaxed. Running his hands through his hair, he straightened.

Love. Sacrifice. Forgiveness. Hope.

He finally understood why Macy trusted in God. Why him clinging to his past, his old life, frustrated her. He had to tell her.

Standing, he sprinted to his car, pulled out his phone, and dialed Jon.

"Kane?"

"I'm sorry I took off, but I need to know her address."

"What? I can't—"

"Yes, you can. Please. I need her, Jon."

"Kane, I'm not sure she needs you."

The comment made him groan. "Everything is different now. I need to see her, talk to her. She wouldn't even let me apologize, and I need to tell her."

"Tell her what?" Jon's tone sounded terse.

A rush came over him as he gripped the steering wheel. "I talked to God."

"What happened?"

Jon's voice hovered between excitement and breathlessness, matching Kane's reactions.

"I guess everything hit me. I remembered what you said about sacrifice and love. I did speak with God, and, well, I asked Him to forgive me."

"I'm so happy for you. I've been praying for years!"

"But I'm not sure what to do."

"Now, you need to find a way to live your life for Christ, just like Paul did."

He shook his head. "How do I do that? I can't do that. I'm not that guy."

"No, you're not like Paul, not exactly. But with God's help, you can do this."

He frowned as Jon chuckled.

"Dig that Bible out of your desk drawer and start reading it. That's how you'll know how to live for Christ."

"That's it?"

"Yes, Kane. God's grace covered Paul's sins, and it will cover yours. 2147 Hooper Lane. Apartment 6A. It's the same apartment building her brother lives in. I'll be praying she lets you in the door."

"Thanks, Jon."

He hung up and pulled out of the parking lot, feeling even more unnerved than earlier. But at least this time, the hope he had seemed stronger, more determined.

Lord, help her to see I'm a new person. Help her to see I'm not the same man. I-I need her more than I ever thought I'd need anyone. Please, God.

His heart pounded as he pulled up to the gate, pressing the code Jon texted him, and pulling his truck through to the right building. He found her car and parked next to it. His gut wrenched. Calming his breathing, he gripped the wheel and got out, throwing the tie and sport coat he'd worn into the seat before shutting the door and climbing the steps.

40

Macy removed her makeup, splashed her face with cool water, and chided herself for getting so emotional.

Drying her face, she pushed away the image of Kane in the ballroom, his dark jeans and sports coat standing out among the suits and khakis. He'd looked pretty amazing, and it took all her will power to walk away from him.

She flipped the light off and padded to her bed. Nausea gripped her stomach once more. All the tremors and nightmares had taken their toll, made her body stiff, and her mood terrible. She'd finally given in and made an appointment to see the therapist Jon had suggested.

Not that anyone else needed to know, especially Kane. She swallowed the lump in her throat.

He'd been trying to apologize, and she pushed him away. She couldn't handle seeing him, knowing even if he'd changed, she wasn't so keen on forgiving just yet. He needed Jesus. *They* needed Jesus. If they were crazy enough to start a relationship, He must be at the center. But, with her body and emotions on high alert, she just couldn't deal with Kane's doubts about his past, about her faith, anymore.

Collapsing in bed, she closed her eyes. It wasn't losing Kane that had done her in. It was the war that waged on her for the past few months, past years maybe. Her capture and then the fallout once she came home, all the run-ins with DeLuca, and then the compound—she'd kept it all inside, making herself physically ill.

Attempting to rest her body, she breathed deeply, slowly in and out. There was no way she could shut down tonight after seeing Kane and wanting him to ignore her attitude and pull her in for a hug.

Her phone beeped, and she frowned.

I want to talk. I need to talk to you.

Sitting straight up in bed, she gripped the phone with both hands, attempting to control the trembling of her fingers.

I can't. Please, just stop.

It's not about you. I need to tell you something. It's important.

Groaning, she fell back in bed. All the calls and messages—she'd hoped he would forget about her and just move on. She never should've gone to Jon's engagement party.

Kane, I can't do this. If you really do care about me and don't want to hurt me, stop.

The bubbles disappeared for a moment, and she sighed, hopeful he finally understood.

She got up and trudged to the darkened kitchen, tossed her phone on the counter, and grabbed a bottle of water from her fridge. Mid-sip, a soft knock stilled her. Surely it wasn't Kane. He didn't have her address, and Jon wouldn't just give it out after everything they'd been through. *Would he?*

Setting down her water, she crept slowly to the door, peered through the peephole. Kane. Her knees went weak. She couldn't talk to him, not now, not like this. The little bit of composure she had dwindled, and she wouldn't be able to hold back her emotions.

He knocked again. "Mace, I know you're there. Please, It's really important."

The urgency in his voice twisted her insides. Saying a quick prayer for strength, she unlocked the door and cracked it open. Gripping the edge, she tried to shield her body and use it for support in case her legs buckled.

"Kane, you can't come here. I ..." She cleared her throat as he leaned into the doorframe.

"Macy, I need to talk to you about something, and I need to come in." His voice raspy, face flushed, smile barely noticeable.

Suddenly, she feared the worst. An illness or moving or going back into the military where he'd be shipped off somewhere terrifying? She opened the door, allowing him inside.

"Just a second." Her voice barely sounded as she locked the door, then darted to her room to grab a sweatshirt.

When she returned, she saw his gaze latch onto her as he waited by the couch.

"What is it?" She clasped her hands and nervously shifted her weight, his calm demeanor annoying her.

"I just, I wanted to, needed to talk about something that happened."

"Okay."

"Sit down. You look like you're going to collapse."

"I'm fine." Her confidence returned as she crossed her arms and waited.

He shoved his hands in his pockets. "I've done a lot of searching lately. I know I've messed things up with us, and I don't expect you to take me back or anything. I just want to tell you, um, something happened tonight."

Her brow furrowed as he chuckled and sat on the couch. She

moved slowly to the opposite end, wincing as she balled up against the arm.

"I was trying to catch up with you so I could find out where you lived. I need to talk to you. I, you looked amazing tonight, by the way." He flashed his grin.

But she held back, needing him to focus on whatever he wanted to say and not on her.

He sighed. "Macy, between you and Jon, I've been given so much information, and I just, well, I think it's taken a long time for me to simply understand. I never understood why you both thought God would want me. Would forgive me."

Kane paused to catch his breath. "But tonight, I'd jumped in my truck, trying to figure out where you went, and I had this ache in my chest. After I lost your car, I went to the park where I first found you. I got out and walked, and I felt this pull. Like someone wanted me to see something or tell me something." He glanced up at her for a moment then leaned forward on his knees.

"It first happened right after the compound, and I thought maybe it was a heart attack. This pull, it wasn't something I could explain. But this time, it was stronger. I sat down, and all of a sudden, this wave came over me, all the things I'd messed up, all the things I regret, all of it just hit me all at once.

"I asked if it was God, and things just started going through my mind. The things you and Jon had told me, the things I'd read. And I wondered if He wanted me or loved me. It's something I've never thought about. I just figured I needed to be better." He looked up at her and smiled.

She grinned back. Joy bubbled in her chest.

"I asked God to forgive me tonight. I can't change my old life, but I can accept the new life He offers."

She wiped her face and attempted to douse her smile but failed miserably.

"I'm sorry for how I treated you. I did think you deserved better. I do think you deserve better. But now, I feel like I'm not in this all alone, like God will help me to do what I need to do. Does that make any sense?"

Macy nodded as a lump formed in her throat. Forgiveness was something she had a hard time with, and this wasn't any different. She still felt the hurt, the pain of being pushed away, feeling left alone. She pulled her knees to her chest. Risking her heart when her whole world was crashing seemed like a bad idea.

"Kane, I—haven't been feeling too well, and I, well, I don't think I can handle going through you walking away again."

"What's wrong? What do you mean you're not feeling well?" He scooted over next to her, gripping his hands together as he leaned on his knees, a frown marred his face.

"Did you even hear the rest of what I said, Kane?"

"What's wrong, Macy?" He touched her elbow.

"Everything is just, well, things aren't good right now. I don't sleep, and the tremors are bad. I just don't think I'm ready for this. For us."

"Why didn't you just tell me? I told you I was worried."

His soft voice and worry on his face put an ache in her heart. *Why was this so hard?*

"I can't go back and forth—"

"I don't want back and forth. I've been trying to apologize since you were released from the hospital. I should never have pushed you away, and I want to fix this, to fix us." He scooted closer, gently easing her hand into his. "I love you too much to walk away. I know you may not believe me after everything, but I'll prove it to you."

She smirked and leaned toward him, her body easing into the couch. "You think you need to prove it after sacrificing yourself for me?"

"I'll do whatever it takes, Mace." His fingers moved gently down her jawline. "I'd do it again in a heartbeat. I want to help. I want to be here for you."

His green gaze met hers, and she felt that same familiar pull, only this time, there was a peace there. She took a breath as a tremor moved through her. Closing her eyes, she leaned her head into the couch but felt him wrap his arms around her.

"Just rest, Mace."

He pulled her in, and she rested her head on his chest, her legs across his lap.

Letting her tears finally fall, she slipped her arms around his neck as he held her, rubbing her back and playing with her hair. Burying her face in his chest, she breathed him in as she sobbed.

"I'm not going anywhere, okay? Let me be here for you."

She nodded as she tried to calm her emotions.

"Macy?" He continued to hold her, caressing her cheek and neck, pushing back her hair off her neck and rubbing her back.

"Umm?"

"I love you. I don't want you to ever doubt that."

Relaxing against him, she whispered, "I'm won't. I love you too."

He pulled away enough to see her, wiped her face dry, then cupped her cheek, his eyes peering into hers. "So, maybe, we can go out on a date?"

She grinned up at him and saw his smile ease back as something much more than heat moved between them.

His gaze shifted to her lips, his thumb moving along her jaw as he gently brushed his lips against hers. She clasped the back of his head, giving him a feathery kiss in return.

"I love you."

His deep whisper made her grin.

He pulled her in as he sank into the couch, with her cheek against his chest. She smiled, closing her eyes as his heart pounded, his breathing as heavy as hers. She found herself drifting into exhaustion as the past several sleepless nights rushed her.

"You need some rest. Maybe I should go."

"Maybe you should stay." She needed his strength, his presence at least for now. "For a little while?"

His chuckle made her heart skip, then settle back into its

normal, quiet rhythm. She felt his legs lift, settling his feet on the ottoman as he pulled her closer, her body slowly shifted into his lap.

"I'll stay just a little longer, okay?"

Macy nodded, kissed his neck, and relaxed. His strong arms moved around her as she drifted into a peaceful sleep.

EPILOGUE

Four Months Later

The whirlwind romance of Lillian and Jon ended in a beautiful wedding on a beach somewhere off the coast of Florida. Macy stood in front of her seat, watching Lillian glide slowly down the sandy aisle. She looked amazing in her fitted white gown, a stunning smile across her face. Jon's grin was just as wide as he accepted her arm.

A small gathering of family and a few friends celebrated with the couple. Macy sat down. Her gaze went to Kane, who stood beside Jon as best man. His eyes hung on hers. He smiled and winked as she grinned back.

The past few months had been wonderful and fulfilling. As a new Christian, Kane's eagerness to learn had put Macy back where she needed to be—in a church where she could learn more about her walk with God.

The months before that had separated her from Christ, allowing her faith to take the hit instead of looking to Him for comfort. Now, after four months of counseling and Bible studies with Kane by her side, she felt renewed, something she'd needed for a while.

As Jon and Lillian kissed, Macy stood with the others and clapped, grinning at the flush that crossed Jon's face.

The reception had all the markings of a black-tie gala, but on a scale for only about thirty people. She stood and waited at the tall pub table, holding her punch.

Between the wedding and the obvious spark between Jon and Lillian, Macy's mind thought about the future. As much as she loved Kane and knew he loved her, her life seemed on hold, as if she had no idea how to proceed.

She loved her job. At least she had loved her career. But now, she wasn't so sure she wanted to deal with it anymore. The only future she could imagine right now was the rest of the weekend here with Kane, falling deeper in love and enjoying their time together.

Applause came from behind her, and she joined in as Lillian and Jon entered, hand in hand, and looking very happy.

Jon quickly made a beeline for Macy and squeezed her tight.

"Congratulations. I'm so happy for both of you." She smiled at Jon and hugged Lillian. "You can breathe now, Jon." She chuckled.

"I know, I'm just not much for being in the spotlight." He took a deep breath as Lillian kissed his cheek. "So, how long do we have to stay?" His grin almost knocked her over.

Jon was always smiling, but that grin was new and intense directed toward his bride.

"Just until we cut the cake, and your brother makes a toast." Lillian giggled.

"I think someone wants your attention, Macy."

She followed Jon's gaze. Kane stood across the room with several men in suits. He looked handsome in his black tux, his hands shoved into his pockets, a broad grin on his face.

"Yeah, I wondered where he went to." She smiled at Jon and headed in Kane's direction.

Jon caught her arm. "What's wrong?"

"You need to let him come to you, Macy."

"What?" She smirked up at him.

"Trust me. Keep him on his toes, and let him come to you. Just remember that for later." Jon grinned as Lillian led him away.

She turned to see Kane sauntering toward her, his hand rubbing the back of his neck. Those green eyes held her hostage as he pulled her to him.

"You look amazing, Mace."

"You're not so bad yourself."

"So, Jon informed me that I'm officially off duty now." His playful tone rang through.

She grinned.

"I heard something about that ..."

"You knew?"

She chuckled. "Well, Lillian mentioned you getting off duty for the rest of their honeymoon, starting today. So, after they cut the cake and have a toast, I'll be standing here all alone with no one around I know." She playfully looked up at him.

"I think we can fill that time." He winked and gave her a gentle kiss, the kind he had perfected in the past few months.

Now and then, he would push for something more serious, but in his quest to keep things above board, something gentler had become the standard—a standard she enjoyed. Breathing him in, she hugged him and closed her eyes for a moment.

The tremors had all but stopped, her nightmares as well. Her sleeping had finally caught up a few months into therapy, but what had helped the most was Kane's eagerness to be involved.

He'd given her strict instructions to call when she had a nightmare or didn't get any sleep. She agreed, knowing full well she wouldn't be able to call him. But after a few nights in a row of no sleep and terrible dreams, he'd come over, talked for a while, and then she'd been able to sleep.

He constantly vied for her attention, making sure she knew

he was there for her. He kept her on her toes as they jogged and worked out together, always pushing her and never letting her give up on herself, something that had plagued her since her capture.

Looking up at him, she saw so much more affection and emotion than she knew what to do with. But right now, all she could think of was spending the rest of the weekend in a romantic setting with the man she'd fallen helplessly in love with.

They moved along with the others toward the front of the small room, toasting Jon and Lillian as Jon's brother made an impressive speech.

They watched the couple cut the cake, and Macy saw the exhaustion on Jon's face. He seemed weak by the time the reception ended, but Kane assured her it was normal.

"He doesn't like being around a large group. It wears him out mentally. That's probably why they're going home. Trust me. He'll be fine." He winked.

She watched the newlywed couple navigate the people in the room until they made it to where she and Kane stood.

"CALL IF YOU NEED ANYTHING." Kane shook Jon's hand and smiled, seeing him happier than he'd ever known him to be.

"I won't, but thanks anyway."

He chuckled as Lillian hugged him.

"Thanks for everything, Kane. I owe you so much."

"Not a thing. Trust me."

Glancing at Macy, his heart flipped. She hugged Jon and Lillian, then waved as they headed for the limo that would take them to the airport.

Gripping her hand, he pulled her in. "I love you, Macy."

"I love you too." She snuggled against his chest, and he didn't think he could make another week without knowing what was on her mind.

Marriage hadn't come up in conversation, but he was there, waiting on her to decide.

"Let's go find someplace to eat." She pushed away enough to grin up at him.

"Okay, let me go change."

"But you look so nice." She winked.

He shook his head. "I'm not a tux kinda guy."

Kane pulled her along and made her wait outside the door of the changing room.

He packed away the tux, slipped his jeans on, and had just pulled his button-up shirt on when a knock sounded on the door. It opened, and Macy came in with the phone to her ear and a wide smile stretching across her face.

"Sorry, but Jon wanted to ask you a question."

She shut the door and moved in front of him, handing him the phone. Her eyes looked him over.

"Hey, something wrong?" He swallowed hard and tried to keep from looking down at her as she moved closer.

"I just needed to ask you a question."

"Yeah?"

"How long do you plan on being gone?"

"I don't know." He smiled. "But don't worry about me coming in unannounced. I have clothes at my brothers' place. Is a week enough time?"

"Give me two."

"Sounds good." He chuckled at Jon's laughter.

He hung up and looked down at Macy. A smile danced on her lips.

"What's that for?"

"Nothing, just admiring the view."

His jaw clenched as he started to button up his shirt, heat filling his face.

"Hey, what's wrong?" She pulled his hands away and threaded her fingers through his.

"Just, I wanted to get ready." He shrugged. "I thought you were hungry."

"You're a terrible liar."

He finally made eye contact and saw another smile.

"Kane, do you think any of your scars bother me?" She stilled his hands.

"They bother me."

"Why?"

"Why do you think?" His tone came out rough, and he sighed.

"Do you think this smile is because I see your scars?" Her grin widened.

He frowned.

"Kane ..." She rolled her eyes as she let go of his hands and put hers on his sides under his shirt. "I see you. I see how hard you work out and how impressive you look. You know, women can be impressed by a muscled man."

Now his face flushed for a different reason. "I guess I never thought of it that way." He gripped her shoulders as her fingers around to his bare back, drawing him closer. "Macy, this might not be the best idea." He leaned down, pressed his chin against her temple as he spoke, smiling at the chill bumps that covered her bare arms.

"Yeah, I just thought that," she whispered.

Her hands worked their way back to his front, finding their way to his chest before dropping. He worked at steadying his breath for a moment, her touching his skin, making him more than a little excited.

"Macy."

"Yeah?"

"Sometimes, I wonder ..."

She pulled back, holding his partially buttoned shirt as she looked up at him. His hands settled on her hips, carefully avoiding her waistline as he saw her blue eyes searching his.

"I wonder what it is you want in life?"

"I guess I haven't thought about it in a while." She swallowed and focused on his chest, then met his eyes with a small smile and pushed away, pulling from his grip as she left the room.

Blowing out, he rested his hands on his hips until he could catch his breath. He'd been hoping for a different answer to that question. Maybe later, they could talk without being so worked up.

With a groan, he finished dressing, praying God had this conversation worked out already because he had no idea what to say.

ESCORTING her back to her room to change, Kane waited in the hall and was pleasantly surprised when she returned with a short jean skirt on and a snug-fitting tank top.

After a quick dinner, he took her back to the beach as the heat of the day cooled. Holding her hand in his, he searched for a way to broach the subject once more.

"Mace, are you planning on going back to work?"

She shrugged. "I don't know. I enjoy my job. I just, I feel a little lost." She cleared her throat as they walked.

"Lost? What does that mean?" He led her to a bench, sitting down close enough to wrap his arm around her to help her warm up from the cool ocean breeze.

"I don't know." She shook her head, lowering her gaze to the sand.

"Macy, what's going on? I know you have something on your mind."

He caught her chin until she finally relented, leaned back, and focused on him.

"We haven't, I mean, what we want and future plans, it's not something we've talked about. Everything seems just, up in the air right now."

He grinned and kissed her forehead, leaning close and breathing in the perfume that surrounded them.

"Why do you think I'm asking Mace? I have a few things in mind, but I kinda wanted to know where you were first."

The surprise on her face made him chuckle.

"Did you really think I haven't been there? Thinking about what our future holds?"

"I guess I didn't know you thought about that." She looked out toward the water.

"You haven't answered my question."

"I don't know. We've been talking in therapy. But my future, I'm not so sure what I want anymore."

He paused as worry flooded him. "Is everything all right?"

"I'm not sure. My future seems limited." She wiped her face and stood, hands propped on her hips as she looked down at him. "I can't even think about going back to work right now, and that's, I mean, that's who I am."

"That's not who you are—it's what you do." He stood and rubbed her arms. "There's a big difference. You are an amazing, strong, and beautiful woman. You can accomplish whatever you want to do. You don't have to go back to work right now."

"Then what, what am I supposed to do?" She pushed her hair back.

He smiled and pulled the ring from his pocket as he knelt in front of her.

"Kane, what are you doing?" she whispered.

He took a deep breath.

God, You're going to have to help me out on this one.

"Macy, I've loved you longer than I want to admit. I would say it was when you moved into Jon's, and everything just hit me at once about who you are and how much I wanted to protect you. But to be honest, I knew it when we were in that hole, when everything in me wanted to rescue you, carry you away to safety." He cleared his throat. Emotions welled up inside him.

"I watched you every moment you were in the cell with me and when you were in the next cell. I still see your face, hear your voice, and it brings me back to earth. I want to do everything I can to make you happy, to protect you, and to love you with everything in me. Please marry me."

Her eyes went wide as he held her trembling hand, pushing the ring onto her finger.

"I kinda need an answer, babe."

"Yes!" She nodded. "The answer is yes."

He stood and blew out a relieved sigh as her arms slipped up his chest and around his neck.

"You scared me for a minute," he whispered into her ear.

Lowering from his grip, she kissed him firmly, moving the kiss from deep to passionate quickly. He let her pull back first, staring into her blue eyes.

"Mace ..."

"After New Year's. I want to start a new year with you, Kane."

"That's only a few months away."

"I know. But you asked what I wanted earlier. I wanted to say that I wanted a new life, a new place to live, a home with you. I don't want to wait. I may not know what I want to do with my career, but I do know I want my life to include you as my husband and my best friend."

He swallowed the lump in his throat at hearing the word husband on her lips. He gently kissed her, pulling back to rest his forehead against hers.

"Only if you promise to kiss me like you did earlier more often."

"Every day." She playfully whispered, making him groan. "And I expect our honeymoon to include somewhere you can take that shirt off." She grinned big as he threw his head back and grimaced.

"Macy ..."

"Well, even if we don't, I guess I'll have to enjoy the view from our room."

He took another deep breath, imagining a life with this amazing woman he'd come to love and desire. It would be perfect. And, with God's help, it would be.

AUTHOR NOTE

Thanks for purchasing my first novel, Hostage. I hope you enjoyed it! As I wrote this story, I wanted to convey just how important God's grace is. You can never be too far gone. Just like Kane realized, God doesn't want you all perfect and complete; He makes you that way.

Join me at CindyBonds.com for updates on my writing journey!

ABOUT THE AUTHOR

Cindy lives with her husband Garrett in rural Arkansas. They have two children, Conner and Kenzie, and are surrounded by farmland and cattle. With a full-time job, a part-time job and being a mom, carving time for her writing has become an art!

Cindy is a past semifinalist in the American Christian Fiction Writers (ACFW) Genesis award contest with this novel, *Hostage*.

She enjoys writing strong female characters and has a heart for military stories. Her creative streak a mile wide, she dabbles in photography, scrapbooking and anything else that lets her creativity loose!

facebook.com/CindyBondsAuthor

MORE ROMANTIC SUSPENSE FROM
SCRIVENINGS PRESS

Deadly Guardian

Book One of the *Trouble in Pleasant Valley* series.

When the men she dated begin dying, Madison Long must convince the police of her innocence and help them determine who has taken on the role of her guardian before he kills the only man she ever truly loved, Detective Nate Zuberi.

Madison Long, a high school chemistry teacher, looks forward to a relaxing summer break. Instead, she suffers through a nightmare of threats, terror, and death. When she finds a man murdered she once dated, Detective Nate Zuberi is assigned to the case, and in the midst of chaos, attraction blossoms into love.

Together, she and Nate search for her deadly guardian before he decides the only way to truly save her from what he considers a hurtful relationship is to kill her—and her policeman boyfriend as well.

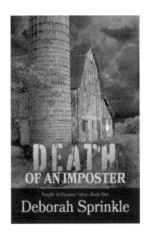

Look for Book Two of this series, *Death of an Imposter*, coming in December 2020.

Rookie detective Bernadette Santos has her first murder case. Will her desire for justice end up breaking her heart? Or worse—getting her killed!

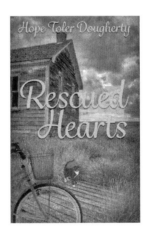

Rescued Hearts

Mary Wade Kimball's soft spot for animals leads to a hostage situation when she spots a briar-entangled kitten in front of an abandoned house. Beaten, bound, and gagged, Mary Wade loses hope for escape.

Discovering the kidnapped woman ratchets the complications for undercover agent Brett Davis. Weighing the difference of ruining his three months' investigation against the woman's safety, Brett forsakes his mission and helps her escape the bent-on-revenge brutes following behind. When Mary Wade's safety is threatened once more, Brett rescues her again. This time, her personal safety isn't the only thing in jeopardy. Her heart is endangered as well.

Scrivenings
PRESS
Quench your thirst for story.
www.ScriveningsPress.com

Stay up-to-date on your favorite books and authors with our free e-newsletters.

ScriveningsPress.com

Made in the USA
Middletown, DE
11 April 2021